Suburbia

(the sequel to *Desmond*)

by Ulysses Grant Dietz

Lightbane Publications

LEGAL DISCLAIMER: This is a work of erotic fiction that includes graphic depictions of sexual intercourse. All characters involved in sexual acts are 18 years of age or older. This novel is not recommended for anyone under the age of 18.

All characters herein are fictional. Any resemblance to real persons living or dead is purely coincidental.

All real life companies and products are property of their respective copyright owners and their appearance in the story is not meant to indicate any affiliation with or endorsement of the author or this work.

Vampire in Suburbia is entirely the product of its author's fertile imagination and Ivy League education. It includes scenes of gay lovemaking (mortal and immortal), blood-drinking, descriptions of museums, thoughts about New Jersey, and substantial chatter on the topic of interior decoration.

All rights reserved. With the exception of excerpts taken under Fair Use to be utilized in articles, reviews or interviews, it is illegal to reproduce this work in part or as a whole by any means without permission. Please do not transfer, sell or copy without permission of the author.

ISBN: 978-1500172572
Copyright© 2012 by Ulysses Grant Dietz
Lightbane Publications
E-Book Originally released September 2012

Cover Art by Jeffrey Apgar

Dedications

For Gary, my rock.
For Alex and Grace, my better angels.
For Jeffrey, my first inspiration.
And for Chris, who kept me from giving up.

Prologue

Desmond Beckwith pushed the shopping cart across the tiled floor of Eden Gourmet. A gray Vampire Weekend t-shirt clung flatteringly to his torso. Along with the cargo shorts and flip-flops, his wardrobe was like that of any suburban husband wandering aimlessly in a supermarket, reluctantly doing errands. The t-shirt had been a gift from Janay; a tween's idea of irony. He was wearing his hair longer these days, and its dark waves set off his pale skin, dusted with Saturday afternoon stubble. Large lash-fringed hazel eyes and a high forehead gave him an uncanny beauty that was at once masculine and delicate. His looks and his youth set him apart from most of the other men out shopping for their wives. Absorbed in scanning the shelves, he didn't notice the heads turning as he passed.

The cart's wheels jumped and rattled over the uneven terra-cotta surface. Desmond was grateful that the molded plastic of the cart's body remained blessedly silent, unlike the old all-metal carts still used in less upscale supermarkets.

Stupid tile floor, he muttered to himself, yearning for the silent smoothness of the linoleum at Pathmark. He eyed the shelves for things on the long list of foodstuffs, ordinary and esoteric, that Dotty had forced him to bring with him, presuming his memory wouldn't be up to the task. He harrumphed internally as he spotted two more items from the list without having to actually take it out of his pocket. His tiny sense of triumph was replaced with an equally tiny thrill of shame.

This is stupid. Why am I making such a big deal out of this? It's only grocery shopping. And I'm not even going to get to eat any of it.

Desmond had never been in a large suburban supermarket until a few months before. Other than quick trips to the neighborhood Gristedes in New York City when he was cooking for Tony and their friends, there had never been any reason to visit such a place. Now, he knew virtually every market in this part of suburban Essex County, New Jersey. He knew the selection variations; he knew the comparative price points; and he knew where to find the really unusual stuff that Dotty loved to fool with when she experimented in the kitchen. ShopRite in West Orange for the ordinary stuff; Whole Foods in Montclair for really good (and really expensive) meat; Trader Joe's in Millburn for funky interesting things; Eden Gourmet in South Orange for the hard-to-find ingredients and the best produce. And all this knowledge was useless to him, except that Dotty needed his help so she could cook for Jane and the girls.

Jane and the girls and Ollie too. Before.

In spite of the fact that Dotty worked *for him,* Desmond had volunteered early on to help with keeping the house supplied. Dot may have been his employee, but she was also part of his family, as he saw it. Pitching in had helped Dotty understand his commitment to them, and had gradually helped wear away the suspicions she harbored as to why this rich white man had taken an interracial lesbian couple and their children into his life the way he had. But once he had stepped up, she made him follow her family's budget, not his own. She gave him coupons and made him use them. Jane and Dotty were willing to take his help with the chores, but not his money beyond the salary he paid them. Dotty was his housekeeper; Jane his executive assistant. But they and their girls were much more than that to him.

Desmond's eyes unfocused and his thoughts drifted as he continued to guide the cart through the narrow aisles.

A sharp tug at his shirt hem brought him back to himself, and he looked down into the wide hazel eyes of Janay, Jane's eleven-year-old daughter. She proudly held up to him a stout, thick-necked bottle full of deep red liquid. It bore a black label with the words TRU-BLOOD in large red letters.

"Look what I found, Uncle Des." She beamed up at him. "Looks good, don't it?"

"Doesn't it," he gently corrected, as he took the bottle from her delicate brown hand. He studied the label for a moment, then smiled and handed it back to her.

"Sweetheart, that's just blood-orange soda pop. It's from a TV show."

Janay's smile faded, but her eyes stayed wide, her long lashes framing a look of disappointment.

"Oh. Then you can't drink it?"

"No, honey. It'd make me sick."

Actually, I could probably tolerate it. But it looks disgusting.

"Damn," she swore, "I thought it was real blood, and that would be so cool."

"Language, Janay. Do you know about the TV show?"

"Sure, *True Blood*."

"Your mama doesn't let you watch that show, does she?" Desmond had seen it, and fun as it was, it certainly wasn't fit for a pre-teen.

"Course not. Mama and Dotty say that show's way too nasty for an angel like me." She beamed up at him again, disappointment apparently behind her.

"That's a relief." Desmond smiled down at the little girl, then, frowning slightly, looked around.

"Where's your sister, Janay?"

"Speck? Oh she's somewhere over there," she answered, pointing vaguely in the direction of the cheese counter.

"Well don't go leaving her on her own—you know she panics."

"Don't worry Uncle Des, Speck knows where we are. She knows we won't ditch her."

As if to make her point, Speck chose that moment to appear around the end of the aisle, a large block of plastic-wrapped cheese in each tiny fist.

"Look, I got some yummy stinky cheese, Uncle Des." She held up her prizes for Desmond to take.

"You sure you're gonna eat these? You like that stuff?"

"Yeah, really. I do. Pleeeease?"

He read the labels and, shrugging, put them in the cart, looking at the younger Ashmun girl. Cassandra, known as Speck because she was so little, was a smaller version of her sister. Her skin was a bit lighter; her hair had more golden highlights; but the wide hazel eyes were the same. Her father's eyes. A faint shudder twitched down Desmond's back, and he shook his head slightly to disperse the unwelcome memory.

He reached out and took the bottle of Tru-Blood soda from Janay's hand.

"You want this? I'll bet it tastes pretty good, even if not to me."

Janay gave him a knowing little smile. "Could I?"

"Sure. Cassie got her stinky cheese. You can have your special drink."

He high-fived both girls, and the trio set off slowly, cart chittering over the tiles, all eyes alert to find the last things on Dotty's list for tonight's dinner.

Desmond smiled a wry smile as he watched the two beautiful little girls skip ahead of him, treating the chore of shopping as if it were a treasure hunt.

Hm. He thought to himself. *How on earth did I ever get here?*

And they all moved on together.

Chapter One

"I know I haven't an appointment, but I was wondering if the curator happened to be available." Desmond offered his most dazzling smile, noting that the receptionist stared at him for a full five seconds before reacting.

"I'll have to see if Mr. Cameron is able to come down. We're not normally supposed to disturb the curators without appointments." The young woman gasped softly. "I'm sorry, that sounded rude. What I meant was … "

"Please don't apologize. I completely understand." He smiled again, reassuring her. "I'm new to Newark and this is my first visit to the museum. I figured it couldn't hurt to try. Could you give him my card?" Desmond pulled a small white business card from his inner pocket and handed it to her.

Jeez, Desmond, pile on the British accent, why don't you?

The receptionist read the card, her brows rising slightly. "Desmond Beckwith, Beckwith Investments? You're over in the Gateway Center?"

"Yes, that's right."

"I'll call the curatorial assistant and see if Oliver's around. Did you want to wait?"

"Actually, I thought I'd go see the Ballantine House. I assume I can get to it from inside the museum?"

"Of course. The museum's north wing is attached to the Ballantine House at the back. Here, let me show you." Tossing her dark, curly hair over her shoulder, the young woman pulled out a brochure with the museum's floor plan printed on it. She showed Desmond the route through the museum's complex of buildings to the place where it joined the servant's wing of the 1885 Ballantine House.

Beaming as she handed him the brochure, the receptionist seemed to have become Desmond's new best friend.

"I'll tell Oliver he can find you in the house."

"Lovely. Thanks ever so much."

He worked his way through several buildings full of galleries that hadn't existed the first time he'd come to this city. Although it was tucked away in the museum's north wing, he easily found the entrance to the restored beer baron's mansion that had long been one of the museum's most popular attractions. As he stepped through the back door into the long, paneled entrance hall, he was startled by the sudden feeling of recognition that swept through him.

Yes, there was an illuminated EXIT sign over the stained glass transom of the double front doors opening onto Washington Park. And the glass and bronze barriers that kept people from walking very far into the rooms were a clear reminder that this was a historic house and no longer a private residence.

Desmond wandered from room to room, reading the texts provided to explain the house and its historical context. He perused the furnishings, which were for the most part things that had been acquired by the museum, and had not belonged to the family who built the house. It was a far more eclectic mix of styles than his own rambling Victorian flat in the Dakota on Manhattan's West Side. But he remembered the intricate mosaic table in the gold and white drawing room, purchased by the Ballantines on a trip to Florence; as well as the Tiffany window in the cherry-paneled library. That, he recalled, was an allegory of the Ballantine name in ancient Scottish Gaelic. A russet-haired priestess in an olive-green tunic knelt before a smoking censer, as fragrant blue-white tendrils swirled around a sun made of opalescent glass. He could remember Robbie explaining the meaning of the window to him, full of the enthusiasm of youth and pride in his family's wealth.

Climbing the carved oak staircase to the second floor, Desmond instinctively turned to the right, into what had originally been the best guest room.

They've gotten the color wrong.

The plaster walls were glazed a deep coppery bronze. Reproduction draperies of maroon velvet hung at the tall windows. Placed in the recessed niche on the southern wall of the room was a double bed with a tall, rectangular headboard. The complex paneled design in Brazilian rosewood was inlaid with an elaborate tracery of lighter wood and mother of pearl.

It's the same bed.

As he stood, transfixed, staring at the shimmering surface of the bed, Desmond's mind let go....

The hack rattled over the cobbles, making its way up Broad Street to the acute angle forming the north end of Washington Park. The interior of the carriage smelled distinctly of sweat and moldy leather, horse dung and coal soot, making Desmond wish his senses weren't quite so keen. Under everything, like a quiet continuo, was the constant scent, warm, animating, vital, of blood, both equine and human. This never troubled him.

The mild October day was turning chill as evening set in, and mist rose from the damp pavement, blurring the outlines of streetlamps, pedestrians and traffic. Desmond lurched to the side as the driver guided his team in a sharp left turn into Washington Street. Passing a long row of large attached houses and a stone church facing the triangular park, the carriage stopped in front of a tall brick mansion. Handing Desmond down onto the flagged sidewalk, the driver tipped his hat and received his fare with a look of surprise. Desmond tended to tip generously, and was rewarded with the driver's enthusiastic assistance in carrying his cases up the steps of the front portico. Desmond waited until the hack-man had clattered off into the gathering twilight before pulling the doorbell set alongside the tall oak doors.

The butler who opened one of those doors and ushered Desmond into a tiled vestibule efficiently removed his overcoat and asked if Mr. Beckwith would wish to wash up after his journey. At Desmond's murmured assent, his luggage and coat were handed off to a pair of indistinct young women who gave off a faint scent of fear as they curtseyed in the dim recesses of the hall. The butler showed him down the hall—plush-draped doorways offering glimpses into reception room and library, parlor and dining room—and into a billiard room opposite the elaborate staircase. The location of the marble-lined washroom having been indicated, Desmond was left to his own devices. He washed the city soot off his face and neck and stepped back into the billiard room, where he stood uncertainly.

Pinpoints of gaslight flickered in sconces, and pushed the ceiling and corners of the room into shadow, making it seem larger than it was. The fading light illuminated the stained glass windows at one end of the room. Thick, new Turkish carpets glowed richly on the parquet floor. The smooth green baize surface of the table shimmered in the warm gloom. The effect was, overall, one of carefully restrained modern luxury. How different it was from Desmond's own old-fashioned row house across the three rivers in lower Manhattan—which seemed a world away from this bustling, soot-filled industrial city of Newark.

Desmond was trying to remember how he'd been talked into this weekend visit, when Robbie Ballantine pushed open the door from the hall and swept into the room. He quickly moved over to Desmond, lifted his face and kissed his lips, laughing softly at the look of panic that flashed in Desmond's eyes.

"Don't worry, Des, there's no one to see. The family is still upstairs. Couldn't resist. I'm just so glad to see you." Robbie straightened up and smoothed the front of his dinner jacket with slender white hands. "How do I look?"

"Lovely," said Desmond, his face relaxing into a smile.

Indeed, Robert Ballantine, at twenty-three, fourteen years younger than Desmond, was unquestionably a pretty young man. They had met earlier that year, at a ball, amidst the overweening splendor of Cornelius Vanderbilt's palace on the Fifth Avenue in New York. Robbie's parents had been hoping for him to meet an appropriate young lady from among the glittering seasonal offerings of New York's elite; but he had instead met the handsome, serious Desmond Beckwith.

Desmond was not unknown in New York society, for in spite of his modest house in an unfashionable downtown neighborhood, he was evidently wealthy, and as mysterious as he was good-looking. No one really knew any great detail about Desmond's history, but faint rumors of a titled English family and the early death of both of his parents gave him a romantic aura that drew both men and women to his side. It was the young men, however, who tended to remain at his side, and New

York's matrons had long since given up trying to match their daughters with the sole heir to the Beckwith investment interests.

Beckwith and Ballantine had slipped away from the Vanderbilt festivities unnoticed. The ensuing liaison had gone on for several months, and had most recently included Robbie's begging Desmond to come and spend a weekend in Newark and meet his parents. Thus Desmond found himself reeling slightly from the sensation of the unexpected kiss, and placing his hands on Robbie's shoulders.

"Behave yourself," he told the younger man. A half smile softened the chastening tone of the words.

Robbie beamed at him, then turned at the sound of a door closing in the distance and motioned Desmond to follow him. He took Desmond's hand and pulled him up the staircase, then quickly into a room at the right of the upper hall. Shutting the door behind him and turning the latch, Robbie stepped closer, placed his long-fingered hands on either side of Desmond's face, and pulled him into another kiss. This time the soft lips lingered, and the younger man's tongue probed, finally forcing Desmond to relent and let him in. He felt the blood rise in hot waves up his neck as Robbie groaned softly, deepening the kiss and lowering one hand down to caress the front of Desmond's trousers. Robbie's groan turned to a muffled sigh of pleasure as he felt Desmond's arousal.

Suddenly Robbie pulled away and dropped to his knees on the thick figured carpeting. With expert fingers he unbuttoned Desmond's fly, pulled down his trousers and the knit underclothes, engulfing his cock in one swift movement. Desmond had to bite his lip to keep from crying out as Robbie's mouth moved up and down the shaft, his lower teeth faintly grazing the underside, his full lips caressing velvet skin, his tongue teasing the slit. Desmond put his hands on either side of Robbie's head, guiding him gently, shivering with pleasure.

A soft tap at the door broke the spell. Both men froze, Desmond's cock still in Robbie's mouth, their eyes locked in sudden alarm.

"Mr. Beckwith?" queried the butler's voice. "I have not yet had the opportunity to unpack your cases, please forgive me."

Robbie sat back on his haunches, wiping his mouth with the back of his hand, and smiled up at Desmond.

"It's all right, McAllister, I'm helping Mr. Beckwith put away his things." Desmond had to bite his lip again to keep from laughing.

"Mr. Robert?" The butler's voice sounded confused. "Oh, very well then." Silence indicated that the puzzled servant had left.

Desmond leaned over and pulled Robbie to his feet.

"That was very bad," he chided softly.

"I know. Sorry." Robbie didn't look sorry at all.

"I think you need to leave me, since now I must unpack without assistance and dress myself for dinner."

Robbie gave a petulant sigh, and then smirked before giving Desmond a peck on the lips.

"Then you'd better pull your clothes up." And with that he turned and, before Desmond could move, unlocked the door and slipped out into the quiet hall.

Desmond rearranged himself, putting aside his frustration and quelling his anxiety. As he put away his things and dressed, he pondered his unlikely situation. Robbie's forwardness both excited and upset him. The youth's evident need was flattering, but it concerned Desmond that his own feelings didn't seem to attain the same intensity. He had never let himself be so drawn into an affair before. Not since Jeffrey Chapman's death long before had he given his heart to anyone.

Robbie was a charming lad, and a beauty, but that was all. Desmond disliked the idea that he was leading the boy on. In the months they had known each other, they had spent a good deal of time together. Robbie's little bachelor flat in the Hotel Chelsea had become a frequent retreat where they could spend quiet nights in each other's company, far from the prying eyes of both New York society and the solicitous parents in Newark.

Desmond had never taken Robbie to his house on Fourth Street.

Robbie was intelligent enough and unfailingly thoughtful when it came to Desmond's wishes. Desmond, as the elder, was treated with devotion and deference. Their physical intimacy was gratifying, extremely so. But Robbie was also – there was no other way to put it – superficial. He loved parties. He loved champagne, which at least Desmond could share with him. Robbie loved going to balls and dancing with debutantes and flirting with heiresses, for all that he had no intention of ever attaching himself to one of them. He told Desmond that he had said as much to his parents. That bit of honesty, at least, was admirable. But in the end, after the lovemaking and the party-going and the horseback riding in the Central Park, there was nothing for them to talk about. Jeffrey Chapman had been his manservant, yet they had never lacked for conversation. Robbie didn't seem to notice this gap in their rapport, but it weighed heavily on Desmond's heart as he dressed for dinner.

The meal passed in a pleasant enough blur. There was Robbie's sister, Alice, a slender figure in pale blue. His parents, Jeannette, glittering in jet-trimmed black silk, her snow-white hair piled high on her head; and John Ballantine, every inch the proper industrialist, from his patent leather pumps to the neatly-trimmed beard streaked with grey. Desmond found the senior Ballantines intelligent company. Mrs. Ballantine, with her soft, melodious voice, was the more gregarious of the two, benignly ruling the table from her seat opposite the pantry door. She kept a sharp eye on the butler and the young waitress who served the meal. Her husband, smilingly taciturn, made only occasional comments as the conversation moved from one suitably neutral topic to the next. They talked of the great World's Columbian Exposition taking place in Chicago. Desmond offered general allusions to the world of investment and real estate. Mr. Ballantine set forth the virtues of Newark as a thriving industrial center. Desmond played this game deftly, trained as he was by many years of acting as host in his own way, within his own small circle of acquaintances.

Dealing with the four-course dinner was another thing. Since this was a simple family meal, there were only two wines served, as well as iced water. Desmond drank generously, hoping to distract his hostess from the fact that he picked at the soup and the fish and the roast lamb. He encouraged Robbie and Alice by asking questions and drawing them into the conversation, hoping thereby to disguise the fact that he wasn't really consuming anything solid. He rarely attended dinner parties, and those he did were usually large formal affairs, where his eating habits (or, more accurately, non-eating habits) were less likely to attract notice. Here, under the watchful eye of the white-haired lady on his left, he was fearful of causing offense.

Desmond managed to get through dessert and, pleading fatigue, avoided brandy in the library and escaped to his bedroom. He shut the door behind him, all but collapsing into a deep plush armchair pulled up by the fire. There was no need for fires in this modern house, but the coal furnace had apparently not been started due to the warm weather, and the crackling wood shed a welcome glow into the room. It was a handsome room, furnished in the same restrained richness as the rest of the house. The dark rosewood of the matching bed, dresser and nightstands was all elaborately inlaid in swirling patterns of stylized flowers in lighter woods. It was attempting, Desmond reckoned, to look Japanese, as had been the mode when the house was built in the 1880s. With its heavy teal-green draperies, Morris wallpaper and figured carpeting, the room was luxurious, if slightly out of style. Desmond's little house in New York was so far out of date that it seemed timeless, at least to him. He had rarely had guests, even less so in the past decades, and thus had never concerned himself with fashionable decoration.

He pulled a book from one of his bags: Sheridan Le Fanu's *Carmilla,* published in Dublin in 1872. How pleased he had been to find this volume in a dusty New York bookstore a few years back. Its publication had escaped his notice, possibly because it would have been largely ignored by the City papers due to its scandalous nature. Not only was the eponymous Carmilla a vampire, but her favored victims were of her own sex, shocking Le Fanu's readers doubly—and no doubt titillating them doubly as well—Desmond thought cynically. It was one of his favorite books, for all its absurd notions, and was honored with a favored place high on one of the mahogany bookcases in Desmond's snug Gothic library.

Lost in rereading his novel, Desmond didn't hear the gentle tapping at his door, but looked up with a start when Robbie entered the room and, once again, turned the latch as he pulled off his white tie.

"There," he said. "At last. They've all gone to bed. I had a devil of a time getting Alice to stop asking about you." He turned to Desmond with a wry smile, shrugging out of his dinner jacket and letting it fall to the floor. "She's quite smitten with you, you know, in spite of the fact that you hardly touched your dinner."

He began to unfasten his shirt studs as he moved to the opposite side of the room and locked a second door. He finished, and pulled off the starched white linen, dropping it in a heap at his feet.

"That's the sewing room. I've also locked the connecting door into Alice's dressing room, should she get it into her head to come snooping." He toed off his black pumps and bent over to pull off the silk stockings, leaving his bare feet pale and elegant against the dark carpet.

"Oh, we wouldn't want that, would we," Desmond responded with a low chuckle. He stood and moved to wrap his arms around Robbie's slim shoulders, drawing him into a deep kiss that drained away all of the evening's anxieties. It was a solidly built house, he imagined. Good thick walls. No one would hear anything.

As he fumbled blindly with Robbie's trouser buttons, he felt the younger man's hand move to his pocket and pull out something. Breaking the kiss, Desmond looked down, to see a dark blue glass jar in Robbie's hand.

"Pomade," Robbie whispered. "For, you know."

Seeing Desmond's quizzical look, he added, "I want you to fuck me."

Desmond took the jar and tossed it onto the bed, then knelt on the carpet and unbuttoned Robbie's trousers. Shoving them to Robbie's ankles, he took the half-hard dick into his mouth, swallowing it right up to the root, his lips nuzzling the musky thatch. Robbie held Desmond's head as he kicked out of the trousers, making him gag slightly as the swelling cock filled his throat. Desmond pulled back to catch his breath, looking up with a brief smile before resuming. As he moved his mouth up and down the slender shaft, he cupped the velvety balls in one hand and began to massage the perineum with a finger, gradually working his way back until his soft pad was gently rubbing the tight sphincter. Robbie moaned softly, and Desmond continued the pressure. When his fingertip breached the ring of muscle, Robbie gasped, but Desmond pushed further, pressing up to find the younger man's prostate. Robbie's breath caught as Desmond found his target; his hips bucked with the continued prodding and within a minute, his knees shaking, he groaned out his release, filling Desmond's mouth and throat.

Desmond continued until Robbie's cock was soft in his mouth, then stood, gathering up his lover in his arms and laying him gently on the cool white sheets. Then he stood and quickly stripped off his own clothing. Robbie looked at him from the pillows with lazing admiration for Desmond's trim muscular frame. What he saw in those large brown eyes, shimmering up at him in the soft light, made him uneasy. He knew Robbie wouldn't see the same thing in *his* eyes.

He applied the pomade to the little ring of muscle of Robbie's entry. The cloying floral scent momentarily masked that of his lover's sweat and the underlying fragrance of his pulsing blood. Having prepared him well, Desmond took Robbie gently, almost tenderly, pushing him back onto the pillows and, grasping one of his ankles, lifting it up as high as it would go. Holding onto Robbie's calf with one hand, the other pressed against the marquetry to keep his balance, he closed his eyes and rubbed the soft pink instep against the evening stubble on his cheeks. As his orgasm built to the point of no return, Desmond drove faster and deeper, bringing himself to a satisfying climax, choking back the cry that tried to force its way from his throat.

As his heartbeat began to subside, his cock still inside Robbie, Desmond opened his eyes and looked down, gasping slightly for breath. A thrill of pain shot through him as he saw the wide-eyed yearning on the younger man's face, and blushing with shame, he shifted his gaze slightly, focusing not on Robbie's face, but on the inlaid pattern of flowers that swirled across the headboard.

Chapter Two

A quiet voice pulled Desmond from his reverie, but at first he didn't hear the words. He started slightly, with a confused "I beg your pardon?"

"I'm sorry, I didn't mean to startle you. You seemed so fascinated by the bed."

Desmond turned, his eyes lighting on a man standing next to him.

"The bed?"

"Yes, it looked like you were quite mesmerized. I don't often see visitors so captivated, and I thought I might be able to answer any questions you had."

Desmond took a moment to study the man. A couple of inches shorter than he was. Fair skin, a smattering of freckles across the short, rather pretty nose. Bright blue eyes, set wide in a delicate oval face above a square jaw; coppery-bright red hair, wavy rather than curly. A narrow, neatly groomed mustache and beard, also ginger, framed full pink lips. A hesitant smile showed even white teeth.

"It's by Herter Brothers," the man offered. "They were a New York firm."

At Desmond's staring silence, the redhead seemed to falter. "Um, uh, the entire bedroom suite was made by them."

"What? Oh, I know the bed," said Desmond, feeling foolish even as he spoke.

"Know it?"

"I, just–I mean I've seen it before."

"But we only just put it out." The confusion on the man's face must have echoed Desmond's own disorientation. His fair cheeks were crimson with embarrassment. Desmond felt awkward and had no idea what to say. It was unlike him to be so tongue-tied.

"I–I guess you must have seen it at auction. At Bonham's in New York. Last year." The redhead's voice was getting softer, as if his battery was running down. "We were awfully lucky to get it. It's the only Herter furniture documented to a family in Newark ever to surface."

"Yes, that must be it. I saw it at Bonham's." Encouraged by the relieved smile that lit up the other's face, Desmond forged ahead with renewed confidence. "I love prowling around the auction houses. I'm a collector myself. I, uh, was just startled to see the bed here." Then he added, rather lamely, "It's my first visit to the museum. I'm sorry to say I didn't know there was a museum in Newark."

The man's smile quirked into a wry grin. "Ah, well yes, I'm afraid I get that a lot, especially from New Yorkers." Then he extended a neat, well-groomed hand, and Desmond shook it, noting the smooth, dry skin and the warmth of his touch. He also noticed that the redhead's eyes widened at the contact.

"I'm Oliver Cameron. I'm the decorative arts curator here."

"Hello, Oliver. I'm Desmond. Desmond Beckwith."

"Desmond Beckwith?" The curator's surprise was clear. "But you seem too young...." his voice trailed off, although whether from confusion or embarrassment Desmond couldn't be sure.

"Possibly you knew of my father." Desmond had never liked the awkwardness of these transition times after his regeneration. "I'm afraid he died this past summer, quite suddenly. I've come to Newark to settle his affairs."

A blush once again flooded the curator's neck and cheeks. Desmond could smell the soft coppery fragrance of his blood radiating from that pale skin. He wanted to put his hand out and feel that warmth with his fingers. Instead, he fixed his eyes on the curator's slightly panicked face.

"How *do* you happen to know my name?"

"I'm so sorry. I had no idea." Oliver lowered his gaze, and Desmond could see that his long lashes were a pale red-gold. Then he looked up, meeting Desmond's gaze. "The receptionist gave me your card. But your father was a good friend of a colleague of mine, Vivian Lake. I've been to Beckwith House in New York any number of times. It's a remarkable place." He went silent again. "I'm really terribly sorry. Vivian spoke so highly of him."

"Oh, I see. Of course you would know Vivian." Desmond's words were full of warmth as he tried to reassure the redhead. "I forget what a small profession you're all in." Desmond had a momentary flash of a handsome face with brown eyes beneath a mop of dirty blond hair. Tony had worked with Vivian. "I'm ashamed to say I haven't spoken with Vivian in some –" he caught himself. "– since I arrived in the states." He hesitated. "How is she doing?"

"Well, you probably know she'd been let go by the Museum of the City of New York; but she's still the director at Beckwith House. I assume you know all about that." Cameron's expression was puzzled, as he watched the younger man closely.

"Yes, yes – I'd been informed by my father. I suppose I should have gone right to Beckwith House to see Vivian when I arrived, but I guess I was too distracted."

"I'd imagine she's getting close to retirement age," added Cameron, "but she loves that place, and I imagine she'll hold on as long as she can." Another look flickered across his features, and his eyes narrowed slightly. "Have you ever seen Beckwith House?"

Desmond hadn't been prepared to engage in a conversation like this. He knew every square inch of Beckwith House like he knew his own face. He himself had purchased every object within its walls. A huge part of his life before Tony's death was in that house. But he had left it behind, turned it into a museum, and made Vivian its director. Or, he should say, his *father* had. He, the twenty-one-year-old Desmond Beckwith, had never been in New York. Had never met any of his friends. Had never met Tony Chapman. This thought triggered an impulse he couldn't resist.

"Did you by chance ever know Anthony Chapman?" As soon as he asked, Desmond groaned inwardly. Of course young Cameron wouldn't have known Tony. He would have been a teenager when Tony died, and Desmond had been in his mid-forties then, in the middle of his life cycle.

"No, but I know who you mean. He worked with Vivian, at the museum of the City of New York. And I know he did a lot of research on the Beckwith house. He died before I came to New York. Vivian spoke of him sometimes." Then Oliver's eyes widened, as if he suddenly recalled something Vivian had said about Tony. "I believe it was your father who introduced Chapman to Vivian."

Desmond began to feel a blush creep up his own pale cheeks as he searched for something to say to fill the awkward silence that followed this last statement.

"Yes," he started, stalling lamely. Then, deciding that candor couldn't be any more uncomfortable than prevarication, he pushed forward. "I never met Tony myself. I know my father loved him very much. I know he suffered terribly at his death." He was surprised at how good it felt to speak the words, as if acknowledging something he hadn't dared think of since his regeneration.

A look of polite concern flickered into Cameron's face. Desmond had calculated correctly. "Yes, I always assumed. Vivian must have cared a lot for Tony, too. She spoke of him almost as if he were her younger brother as much as a friend and colleague."

This was something he hadn't expected to hear. He had known of Vivian's sorrow over Tony's death nineteen years earlier, but it had never occurred to him that Vivian might have suffered more than just the loss of a colleague. So caught up in his own grief, he hadn't given much thought to the other people that Tony's life had touched. He would have to find some way to speak to her about it—when he introduced himself to her in his new state.

A gentle clearing of the throat brought Desmond out of his reverie. He found Cameron's wide blue eyes fixed on him.

"Could I show you more of the house, Mr. Beckwith? Perhaps some of the other galleries in the museum if you haven't visited before. This is my department, but I know the other exhibits here pretty well." His tone was quietly eager. The sweet tang of his blood seemed to fill the small space between them. At Desmond's silent gaze, he once again faltered.

"If you're busy, of course, I don't mean to take up your time...." The blue eyes were cast downward; another blush intensified the scent of blood. Desmond had a sudden revelation.

He's flirting with me.

"Mr. Cameron...." he started.

"Oliver, please."

"Oliver, then, I really do need to get back to my office. I'm looking for a house here in New Jersey and I have to meet with a realtor this afternoon."

He could see the disappointment in the curator's eyes and, unaccountably, wanted to comfort him in some way.

"But I do have some time before I need to retrieve my car. I'd very much like to see the American pictures and sculpture. Would that be possible?"

"Of course. It would be my pleasure. Here, let me give you my card." Cameron reached into the inner pocket of his jacket and withdrew a business card with his contact information on it. His eyes met Desmond's briefly as he handed it over, then dropped his gaze again, showing off the ginger lashes to advantage.

"Shall we go have a look, then?"

"Yes, indeed."

Cameron escorted Desmond back to the museum's north wing and gave him an efficiently professional tour of the American art galleries, starting with Colonial portraits and ending with contemporary works by living artists.

"I was on the curatorial team when we installed these galleries, and I convinced my colleagues to include decorative arts objects to amplify the context of the art."

He looked shyly at his guest.

"They were a little dubious at first, but I think it works pretty well, if I do say so."

Desmond smiled at him, tickled by the mixture of pride and modesty that radiated from the handsome bearded face.

"I love the way you've interpreted the furniture and objects to echo the themes presented in the pictures. The fact that you've actually explained what things mean and not just described them is very interesting."

Again, Desmond was oddly pleased to see that his

praise provoked a strong blush that suffused Cameron's pale complexion.

Redheads can never hide their emotions, can they? Just like Roger.

But it was not the intelligence of the labels or the quality of the works in the galleries that most impressed Desmond during the half hour he spent with the curator—it was the way Oliver interacted with the museum staff they encountered during their tour.

The security staff in the museum was a diverse crew, men and women of varied ages and ethnicities. They were paid minimum wage to stand in the galleries and protect the irreplaceable artworks on display from over-enthusiastic visitors. Whenever he and Desmond entered a gallery in which an attendant was stationed, Oliver always spoke to them, greeting them by name. He seemed to know a remarkable amount about their lives and families. He always introduced Desmond and explained that he was new to Newark and visiting the museum for the first time. Oliver's broad smile and bright blue eyes lit up with each meeting, and that warmth was reflected back in the attendants' expressions.

These people adore him. They're not just fixtures to him, and they know that.

What also came through during their brief tour was Oliver's love, both of this institution, and for the works in its care. He spoke of paintings and teapots with equal affection, underscored by a profound understanding of their beauty as well as their meaning. It was not a collector showing off things of value; it was a scholar sharing his passion for things that mattered to him.

When Desmond finally had to excuse himself, Oliver escorted him back to the lobby through which he'd first entered. There they said their goodbyes.

"I'll give you a call sometime," said Desmond using his plumiest accent and brightest smile.

"I'd like that very much," Oliver answered, returning the smile.

As they shook hands in parting, Desmond noticed again the firm, warm grip, and also the slightly startled look on the curator's face at their touch.

Was the boy so smitten already?

As he walked back to the complex of office towers adjacent to Newark's Pennsylvania Station, Desmond pondered the slightly unsettling visit to the museum. He was oblivious to the noise of the traffic and the jostling of other pedestrians on the sidewalk. He thought about seeing that house again after so many years. About poor Robbie, with whom he had broken it off shortly after the dinner with his family. A decade later, still unattached, living alone in New York City, Robert Ballantine had taken his own life. He had returned to that very house, where he had put a gun to his head, leaving his family and friends heartbroken and confused. He had been handsome, intelligent and rich. How could he have done this? Desmond thought he knew, and had tried hard to reassure himself that he was not to blame.

And now, in that very room, looking at that same bed, his thoughts had been muddled by a good-looking bearded curator. And not a boy, he chided himself ... probably in his late thirties at least. Older than Desmond—at least as things stood now. The memory of his eyes, of the touch of his hand, of his rich, thrumming fragrance, all swirled slowly in Desmond's brain as he headed back to the headquarters of Beckwith Investments in the Gateway Center.

After September 11, 2001, Desmond had moved his staff out of Manhattan and into a newly built tower in downtown Newark. Although the building in which his offices were located had not been damaged, it had been very close to Ground Zero, and he had been in the office that day. The decision to move to Newark had been made as much to assuage his own fear as that of his employees. He could have just as easily died in one of those towers as they fell—or on one of the jets that had caused the havoc on that awful bright September morning. His oldest friend in the world, Roger Deland, had called in a panic, almost sobbing in fear over what might have happened to Desmond. He had never heard Roger so distraught, at least not since the night in a Paris prison when Desmond had saved his life.

Bill Lawrence, Desmond's oldest friend in New York City, whom he had known since his official coming out days in the mid-1960s, had covered the unfolding drama for the *New York Times*, and had shared his terror and grief with Desmond as they comforted each other and helped each other through the ensuing difficult days. Of all his New York friends, only Bill knew the whole truth of Desmond's life, and the value of his presence had been incalculable. Together they had mourned the loss of many friends as AIDS had spread its fog of despair in their community in the 1980s and 90s. Together they had faced this nightmare as well.

Approaching the black glass skyscraper, Desmond skirted the main entrance and walked around to the garage on Mulberry Street. He slipped in through the side door, making his way directly to the elevator at the back of the entrance bay. He waved to Luis and Hector, the daytime garage attendants, as he passed the glassed-in cubicle where the attendants took shelter from heat and auto exhaust. Luis smiled at him in a way that was unmistakably flirtatious.

Hmm, he never smiled like that when I was older, Desmond thought wryly.

The elevator took Desmond high up in the building, and he stepped off onto the pale travertine floor of the reception area of Beckwith Investments. The young woman at the front desk offered him a tentative smile as he walked by. As he made his way to his office at the back of the suite, its windows looking out both over Newark and the Manhattan skyline ten miles distant, Desmond could see people looking up from their work; pausing in conversations to glance at him. One or two raised a hand in greeting, and he responded in kind, saying names aloud to those who made the effort to use his. The staff still wasn't entirely sure about the young

Mr. Beckwith, Desmond noted, and not for the first time. Since his sixty-five-year-old self had suddenly disappeared in early August, replaced by this uncanny younger version of the man they'd all come to know and trust in the years since 2001, Desmond could feel the anxiety that still rippled through his employees, in spite of his attempts to assure them that he was a good guy, too.

Hell, having to live up to your father is one thing. Having to live up to yourself is incredibly annoying.

He sighed as he approached the desk outside his office door, where his assistant, Jane Ashmun, sat peering at her computer screen. She looked up.

"Rough day?" she asked in faintly mocking sympathy.

He merely raised his eyebrows in response to her tone. "No, nice one in fact. I'm afraid I still find it rather irksome that the staff here continues to be unnerved by me."

Jane rolled her big dark eyes at him. "Wow, Desmond, I love it when you get all Basil Rathbone that way. Look, just try to cut the staff a break. They loved your father, and you look about eighteen. They haven't figured you out yet."

Jane Ashmun had figured him out; that was certain.

Chapter Three

Desmond had first run across Jane while she was temping at the recently relocated offices back in 2003. At first it had simply been her looks that caught his eye. She was small and slender, and strikingly pretty. Light cocoa-colored skin, wavy dark hair that reached to her shoulders, and huge dark eyes that could laser right into you. Her smile was terrifying, because it gave the impression she wasn't afraid of anything, and that she was equally willing to either embrace you as a friend or cut you off at the knees. And it didn't matter if you were the owner of the company or not.

Once his notice had been drawn to Jane, he had kept track of her; and he soon realized that she was not only very smart, but a hard worker and scrupulously honest. He learned from snatches of office gossip that she was divorced and was raising two small children–girls–on her own. Born and raised in Newark, she'd graduated from the Rutgers University's Newark campus, and had married her college sweetheart—a marriage that had too quickly soured with drug abuse and alcoholism. The temp work had been a necessity, helping her hold onto her kids, even as her husband continued his bad habits. None of this had mattered greatly to Desmond, but he had made sure she got a permanent position as soon as one opened. It was only after about a year that his ears had pricked up at overhearing that she was living with another woman, and that their relationship was more than just practical. This had made her even more interesting, and when Cathy, his old secretary – a title she had used since starting to work for him two decades earlier – retired, he had decided to offer Jane the position as his assistant.

He was amused by the look of suspicion on her face when he'd found her in the file room, digging in drawers full of old, pre-computer paperwork, and had invited her to have coffee with him.

"What would you want to have coffee with me for?" she had challenged him, flashing him a smile that was as much a warning as anything.

"You'll find that out over coffee." He grinned back at her, making her smile falter.

Slightly cowed by his unflinching gaze, she countered, "What if I say no?"

"Then we won't have coffee. I'm not going to strong-arm you. I promise you I have no sinister motives."

She gave in with a wry smirk and joined him at a nearby diner.

Newark was hardly a city of gourmet brasseries, but it had any number of excellent diners that served surprisingly strong coffee. As they settled into the worn vinyl booth, surrounded by expanses of beveled mirror that reflected a mauve-and-gray color scheme from the mid-1980s, Jane took the offensive once more.

"I wonder what the people in the office are saying about this."

Desmond suppressed a grin. "They'll say I'm going to offer you a job."

"Or that you're going to fire me."

"Over coffee? Not possible. Maybe they'll think I'm hitting on you."

This stopped her, and her brow furrowed in something approaching anger as the waitress brought them their cups of coffee. Once they were alone, she spoke.

"You'd better not be planning to hit on me."

"That's even less probable than my firing you. Not all fifty-nine-year-old executives chase after younger women. Let's go back to the first option."

"Cathy's job?" She huffed softly. "I haven't worked here that long and I have no experience as an executive assistant. I'm a glorified intern for God's sake." She sighed heavily, shaking her head with comic self-deprecation. "Maybe you'd better go ahead and hit on me."

This made Desmond laugh out loud. "Not bloody likely, since I have it on good authority that you're a lesbian."

That opened her eyes even wider. "And that's a reason to hire me to work for you? Sounds nice and liberal of you, Mr. Beckwith, but not particularly astute as an executive decision."

Desmond had only laughed again, more softly this time. She was exactly right.

"Well, as it happens, I'm gay myself. I like the idea of having a gay assistant."

He saw her start to object, and held up a hand to cut her off. "And it's not just that. I've watched you and asked about you. You're good. You're smart. You'll learn what you need to do." He paused. "And I'm sure you wouldn't be adverse to the rise in salary, with two little girls to care for."

Jane stared at him silently, as if trying to determine whether there was something less than generous behind his overture. "It's weird how English you sound sometimes. Why do you do that?"

It was his turn to be surprised. "No fair changing the subject. I've lived here a long time, but I was born in England."

In 1724, to be sure, but that's just a detail.

Then Desmond decided to take the bull by the horns to get them back on track. "Would you tell me about your partner?" Hesitating, he added: "And your children?"

Another long appraising stare, and Desmond saw her face change, soften; as if she'd made a decision to trust him.

"Dot – her name's Dorothy Brown – works at a warehouse here in Newark." She smiled shyly, looking down at her hands wrapped around the cup. "She's very different from me. She was at Millburn High while I was at Science High in Newark. We never knew each other growing up. She's beautiful...."

"Is she, would you say, pretty the way you are?" Seeing her expression darken again, Desmond gave Jane a look of complete innocence, spreading his hands in a gesture of surrender. "Gay, remember? Just trying to create an image of her. Really."

She smiled in spite of herself. "You are one inappropriate old white man, you know that, Mr. Beckwith?" Her smile broadened when she saw him wince at the age reference. "Dot is smaller than I am. And she's blonde and blue-eyed. I'd say her features are sharper, more chiseled than mine. Her eyes are big like mine are. She's also way fiercer than I am. I'm no slouch, as you might have noticed, but Dotty is ... she's a scrapper."

"I think I get the picture. And the girls? They must be pretty young still."

"Janay is five, and way too smart for her own good.

She started kindergarten this fall and is already terrorizing the teacher. Not that she's acting up or anything, but she likes to ask questions that tend to be a little off topic." She smiled with pleasure at this thought. "I keep getting these confused notes from school, but Janay won't talk about them and there's not much I can do."

"So your younger daughter must be what, three?"

"Right, Cassandra is three. She's the opposite of Janay. Sweet, compliant, easy. She's small for her age. Janay, of course, focused on that early and started calling her Speck, which makes her whine." She rolled her eyes and gave the sort of sigh Desmond imagined every long-suffering mother must give.

"Do they look like you?" Desmond knew he was stepping into tricky territory here, but he wanted to know.

She met his gaze for a moment. Apparently satisfied that his interest was genuine, she answered: "Yes, but they also favor their father. He's blond and blue-eyed, so the girls are fairly light-skinned – honey-colored. Gorgeous, really. They've got my curly hair, but with gold highlights from their dad." She looked at him again, squinting a bit as if studying his face. "And hazel eyes, sort of like yours."

Desmond took a small breath before continuing. "Sounds like the children you and Dorothy would have produced together, if you could have." Since this made Jane smile, he braved one more question. "Is their father – your ex – handsome?"

To his surprise, she smiled at this as well. "Is this a gay thing, Mr. Beckwith?"

It was his turn to roll his eyes. "No! You needn't answer. I realize this isn't very professional of me. But it's more than idle curiosity. I'm just trying to complete the picture. It's unforgivably nosy of me, sorry."

Pleased at her employer's discomfiture, Jane became confidential. "He is handsome. Or was, at least. You probably know that we broke up over his drinking. We partied pretty heavily after we were married. Not much in the way of drugs, but plenty of liquor. I stopped drinking after I got pregnant, but Dane kept on struggling. Finally, after Cassie was born, I couldn't take it any more. We split."

"I'm sorry. This must be painful."

She shrugged, but her eyes stayed on his. "It's history. He still sees the girls now and then. I give him credit – he's incredibly good with them. Other than that, he has his good moments and his bad ones. Mostly, I feel sorry for him."

The waitress poured them each another cup of coffee. Desmond inhaled the scent of the coffee, mingled with Jane's blood-fragrance and all the other smells the diner offered. He could feel the warmth radiate off her across the booth from him. The silence between them should have been awkward, but somehow it wasn't.

"So now, do I get to ask you intrusive questions about your private life?"

Had he not already been so pale, Desmond would have blanched.

"I suppose that it's only fair." He swallowed.

"Have you got a boyfriend? You're handsome. Must have been pretty hot when you were younger. I don't see you being alone somehow."

Desmond tried to smile, but found he couldn't. There was no malice in her question, but it had touched a tender spot. "I have been alone for rather a long time now. There was someone. A young man named Tony Chapman."

"A young man. Sounds like there was an age difference."

"Quite. Twenty years or so between us. But it's all moot now. Tony died nine years ago."

"Desmond. I'm sorry." Jane looked suddenly abashed, pained that her one dart had hit such an unfortunate bull's-eye.

Desmond reached over and put his hand on hers, giving it a gentle squeeze before letting go.

"And I have a son in England. He's still a teenager."

"A son? Um, how?"

"Why so surprised, Jane? After all, I might have once slept with someone of the opposite sex, as you have. But as it happens, this son was by arrangement. I've never been married."

"Why?"

"The same reason any man wants a child – an heir."

"What if it had been a girl?" Her eyes had narrowed again.

"Then she would be my heir. But he's a son. Also named Desmond." After a pause, he added, "Looks rather like me, too."

"Why not raise him yourself, here in New York?"

"I'm not really the fathering type, Jane. I fear I would have made a bad job of it."

An amiable stillness settled over them. Desmond realized that he felt strangely light. How long had it been since he told anyone about Tony?

Jane broke the silence first. "So, is the job still open?"

Without another word, she put out her hand and, shaking his, accepted the position. From that moment on she was his friend as well as his assistant. His gamble turned out well, and Desmond sometimes wondered how he'd managed without her.

Chapter Four

Of all the employees at Beckwith Investments, only Jane had gotten any forewarning of the elder Beckwith's pending demise in the summer of 2009. Having organized the usual legal and financial scheme which turned everything he had over to the fictitious son living in England, the sixty-five-year-old Desmond had spent a good deal of time dropping hints about feeling unwell; about mysterious doctor's appointments and late arrivals at the office. He had expected her to spread the rumors of poor health, but he had underestimated her fierce loyalty. She had kept his secret, guarding his privacy to the very end. His well-choreographed passing had been a shock to the company and had devastated Jane, much to Desmond's regret.

It had been Bill Lawrence who had called to break the carefully scripted news of Desmond Beckwith's sudden death at the age of sixty-five from an unnamed illness; and it had been Roger Deland, director of the firm's West Coast office, who had come east from San Francisco to take up temporary residence in the executive office and manage the transfer of power.

It had also been Roger who, familiar with the process after five lifetimes as Desmond's closest friend, had spent three days in the New York apartment with the prostrate Desmond. Roger had watched over him as he lay comatose in his carved ebony bed, seething with internal fire as his body regenerated to the age at which he had first been transformed. But, when Desmond had awoken from the ordeal, it was to Bill Lawrence's lined brown face and close-cropped gray hair. Roger had needed to tend to business matters related to Desmond's transitional finances, and Bill had volunteered readily, his love for Desmond jostling with his journalistic curiosity at being the only mortal ever to witness a vampiric rebirth.

As he had once before, right after Tony's death, Bill had offered his own blood to the newly reawakened vampire. Disoriented and hungering, Desmond had drunk from him gratefully. The taste of his old friend's blood, spiced with his humanity and heightened by the memories they shared, had filled Desmond's soul as well as his veins. Aware of his friend's age and relative frailty, Desmond had not taken a great deal of blood, but had clung to him after drinking, shuddering away the effects of the transformation in the arms of this loving comrade.

Roger, having made sure to feed the night before, gave Desmond a full measure of nourishment on his return from Newark that day. This, too, was part of their ritual, and in this way they had comforted each other into renewed youth time and time again. Roger's had been the first vampire blood Desmond had ever tasted, and its savor was precious to him beyond measure. Its power gave him the strength he needed; and its source assured him of the love he thought he needed almost as much.

When the twenty-one-year-old Desmond had first appeared at his father's Newark office to take up his position a week after his father's supposed death, Jane Ashmun had greeted him by the front reception desk and had shown him in. Trim and elegant in a tailored jacket and skirt, she had shown no trace of distress as they walked down the glass-walled corridor, turned heads and whispers following them as they proceeded.

When Jane had shown him to his desk, she had closed the door and turned to face him.

"Mr. Beckwith."

"Yes, Ms. Ashmun?" He looked at her, unsure what he was supposed to do.

"I just wanted you to know that I was very fond of your father, and I'm, um, very sorry that he's gone." Desmond could see the shimmer of tears in her eyes, and was about to speak when she continued.

"I was a good assistant to him. He trusted me when he had no reason to, and I think I repaid that trust."

"Yes, Jane, go on." Desmond noted her smile at his use of her first name.

"I know I have no right to expect to remain in this position, but I at least hope you'll give me a chance to prove myself." She swallowed and fell silent, eyes on her new boss. There was no fear in her face, but no defiance either.

Desmond had stood and walked around the desk, extending his hand as he went.

"Jane. My father adored you and relied on you. I wouldn't consider replacing you for anything."

And just like that he'd gotten her back again.

Returning from his visit to the museum, Desmond went into his office to check his email and phone messages. Not bothering with the interoffice phone, he called out to his assistant's office.

"Have them bring my car up, would you, Jane? I'm driving out to West Orange to see a house. I'll see you tomorrow."

"A house? In the suburbs?" She looked at him incredulously.

He beamed at his assistant through the open door as he sat down at his computer.

"Yes. In the suburbs. I'm beginning to think I need a little more greenery in my life."

Rather than take Route 280 to West Orange, Desmond decided to use surface roads to the gated enclave of suburban quiet known as Llewellyn Park. He had been reminded of the Park's existence just after the firm had relocated to Newark; an oasis of spacious properties and old houses in the middle of Essex County's densely developed suburban sprawl. Llewellyn Park had the distinction of being the first garden suburb in the nation, developed in the 1850s for New Yorkers and Newarkers who wanted to get away from the dirt and crime of the city. That much hadn't changed, but the Park itself was no longer out in the country. It sat a scant few miles from downtown Newark, and less than twenty from Manhattan. From Beckwith Investments it was a short drive up to Bloomfield Avenue in the city's north end, and thence into the sprawling complex of hills and lakes known as Branch Brook Park, designed by the Olmsted Brothers in the early twentieth century. From here, Park Avenue made a stately progress through the blue-collar neighborhoods of Newark and East Orange before terminating opposite the stone entrance gates to Llewellyn Park on Main Street in West Orange. Thomas Edison and his children had all lived in this park, and had once been driven in their carriages on this very same route to shop in Newark's great department stores.

The dark blue Volvo S70 was the first automobile

Desmond had ever driven himself. Having always ridden horses or been driven in carriages, Desmond had hired chauffeurs and rented limousines during his twentieth-century urban life. The move to Newark had made a personal car seem more logical. Learning to drive in his late fifties had been exhilarating and terrifying, and he had come to enjoy the challenge of negotiating city traffic. For the most part, he left his car in the Newark garage, taking the trains and subways into the city. When you hunted for blood in the late night shadows, wasting time finding a parking space was not in the program.

Desmond confirmed his appointment with the guard at the Park's whimsical turreted entry pavilion and made his way down winding tree-shaded lanes, craning his neck to see the unobtrusive street signs that seemed more designed to confuse outsiders than to assist residents. As he came around a bend, he spotted a small sign reading Oak Lane, just as the trees fell back and he found himself facing a long stone house across an expanse of clipped lawn.

Oakwood, as the realtor had rather breathlessly told him the house was named, was set a few hundred feet back from the road. Desmond had known its name since before the realtor was born, even if he hadn't seen Oakwood in nearly eighty years. As he approached the house along a graveled drive at one side of the main lawn, a drive lined with tall oak trees, he saw it from a historical distance he hadn't possessed on his first visit. It was intended to look English, but in a way that was filtered through the taste of 1920's America. The slate-roofed house was built of rough-cut light brown stone, which contrasted with severe dressed stone window frames and a fanciful pedimented entrance topped with an oval window. The effect was a mixture of Scottish highlands and Italian baroque that somehow worked. The drive divided, one branch curving behind the house to an attached garage; but Desmond took the left turn to the front entry. Here it passed beyond the house to a turnaround, where, Desmond noticed, a small castle-like playhouse had been built out of the same stone as the house.

That wasn't there before.

As he got out of the car, he looked back to the road. Not another building was visible. There was only grass and trees, and a barely audible thrum of Route 280 in the distance. Six miles from his office and it was like being back at Beckwith House in England where he had grown up. He took a deep breath, savoring the smell of mown grass and warm late-summer foliage, as well as the sharp undercurrent of scampering creatures filled with blood and life. Not even the Ramble in Central Park, one of his favorite hunting spots, was like this.

The last time Desmond had been to Oakwood, it had been brand new....

Chapter Five

Clutching the passenger door, Desmond leaned back into the tawny leather seat as Corbin Fletcher steered the massive Duesenberg into the narrow gravel drive and roared far too quickly down the allée of young oaks, scattering pebbles like buckshot. He deftly wheeled the glittering red machine into the sweep before the front doors of the house, and was out of the car before Desmond had a chance to catch his breath.

The tall front doors of the stone house opened, and a butler hurried down the steps to the convertible, greeting Fletcher as he went around to open the boot and lift out the young men's valises.

"Good afternoon, Mr. Corbin."

"Afternoon, Horton," Fletcher answered breezily as he surveyed the house, then turned and beamed at Desmond, who was climbing stiffly from the passenger seat of the Model J.

"Mrs. Fletcher has put you and Mr. Beckwith in the blue suite."

"Fine, fine." Fletcher, his wavy blond hair glinting in the autumn sunshine, fixed a smile on Desmond, his sky-blue eyes mischievous and happy.

"Don't mind sharing a bath, do you, Desmond?"

Desmond made a face at him, but said nothing until the butler had disappeared back into the house, staggering under the weight of the two heavy leather suitcases.

"You drive like a madman, Fletch. Were you trying to scare me to death?" For all his immortality, Desmond was still not entirely comfortable with automobiles. Even a vampire's body could be charred in the wreckage of one of these contraptions, were there to be an accident. Young Fletcher had broken every speeding limit between here and the exit from the Holland Tunnel, terrifying pedestrians and other motorists alike as they roared through Jersey City, then the reeking pig farms in the New Jersey meadows and the industrial outskirts of Newark, finally winding their way at full speed into the blessed cool and freshness of the suburbs.

Fletcher came over to him and wrapped him in a bear hug, kissing his cheek in a decidedly un-brotherly way, giggling as Desmond pushed him away.

"Don't, Fletch. You have no idea who's looking."

"Who's to look? It's only mum and dad and they'll be in the library drinking already." The younger man took Desmond's arm, and steered him into the house.

They proceeded straight across the entrance hall, dodging a French marble-topped table in the center, and into the paneled library. In spite of the warm day, there was a wood fire burning merrily, and Desmond just had time to register the room's similarity to his father's private study at Beckwith House before turning to greet his boyfriend's parents.

The senior Fletchers were elegantly dressed, beautifully groomed, and not a little tipsy already, although the hands on the ormolu mantel clock showed it to be just past five-thirty. They greeted Desmond with faintly slurred cordiality, and offered him an illegal gin martini, which he accepted thankfully.

Prohibition doesn't exist if you have enough money.

He drank his cocktail in silence, observing his hosts as they nattered amiably with their only son, outlining the social activities planned for the weekend. Apparently there was some sort of a big do at a neighbor's house later this evening, and then tomorrow they were motoring west out to Far Hills for the Essex Hunt. Desmond mentally rolled his eyes. He'd thought he'd left that behind in England in 1810. Outwardly, however, he maintained a bland serenity, until, martini finished, he and Fletcher were dismissed to their rooms to bathe and rest before the soiree at the Edisons.

As they climbed the curved staircase, Desmond suddenly registered the name that Mrs. Fletcher had spoken so offhandedly.

"What? *The* Edisons?"

"The very same. Old Thomas Alva is still kicking, but getting frail. His wife – Mina, the second Mrs. Edison, although she's been Mrs. Edison since long before I was born – is a lot younger and quite a charming hostess. You'll see."

"Heavens, I'm not sure I'm up to meeting a legend."

"Nonsense, Desmond. You never know who you'll meet at these Llewellyn Park parties. It's like a whole little village of rich people who are all in and out of each other's business. Given the economic conditions, it couldn't hurt to find a few more investors for your firm, am I right?"

"I suppose," Desmond answered softly, unnerved at the thought of this party turning into a working event.

As Fletcher led him down the long carpeted

corridor, Desmond studied the back of his handsome, athletic paramour of the moment. At twenty-five, Corbin Fletcher was four years Desmond's junior, a few years out of Yale, and spending most of his time enjoying the novel position of being unemployed and rich at the same time. He was smart, but thoughtless, seemingly unaffected by the increasing financial disaster that was overtaking their world. Meanwhile Desmond was in his small downtown offices daily, desperately holding together the financial enterprise he'd managed since the 1740s when his father died. The telegraph between the New York, London, and Paris offices had been clattering wildly for the better part of a year, as stock markets plunged and banks failed. Only Corbin Fletcher sailed on, cocooned in his parents' substantial fortune, which apparently had not been compromised by the Crash of '29 or the subsequent chaos in the financial world.

The Fletchers had moved into their newly completed Georgian mansion the summer before the Crash, papa Fletcher having fortuitously sold his substantial chain of retail outlets to a burgeoning national chain for a tidy twenty million dollars. In the year since, the new owner of the Fletcher stores had been forced to close half of them, thus cutting rather deeply into his investment. Desmond had been very useful to Fletcher in diversifying some of his family's windfall from the sale – funds, he reminded himself, that had remained remarkably solid in spite of the general upheaval. Desmond was good at what he did, and had the advantage of having more than a century and a half of personal experience in the vagaries of human financial history. After all, he had kept his bank afloat all through the French Revolution in the 1790s, and through every subsequent financial crisis in England and the United States as well.

Fletcher turned as he reached a doorway, and taking Desmond's hand, pulled him playfully into a small vestibule. A large bedroom opened on one side, a smaller one straight ahead, directly over the front door. To the right was a sparkling modern bathroom, its white tiles and nickel-plated fixtures aglow in the bright electric light. Desmond was impressed in spite of himself.

I really must update the bathrooms in the 4th Street house.

His train of thought was interrupted by Fletcher's embrace and a hard, hungry kiss. Desmond allowed himself to be carried along, running his tongue across his boyfriend's soft lips until Fletcher pulled away slightly and let go of him.

"Go mess up your bed and get undressed," he whispered conspiratorially. "And meet me back here in five minutes. I'll start the shower."

Desmond did as he was told, artfully disarranging the expensive linen sheets and rumpling the pillows on his bed as if he'd taken a nap. Then he stripped off his clothes and tossed them across a side chair by the dresser.

Padding into the bathroom, he found it already steamy from the hot water, and Fletcher standing in the tub, his head bent under the powerful stream coursing from the large nickel showerhead. He climbed in and wrapped his arms around his lover's torso, letting the heavenly wetness pour over him, easing his muscles and relaxing his jangled nerves.

Fletcher's body was softly muscled and golden-pink, the pale hair on his arms and legs all but disappearing in the flow of the shower. Desmond's own ivory-pale skin and dark hair stood in contrast against his lean, less opulent frame. Vampires didn't build muscle, but they didn't get fat, either, unless they were that way when transformed.

Desmond leaned into Fletcher's slippery back, nuzzling his shoulder and inhaling the intoxicating fragrance of lavender soap and hot coppery blood. Oh, how he wanted to release his canines and drink from his lover then and there. But he had never taken blood from Fletcher, and generally didn't like to drink from anyone with whom he had any sort of ongoing relationship. It just seemed too awkward. But he was sorely tempted. He felt his cock rise at the thought, filling at the closeness of Fletcher's body and encouraged by his scent.

Fletcher turned his head, his blue eyes locking onto Desmond's over his shoulder.

"Take me, Des. Now. Please." There was hunger in those eyes. Different from Desmond's hunger, but no less real for that.

Of course Desmond obliged him.

Dressed in evening clothes – it was only black tie, for this was an informal evening – the two young men walked, coyly hand-in-hand, through the deepening shadows of Llewellyn Park, along the winding lanes that passed for streets here. The parental Fletchers had decided, in consideration of the amount of gin they had consumed, to be driven the scant half-mile to Glenmont, Thomas and Mina Edison's estate, leaving the boys to walk. Fletcher was in a playful mood, having been well and carefully fucked by his dark-haired lover, who himself was feeling mildly anxious at the prospect of an entire evening among celebrated strangers looking for business prospects and worrying about his friend's potential indiscretion.

His eyes widened as they rounded a curve in the road and came upon the ungainly, fully illuminated Victorian bulk of Glenmont. It was painted muted terracotta red, visible only in the pools of electric light that flooded the porte cochère at the entrance. Numerous gables and tall chimneys serrated the fading twilight in the sky. Every window in its riotous profile was lit, from cellar to attic, and the sound of a small jazz orchestra could be heard coming from a large glassed-in verandah to one side of the house. Lots of people. Desmond shuddered slightly.

I can handle this.

As they pushed into the crowd of bodies filling the entrance hall, the visual complexity of the place mingled with a flood of human blood-scent that made Desmond feel slightly giddy. It always took him a moment to focus his senses in a mortal crowd, and he clutched at Fletcher's arm as they made their way through the throng. Eventually they found Mina Edison, a vivacious sixty-four, wrapped in a Fortuny gown and ensconced in a velvet-covered armchair in the reception room. She beamed at them warmly, lifted her powdered cheek with neighborly familiarity for Corbin to kiss and shook Desmond's hand with a surprisingly firm grip. After a little polite small talk, she waved them on. They moved into the long gloomy parlor, cluttered with the eclectic elegance of the past century.

Fletcher snorted softly, whispering in Desmond's ear, "They moved in here in the 1880s. Look at this mess, will you? Where did people find such god-awful things?"

Desmond smiled at him benignly, but bristled inwardly. Some of these "god-awful" things were pretty similar to what he had in his own little house in New York; things he'd chosen himself over the course of a century and had cherished as part of his life. Corbin's unthinking snobbery rankled, and Desmond was angered by this feckless young man's assumption that he recognized good taste based on nothing but an Ivy League education and a lot of new money. This was just one of the reasons Corbin had never been inside of Desmond's house. And, apparently, he realized uncomfortably, never would.

The young couple at last found the august inventor and millionaire seated in a faded chintz armchair at the back of the house in what was referred to quaintly as the "family room." There, beneath a bizarre wood and iron chandelier decorated with what looked like the heads of medieval maces, the Wizard of Menlo Park held grandfatherly court. He twinkled like some old Santa Claus figure rather than an international celebrity who had hobnobbed with presidents and with the likes of Henry Ford and Harvey Firestone.

Having done their social duty, the two handsome

young men had no trouble forging a path politely through the rest of the party, downing proffered glasses of illicit champagne while Fletcher snatched whatever delicacies passed by on silver trays.

Fletcher introduced Desmond to people he knew, and Desmond did what he had always done so well: he was charming and attentive without committing himself to anyone or anything. He smiled and listened and laughed politely when it seemed appropriate. He shook hands with men and women alike, and handed out vague compliments.

He also found himself pushing aside uncomfortable thoughts about Fletcher's complacence. At one point in the evening Corbin whispered a particularly sneering remark about an innocuous young man who had bored them with details of his struggling law firm. Desmond tried unsuccessfully to suppress a rising resentment over his feckless lover's blind presumption of his own social superiority. Desmond had never known a moment's want in his entire long life; but he had never taken for granted his need to work to maintain that security.

Desmond also had always been aware of the need to keep his doubly secret nature obscured from prying eyes. He studiously monitored his behavior around marriageable women lest his attentions be misapprehended and cause any hurt. Sexual discretion was a survival skill, and Corbin's carelessness in this regard grated on him. The handsome blond's easy flirtation with attractive young women at the party took on an almost sinister tint in Desmond's eyes. To quell his growing uneasiness, he drank. Even a vampire could drown his worries, to a point.

Corbin Fletcher, fresh out of Yale, had met Desmond Beckwith at the Oak Room bar in the Plaza Hotel in the summer of 1928, when the economic calamity that would hit the next fall had seemed unimaginable. They had been instantly attracted to one another, commencing their affair within an hour of locking eyes over porcelain teacups filled with tea-colored gin martinis. In those days, Desmond had worn his hair short and pomaded back in shining black waves. Corbin's gilded Arrow-Collar-Man beauty made him the instant center of attention in most social situations, and with Desmond's pale delicacy beside him, they had become a memorable pair in New York's jazz clubs. Desmond had been pleased that Fletcher seemed not to be emotionally needy, in fact rather the opposite.

Fletcher made no real secret of his taste for men, something that shocked and frightened Desmond, used to lifetimes of caution and discretion. On the other hand, Fletcher was also a notorious roué, and his persistent habit of bedding languid debutantes during their three-year friendship had both camouflaged the nature of their bond and had also deeply wounded the young vampire. Desmond had never experienced anything like monogamy with anyone since Jeffrey Chapman; but he had never been one to desire intimacy with more than one person at a time. Corbin chided him for being Victorian in his prudery, and Desmond simply buried the pain.

As the Edison soirée wound down, the young men returned to the Fletcher house the way they had come, although rather the worse for all the alcohol in their systems. Fortunately, Desmond's night vision kept them from doing themselves any mischief as they stumbled giggling through the dark undergrowth of the Park's sylvan setting. They arrived at the house to find it dark; the Fletchers having returned earlier to tuck in for the night. They let themselves in through the unlocked front door and snuck, shushing and poking each other as they tried, with modest success, to get up to their rooms without waking the household.

After locking the outer door and leaving his evening suit in a jumbled mess on the floor next to Corbin's, Desmond climbed into bed naked and snuggled into the strong, warm arms of his drowsy boyfriend. Fletcher chortled softly, swallowing a little belch, and nuzzled Desmond's ear.

"Say, Desmond, you're a pip." His lips moved along Desmond's neck to his shoulder.

"Thanks, Fletch. You're something yourself."

"Wanna have another go? I'll catch if you wanna pitch." The blond man giggled again at his own coy joke, settling his head on Desmond's lightly furred chest.

Desmond was silent, but reached down to caress Fletcher's groin, only to find his prick fully at rest, nestled contentedly against the velvet sac of his scrotum.

"Doesn't seem like you're much in the mood, my dear. Perhaps we'd best wait," he said softly, running his hand gently up the silky skin of the other man's stomach. The aroma of Fletcher's blood, with faint undertones of gin and champagne, was very enticing, but somehow Desmond couldn't bring himself to be aroused even by that. He continued to stroke Fletcher's belly, until he felt the other man's breathing settle into a low, even rumble. Then, gently rolling him onto his side without waking him, Desmond slipped out of the bed, gathering up his clothes, and went into his own room, shutting the door behind him.

Chapter Six

He and Fletcher Corbin had parted, amicably enough, a short while after their awkward weekend. Desmond had just chalked it up to experience, and in fact had been emotionally detached enough to drink from Fletcher on their last evening out. After an agreeably drunken break-up conversation, he had cornered him in a booth at a repulsive speakeasy in Greenwich Village and had taken his fill, surrounded by unlawful partiers, his shimmering regret at the failure of another relationship quenched in the fiery bliss of his now-former lover's blood.

Unlike Robbie Ballantine, however, Fletcher had not succumbed to despair and loneliness. Rather, he had given in to his parents' expectations and had married an appropriately beautiful and well-connected society girl. Desmond had attended their wedding at Saint Thomas's on Fifth Avenue in 1932. He shivered slightly at the memory, remembering the look of ill-concealed sadness in Fletcher's eyes as he greeted Desmond at the reception.

It was Fletcher's son, now in his seventies and retired to Palm Beach, who had offered Oakwood for sale.

As Desmond stood gazing off into the afternoon sun, one of the paneled oak doors opened and the realtor, Janet, came down the broad marble steps onto the gravel to greet him. Athletic and blond, in a Chanel suit and shiny patent leather Ferragamo pumps, she wrung his hand and ushered him into the dark hall like a maitre d' showing him to his table.

"Now, the owners have already moved out. What they've left here is all available as part of the deal – at extra cost of course. And there will be upgrades needed, because the bathrooms haven't been renovated since forever and the kitchen is rather dated, but I'm sure you'll find that with a little work …"

"I think I'd just like to look on my own, if you don't mind," Desmond said quietly, cutting her off. "I believe the brochure said the house was designed by Delano and Aldrich?"

"Um, yes. I think so." She looked at him, a faint panic lighting her eyes. Apparently no one had ever bothered about this detail.

Desmond just put out his hand and smiled at her, knowing that he was good-looking enough to confuse her if he tried. He'd drink her blood to shut her up if that didn't work. "Thank you. I'll meet you out front in, say, an hour?" He locked eyes with her, and she stared at him briefly, before accepting the handshake and suddenly deciding to rifle through the papers in the folder she was carrying. Desmond left her to find her way out and began to explore.

The entrance hall was an oblong octagon, sheathed in Louis XVI paneling of waxed oak. It seemed slightly at odds with the severe exterior, but was very beautiful. Behind him, facing a walled courtyard with a swimming pool, was the walnut-paneled library he remembered from this previous visit, done in the English style of Desmond's own childhood in the 1720s. Down the hallway leading left from the entrance, past a slender spiral staircase, was a vast Georgian living room that would easily hold a hundred people, and beyond that a charmingly peculiar 1920's sunroom with French doors out onto the lawn, Spanish-tiled walls and a tinkling fountain. Down the other hallway, to the right of the entry, was a large Louis XV style dining room with an ornate marble mantelpiece and a huge French rock-crystal chandelier. All of the rooms had fireplaces, wide multi-paned windows and what appeared to be their original light fixtures. A surprising amount of furniture and even bric-a-brac had been left behind. Some of it he vaguely remembered from 1930, but none of it related to what he had collected for his house or his apartment in New York, and Desmond wondered what to do about it. Some of it was quite lovely. Perhaps he should buy it ... And with that thought he realized that he already wanted this place. Badly.

There were two dressing-room-lavatories, his and hers, also off the entrance hall, and a sprawling ugly kitchen made for servants and upgraded badly in French provincial in the 1970s. Desmond had never renovated his own kitchen in New York, so it hardly mattered. Viking stoves and Sub-Zero refrigerators didn't mean much when you drank blood to survive.

The upstairs of the house had lower ceilings, but equally large windows, letting the dappled late-afternoon sunlight flood in. Five bedrooms with fireplaces and private bathrooms – which, Desmond noted, far from being "outdated," were still the beautiful 1920's tiled bathrooms with heavy porcelain fixtures. There was also a paneled dressing room for "him," a mirrored dressing room for "her," and a spacious sitting room with its own fireplace off the master bedroom. The large guest room over the library had a bowed wall overlooking the pool.

This will be Roger's room, when he comes to visit. And the one on the front with the blue wallpaper will be Bill and Alex's.

Over the kitchen was a warren of perfectly nice but small maids' rooms—five in all, sharing a single bathroom and having a narrow staircase down to the service area. Desmond mentally moved a few walls around and figured that he could create a pleasant three-bedroom apartment here – for someone. He certainly wasn't going to have five maids. He had never even had a cleaning woman for his house in New York. He'd done all his own housework for 170 years, little as that was. Bill had finally shamed him into hiring a cleaning woman when he'd bought the huge flat in the Dakota on Central Park West. Bill had insisted that he needed to start trusting people. After Tony's death, Desmond had started listening to Bill more, because he'd been so lost.

Before his hour was up, Desmond returned to the front drive, where Janet was hovering uncertainly. Her face lit up when he came down the broad marble steps from the front door.

"Now, you know, there are seven acres with the house and flower gardens over there." She pointed toward the playhouse. "And there's an attached three car garage with a driveway that comes in from the back road." she added, pointing in the other direction.

"How much was the price again?" Desmond asked politely, make mental calculations.

"Um, what?"

"The price?"

"Oh, well, they're *asking* three million dollars."

"I'll offer two and three-quarters. Cash. I'll need to make renovations. And the left furnishings?"

"Oh. Um. That was another half million above the asking price."

"Three million. Cash. Call my assistant, Ms.

Vampire in Suburbia

Ashmun, at the office, and she'll take care of whatever needs doing. Just let her know when the closing will be."

Desmond held out his card to the startled woman, shook her hand, and climbed back into his Volvo. She waved at him vaguely as he turned the car around and headed down the oak allée.

What in hell am I going to do with a huge house? What the bloody hell am I thinking?

But as he steered the car expertly back down Park Avenue to Newark, Desmond found he couldn't keep the smile off his face.

He pulled the car up to the booth in the garage, left it running, and climbed out. Luis came over, saluting him with a smile, and took Desmond's place behind the wheel.

As he was about to drive off, Desmond asked him, "Where's Hector?"

"Oh, he had to leave early. Take his daughter to the doctor. It's no problem, I can cover till the night shift comes on. Most people have gone home already."

As the car roared into the dim bowels of the garage, Desmond stood and watched it go. Luis was all alone. The garage was quiet at this hour.

And all the excitement about the house had made Desmond hungry.

Moving quickly, Desmond followed the sound of the retreating automobile, descending the ramp to the lower level. He arrived just as Luis cut the engine and opened the door.

"Mr. Beckwith. Uh, hi." The young man stood and hesitated by the open car door. Desmond took in his honey-colored skin, and the long lashes that made his deep brown eyes childlike. Luis was handsome. Almost pretty. His hair was cut short, but it was wavy and longer on top.

"Sorry to startle you, Luis. I, ah, think I left something in the back seat." He moved up close as Luis turned to look into the interior.

"I don't think I see anything in there Mr. Be –" He

stopped short, finding himself face to face with Desmond, whose hazel eyes were focused on his own.

"Never mind, Luis," said Desmond softly, his voice quiet, but focused like his eyes. "I must have been mistaken."

He moved still closer, his eyes never leaving Luis' gaze. He could feel the other man's breath on his face. A mild scent of garlic and tomato mingled with the sweetness of whatever gel he used in his hair and the gentle musk of his sweat and his skin. Desmond breathed in. And there it was, below all the other aromas, the blood. Deep and coppery, pulsing through the endless maze of vessels, into the young man's heart and out again, rich with oxygen.

Desmond's lips brushed the softness of the other man's mouth. He flicked his tongue gently across the opening between his lips, eliciting a faint groan from Luis. But he didn't linger. He moved his lips across the stubble of the jawline and down to the smooth silky skin of his neck. He could hear the blood rushing through the carotid artery. He could feel its beat with his lips as they touched the tender surface.

Desmond's lower jaw dropped slightly, and two delicate ivory fangs extended downward as his canines grew. He moved his head slightly upward, and with a precision learned over centuries plunged his teeth into Luis's neck, clamping his lips over the wounds as the blood began to stream out. Luis groaned again, but Desmond wrapped his arms around him, supporting him as he drank.

The blood filled his senses, filled his body with the sensation of fire. His heart began to beat in rhythm with Luis' own, speeding up with the other man's instinctual fear, then slowing down as their lives merged, as the blood flowed, as Desmond fed his hunger.

This was life. This was the best part of being a vampire. Feeling the life in your host. Feeling his heart beat, feeling him give himself up to you, to let you live. There was no idea of killing Luis in Desmond's mind.

The very idea of feeding to kill was grotesque to him. There were vampires, he knew, who enjoyed the kill; but they were no better than murderers to Desmond, putting the safety of their whole race at risk for a fleeting thrill.

He shuddered. Feeling a body die in your arms. Feeling the life ebb away. There was no pleasure in that. That was hell. Desmond had only experienced that once in his many years on earth, fighting for his own life in a midnight park in revolutionary Paris. He never wanted to feel that again.

It didn't take long. Desmond's fangs withdrew, and before removing his lips from Luis' neck, he ran his tongue lovingly over the openings to close and heal them. Still holding him, he lowered the unconscious garage attendant back into the Volvo's driver seat and settled him comfortably. He made sure the ignition key was in Luis' hand, carefully posed in his lap. Then, leaving a gentle kiss on his forehead, Desmond shut the car door and moved silently away into the shadows.

Chapter Seven

Bill and Alex were waiting for him in their usual booth. The Italian restaurant on the Upper West Side served adequate but unsurprising food to a devoted clientele that had survived the transformation of their neighborhood. The young professionals and urban-hip families who filled the West Side now avoided Solano's. It was too dark, too old-fashioned, the portions too large, the pasta not *al dente* enough. It didn't matter. There were plenty of bright, chic, edgy places for them to eat; plenty of popular chains to which they could drag their perfect children. New York was a big place.

Desmond felt, without looking, heads turn as he pushed through the padded leather door into the fragrant, dim interior. He felt oddly out of place in his old haunt, realizing that he was probably twenty years younger than the next youngest patron. No one recognized the beautiful dark-haired youth who strode purposefully toward the secluded half-round booth in the back. At sixty-five, Desmond Beckwith had been lithe and handsome, elegant and restrained. Rather formal, but not cold. Vampires aged gracefully, and never lost their strength; it was part of the camouflage of survival for his kind. But the old Desmond was no match for the younger model. After each regeneration he felt the exhilaration of his attraction, the power of his looks to bring others within range of his voice and his eyes. He was unsure whether or not being a vampire gave him some intangible allure that amplified his physical attributes. He did know that as he aged, both of his needs, for sex and for blood, grew less urgent, less demanding. This was part of survival as well. But with Luis' blood fresh in him, he felt powerful, almost magnetic. His keen sight could make out the hungry glitter of eyes, male and female, in the relative darkness. He smiled at the odd balance: they made him hungry, he made them hungry – if not for the same thing.

Bill tried to stand as he approached, but Desmond motioned him to sit and slid onto the red-leather banquette next to his old friend. He reached over the table to offer an awkward handshake to Alex Duquesne, Bill's partner. Partner seemed the perfect term in this instance. Boyfriend would have been far too undignified.

Bill Lawrence and Alex Duquesne had been together for five years, more or less since the three of them had turned sixty. They had all been part of the same small circle of gay friends since the mid-1960s, drawn together at first more because of their orientation than any shared interests. Bill had been Desmond's only really close friend, but even one mortal friend had been one more than Desmond had ever had before. Alex had built up a successful interior decorating business in the 1970s, one of the few run by a black man at the time. As a young man in the sixties, trained at Parsons and the New York School of Interior Design, he had struggled to get a job with a New York firm, finally overcoming the ingrained prejudice of rich white clients with his slender prettiness and warm personality. Desmond had always, and to his own shame, found Alex a little too fey for his taste. He and Bill both had teased Alex, nicknaming him Bernard, after seeing the lone non-white character in Mart Crowley's play, *The Boys in the Band.* To his credit, Alex had always been forgiving and friendly, and during the brief happy time when Tony Chapman had been part of Desmond's life, willingly accepted the younger man into their circle. When his own partner – a deeply closeted CPA from Queens – had died right after 9/11, Alex and Bill had started "keeping company," as Bill quaintly put it. That friendship had grown into something deeper, and Desmond found himself envying them now, feeling more alone than ever in contrast to their evident contentment.

Alex was slightly lighter-skinned than Bill, but he kept his head shaved. There were few wrinkles on his elegantly sculpted face, and somehow his trim frame had managed to avoid the drift and sag that tortured older gay men. Thin as a rail, over six feet tall, he was still pretty, even at 64, and still fey; but Desmond had long since gotten over his hang-ups regarding masculinity. When the new Desmond had appeared on the scene, Alex had followed his lover's lead and accepted the handsome young white man as a friend. If he ever wondered at the fact that Bill seemed just as attached to the young Desmond as he had been to his father, he never said anything.

A bottle of strong fruity Chianti arrived at the table, and the three filled their glasses. Bill and Alex ordered appetizers, and turned to look expectantly at Desmond.

"Well?" asked Bill, his voice a deep rumble.

"Well, it appears that I've bought a house in New Jersey." Desmond couldn't help beaming at the startled expressions.

"What kind of house?" asked Alex, suspiciously, as if Desmond had announced that he'd bought something potentially lethal.

"Oh, a pretty large one. In Llewellyn Park. Really beautiful. Built in 1929. Delano and Aldrich. Seven acres. A pool. Three car garage."

"Good God, Des. Just *how* big?" Bill was clearly alarmed.

Desmond hesitated, knowing this would set them both off.

"About twenty rooms."

Bill looked dumbstruck, while Alex just threw back his head and laughed, showing a dazzling array of still-perfect white teeth.

"Oh, my dear young man, you have really embraced the corporate executive role, haven't you," Alex chortled, reaching across the table to caress the back of Desmond's hand. He was touched by the gesture of support for what was clearly an impulsive move on his part.

"And how are you going to manage a place like that?" ask Bill, his voice getting paternal.

"Like I've always managed ..." and then Desmond faltered, seeing Bill's eyebrows shoot up. He had stepped into dangerous territory, forgetting that he was not the man he'd been two months ago. He took a swig of his wine, searching for the right words.

"Um, my father had a house in the city, and he managed."

"Yes, Des, but that was a townhouse. No garden, ten rooms. He did all his own cleaning." Bill knew Desmond's old house on 4th Street well, and Desmond's peculiar housekeeping habits, too.

"Look, I know it was impulsive, but I fell in love with it. I need some space." He turned to Bill, looking him in the eye, hoping that he'd get the meaning behind the words.

"I need to be different from my father. I'll probably keep the apartment, but it's unnerving to live there, surrounded by all of the things he collected. None of it's *me*."

Bill's amused expression told him he was winging it pretty well. He turned to Alex, realizing that he was explaining himself to Bill and creating the backstory of his new life for Alex.

"I want something else, something closer to where I work. And my father always talked about the house in England that the family used to own. This made me think of that."

A light seemed to go on in Alex's eyes.

"Soooo, it looks like you'll be needing a decorator, won't you?" he asked, swirling his wine as he gave Desmond an arch look. Out of the corner of his eye, Desmond saw Bill drop his eyes to the tablecloth and hide a smile behind his hand.

"I suppose so." He grinned at Alex, playing along. "Hey! *You're* a decorator, aren't you?"

"Oh, I'm way too retired to take on a job this big." He took a long pull at his wine. "But there is a young associate I'm grooming. He's sort of new to the firm, but I think he has a lot of talent. He has a great sense of period."

Desmond's attentive silence encouraged him.

"His name's David Parker. Just a couple of years older than you, I'd guess."

Bill perked up at this remark. "I met him at your office, didn't I? Blond boy? Big brown eyes? Very cute as I recall."

"Don't get Desmond's hopes up, Bill, he has a boyfriend."

Oh great, now I have them matchmaking for me.

The fact that he was gay, as his father had been, had never even come up. Bill must have told Alex, and if Alex found it odd, he hadn't mentioned it. Desmond rolled his eyes but didn't comment.

Instead he asked, "Could I set up an appointment to meet with him at the house next week some time?"

"Of course. I'll talk to him on Monday and have him

call Jane to place it on your calendar." Everyone, even Desmond's friends, knew that you had to talk to Jane.

From there the evening progressed as it had before the old Desmond became the new Desmond. They talked. Bill and Alex ate the ample food and drank the comforting Chianti. Desmond drank with them. Just like old times.

Enjoying the cool evening, Desmond walked east to Central Park and headed south toward his apartment. As he approached 72nd Street, the gabled outline of the Dakota loomed, its tawny brick and brownstone mellow in the glare of the streetlights. A subway station emerged right at the corner, a feature Desmond loved about this building. Most of his fellow residents wouldn't be caught dead in the subway, but Desmond used it every day to get to his office in Newark, taking the C down to Penn Station, and then the commuter train to Penn Station Newark. It was the easiest commute in the world.

As he walked through the deep arched carriageway, he waved to the concierge, seated in the little bay window that was his guard post. The massive iron gates released with a buzz, and he crossed the inner courtyard to his entrance in one of the corners.

He'd lived in a sprawling flat here for fourteen years, having tried a modern penthouse in Bill Lawrence's midtown high-rise for several years following Tony Chapman's death. The old townhouse on 4th Street had become a tomb, full of too many memories, too much past happiness and current loneliness to bear. At his friends' urging, he had given it to the City as a museum, endowed it, and moved on. He'd found he wasn't ready for the sleek modernity of the twentieth century, and had instead bought his apartment here, furnishing it in the style that would have been modern in the 1880s when the building was new. Ornate rosewood and ebony furniture, shimmering silk plush draperies and deep-piled Oriental carpets had turned the flat into an opulent retreat, a place where he could start again without entirely abandoning his affinity for the past.

Desmond unlocked the paneled mahogany door and made his way through the dark apartment. Even without the faint glow from outside, he had no trouble seeing; his immortal eyes able to distinguish even color in the gloom. As he passed his library, he saw a blinking red light – his answering machine. He pulled off his necktie as he walked over to the desk and pushed the play button.

"Hello, Mr. Beckwith? Uh, Desmond? It's Oliver Cameron here, from the Newark Museum? I, um, realized I hadn't given you my home number with my card, so I just thought I'd leave it for you." Desmond smiled as Cameron left a number with a suburban Essex exchange and said a slightly flustered good-bye. He jotted it down and deleted the message, noting it had come in during the afternoon. Then he picked up the phone and pressed the numbers in the note.

Cameron answered after two rings.

"Oliver? It's Desmond Beckwith."

"Oh. Hi! Gosh, I didn't expect you to call me back." The sudden silence that followed this remark suggested to Desmond that Cameron was blushing furiously, and tried to imagine the rising tide of warm blood suffusing his fair skin, making the freckles disappear, remembering his scent from their first meeting.

"As it happens, I had been thinking about calling you, so I was glad to have your private number."

"Ah. Good, then. So what can I do for you?" Desmond heard Cameron making an effort to adopt a professional tone.

"Well, it seems I've decided to purchase a house in Llewellyn Park. I was rather hoping you'd be willing to go there with me and give me some advice. I'm afraid it hasn't been updated in quite a while, and I thought your insight might keep me from going astray."

"Really? Which house?"

"Do you know the Park that well? Then again, I

guess you would, after all this time. It's a place called Oakwood."

"Wow, Oakwood? Actually, I do know that house; it used to belong to a trustee of ours. I think his parents built the place. I'd heard he was finding it a bit daunting."

"Well, I'm afraid I'll be living there all alone, and I'm going to need some wise counsel."

"It's an amazing place. I'd love to go through it with you." There was a momentary silence, as if he were checking a calendar. "I'm sort of tied up the next two days. Would Monday work?"

"That'd be fine. I'm in New York for the weekend in any case, but I'll be back in Newark on Monday. Would later in the day be good – so as not to interfere with your real work?"

He could hear the laughter in Oliver's response. "Let's just say that if I can get you to become a member of the museum, I can legitimately call it work-related activity."

They made their good-byes, and Desmond put down the phone gently, wondering to himself whether he'd done the right thing.

Chapter Eight

On Monday afternoon, Desmond picked up Oliver at the museum and together they retraced the old route from Newark to Llewellyn Park. They didn't talk much during the drive, but Desmond felt perfectly at ease. He enjoyed watching Oliver survey the motley mixture of buildings along the way. It was as if he were watching a movie, the way his eyes moved across the scene as it unrolled past them. His only difficulty was that he continued to think of the engaging redhead next to him as a younger man, when he had to be, at least now, quite a bit Desmond's senior. Getting accustomed to being young again always took some mental realignment. It wasn't just the physical renewal; it was also readjusting your perspective on the world. Cameron still *felt* like a young man to the lingering memories of the elder Beckwith.

The sun was heading west as they pulled into the gravel sweep before the front doors. Janet emerged from the house and greeted him with the same vigorous handshake as on their first meeting, which she applied equally to Cameron's extended hand. Desmond introduced his new friend by his professional title, which was met with a tilt of the head and a tight little smile from the realtor.

"I've heard the Newark Museum is just lovely. I really need to get there sometime."

Desmond saw Cameron beam at her. "And how long have you been in real estate?"

"Oh, over twenty years. I've been in the ten-million-dollar club in Essex County three years in a row!" the realtor reported proudly.

"That's fantastic," enthused Cameron, his face alight with what looked to Desmond like real pleasure at her accomplishment.

Janet handed the key to Desmond, telling him that this was his to keep, and that one of the security guards from the Park's private force would come by later and check on the house. Clearly, she wasn't going to risk displeasing the easiest buyer she'd ever had.

As the realtor's black Mercedes sedan crunched down the oak allée, Cameron turned to Desmond, his eyebrows raised and his pretty mouth set in a thin line.

"I hate her."

Desmond couldn't hold back a laugh at this unexpected comment.

"I can't tell you how often I hear that. People who live right here in the county and think of themselves as cultured and art-lovers; and yet haven't bothered to take a look at the largest museum in the state, right in their own backyard. It's all an anti-Newark attitude, and it drives me crazy." Then he flushed and looked down at the driveway. "Sorry, I should hardly be venting this way. It's not appropriate."

"It's okay, Oliver, I understand. Newark's had a hard go of it."

Oliver shook his head as if to clear his thoughts. His russet waves glinted in the lowering sunlight. Desmond felt himself wanting to find out if his hair was as soft as it looked.

Instead, he said, "Let's go in, shall we?"

Together they explored the house just as Desmond had the week before, but this time he reveled in having someone to talk with. Desmond had been in houses like this one when they were new, and he had memories of how they were finished and decorated that filled his imagination as he tried to see this place as his. He was astonished at how well Oliver knew the period as well. He clearly was familiar with the work of the architects – and other architects of the time.

"I have to say, I'm impressed," he remarked as they looked over the dining room.

"Sorry to sound like such a know-it-all," answered Oliver diffidently. "It all had to do with working on the Ballantine House. I got very obsessed with appropriate finishes. It's not just paint color, but the way paint is mixed and applied. It changes over time, both with taste and with technology."

Of course Desmond had witnessed these changes firsthand. But he remembered how intensely fascinated by all of this kind of detail Tony had been, how enraptured with the townhouse he'd been. Eventually, Tony had understood why Desmond knew what he knew. It had been one of the most precious parts of their short time together.

As they came back into the entrance hall, heading for the stairs, Oliver ran his hands across the marquetry front of a chest.

"Have the owners not completely moved out yet? There seems to be quite a bit of furniture left."

"Ah, yes. Well, I sort of bought what they didn't want to move. Apparently some of it was in the house when it was new. But other pieces were brought in by the last decorators who worked on the house in the 1970s."

Oliver didn't seem to react to that last information. He continued to stare at the chest and ran his hands across its ornately inlaid surfaces. Desmond had seen curators and antique dealers get down on their knees and shine flashlights up under furniture to see if it was legitimate, but he'd never seen this sort of hands-on technique.

He watched as the redhead skimmed strong fingers over the ormolu mounts, the marble top, even opening the drawers and passing his hands along the bottom and sides. He looked up, suddenly aware of how closely Desmond was watching him, and once again the scent of his blood reached out as it turned his cheeks pink.

"Sorry. I get very into this." He seemed to falter under Desmond's gaze. "This piece seems like it's mostly of the period, although there was a good deal of restoration early in the twentieth century. The drawer pulls, for example, were made much more recently than the rest of the piece, apparently here in New York. The marble top is original, I think. Some of the drawer bottoms have been replaced, but that's pretty common."

He dropped his gaze again, and moved to another similar chest across the hall. After a few minutes of the same odd procedure, he looked back at Desmond.

"This piece is completely new. I don't think it's any older than the 1960s." He looked over at the chest he'd examined previously. "I suppose this one was found to create a sort of a pair with that one. The decorator – or the client – didn't care enough, or didn't want to spend the money or time to find a period mate."

"Should I get rid of them?" Desmond asked. This was all so different than anything he'd owned in the past 170 years.

"Well, that depends." Oliver hesitated. "Do you like them?"

Desmond laughed softly. "Should I?"

"Please, Desmond, this is *your* house. Are you a

collector? Do you care if everything is perfect, or do you just want it to look right?"

"Just look right, I guess. I really haven't thought it through. I just know I'm not bringing anything from my New York apartment." At Oliver's quizzical look, he continued. "I have a flat in the Dakota. It's all Aesthetic movement, Modern Gothic, Anglo-Japanese. To suit the building." It was his turn to falter at Oliver's wide-eyed expression. "It was all my father's. It wouldn't look right here."

"Wow. That sounds awesome. But you're right. Actually, a 1920's house is ideal to work with, because you can really put any sort of period look in it and it will suit. Reproductions are just as appropriate as antiques. It's just that most decorators have a very modern sensibility, and they don't necessarily understand the 1920's as a period in itself."

"I am using a decorator. Sort of a friend of a friend. Should I be worried that he'll mess things up?" Desmond had never let anyone else decorate for him, and he'd been having second thoughts about his decision to work with Alex's associate.

Oliver granted him a wide smile that embraced his eyes.

"I think you have an uncanny sense of what this house should be. I'm sure you'll honor it, and from what little I know of you, I don't think you'll let any decorator run roughshod over you."

Once more, Desmond was struck with the way his new friend was able to make you feel good, to feel self-assured, without resorting to flattery. There was no coyness in his words; only sincerity. This was not some obsequious curator pandering to a potential donor; this was professional candor, and it was more flattering that any calculated praise would have been.

"Thanks for your confidence," he replied, feeling weirdly thrilled at the curator's tribute.

They continued their exploration, climbing the winding staircase to the bedrooms. Desmond talked warmly of his plans for the various rooms, and the friends he saw staying in them. He reviewed his idea for renovating the servants' rooms into an apartment, and was relieved to see that Oliver didn't object.

"It doesn't make sense to freeze a living house in time, you know. The Ballantine house's maids' rooms were all gutted in the 1920's when the place became offices. There's no way I'd try to restore them. You don't plan on having four maids and a cook, do you?"

"No, of course not."

"These days, a housekeeper or a private chef might expect to be treated more professionally, especially if they have a spouse or a family, even."

"That's good to know. All I have in New York is a cleaning woman who comes in once a week."

"And for parties?"

"Caterers."

"And just your friends?"

Desmond had to smile at the cross-examination.

"For them, I've actually learned to cook."

Their tour finished, they locked the front door and left the keys with the guard at the Park entrance. Following Oliver's directions, Desmond steered the Volvo through the tree-lined streets, heading two communities south until they came to Oliver's town.

"How about we have dinner somewhere?" he suggested. "There's a little place I go quite a lot. Nothing fancy, but the food's good."

"That would be nice." They exchanged smiles, but Desmond felt compelled to be candid. "I need to explain, beforehand, that I have a very messed-up metabolism."

"Oh?" The hazel eyes widened in concern.

"It's rather hard to explain."

Again with the lies. I went all through this with Bill and our friends, and then Tony.

"Basically I eat alone, and drink with friends."

Oliver just smiled at him. "So you'll drink with me?"

"Gladly."

"Good, then."

True to promise, it was a charming little place, and they shared a bottle of white wine while Oliver ate a Caesar salad with salmon. The conversation was light and pleasant. They talked about the new house, their jobs, the Museum, living in suburbia. Oliver had never lived in the city, except his two years in graduate school at NYU. He had always wanted to live in a town like this, with trees and lawns and kids playing in the street. For all of the tender echoes of Tony Chapman, Desmond could see that this was a very different man. Confident, proud of what he'd done with his life, there seemed to be none of the lack of self-assurance from which Tony had initially suffered. Yet Oliver wasn't boastful or arrogant. He was close to his parents and his one sibling, an older brother, who lived a couple of hours away in Connecticut. Everyone was fine with his being gay, and he loved being an uncle to his brother's children.

Desmond felt comfortable with Oliver, enjoying the aura of contentment that radiated in his words, in the way he moved, in the way those ginger-lashed eyes didn't hesitate to meet his own. It wasn't just his good looks; he had a personality that drew you to it, that engaged you and made you feel included. He felt as if he'd known Oliver for a long time, although he knew perfectly well that he'd never met anyone quite like him before.

After the meal – at which Oliver refused any dessert, patting his perfectly flat belly in a way that created a stir in Desmond's own stomach – they drove a short distance to a tidy little colonial-style house. In the fading light, it looked like a postcard. A neat boxwood hedge enclosed the small front garden, and a towering tree arched gracefully up by the sidewalk in front.

"Is that an elm?" Desmond asked.

"You recognize it?"

"Sure. Why wouldn't I?"

"I'm so fond of that tree. Most of the American elms died before I was born. There was a terrible blight in the 1960s. Fortunately, this town had mostly been planted with maples and oaks when it was developed in the 1920's, so this one elm never got diseased."

He looked right at Desmond, his head cocked slightly, his brows raised. He was adorable. "Most people your age don't know what an elm is. Or care. Will you come in for a drink?"

Flustered at yet another scrap of inappropriate knowledge he'd let slip, Desmond agreed and followed Oliver up the front steps and through the dark green front door.

Inside, the house was just what Desmond would have expected. Tasteful, and tidy. There was a mixture of antiques – modest things – and comfortable modern pieces. There was nothing of the bachelor in evidence, and an odd hint of fussiness that didn't seem to jibe with what Desmond knew of Oliver so far.

Watching as the other man disappeared upstairs to put away his jacket and tie, he noted with an internal twinge the movement of the curator's pleasantly rounded bottom beneath the gabardine of his trousers. Alone in the living room, Desmond surveyed a group of china figurines on the simple Georgian mantelpiece. He noticed two framed photographs arranged symmetrically. In one a very young-looking Oliver, beardless and strikingly sexy, his shoulder-length red hair pulled back in a ponytail, had his arm around a handsome dark-haired man a few inches taller than he was. The other showed Oliver more as he appeared now. The same man was with him, looking much older, shrunken somehow, his dark hair mostly gone. A background of palm trees suggested a vacation somewhere warm.

Desmond was startled by a nudge at the back of his leg, and looked down to see a small black-and-white dog wagging its tail tentatively at him. At his gaze, the dog sat and cocked its ears expectantly, still watching him, its tail still sweeping the floor. Hesitantly, Desmond bent down and reached out a hand, which the dog licked before rubbing it with his head. The little brown eyes closed in bliss as Desmond softly caressed the silky black fur.

"I see you've met Katrina." Oliver walked into the room and crouched before the dog, who put its head on his knee for more rubbing. Desmond straightened up, eyes still on Oliver.

"Cute name."

"I'm embarrassed to admit that I named her after the hurricane. It was the fall of 2005, and we found her cowering in a park during a thunderstorm. She was terrified and wet, hardly more than a puppy still."

"You said *we.*" Desmond gestured with his head toward the pictures on the mantelpiece, his brows raised.

"Yes. Asa and I. Asa was my partner." At Desmond's silence, he stood, dropping his gaze and putting his hands in his pockets.

"Would you like a glass of wine?"

"That would be nice."

Together they went into the neat kitchen, Katrina trotting hopefully behind them. Oliver pulled a bottle of red from a cupboard, uncorked it, and poured them two glasses. They offered each other a silent toast and drank, not quite looking each other in the eye. Desmond pretended to study the kitchen, which revealed little about the other man beyond the expected neatness. Katrina sat between them, and began to whine softly.

"Oh, gosh, I need to walk her." On hearing the word 'walk,' the dog began to wag her tail furiously.

"I'll go with you. Let's take our glasses." Desmond finished off his wine and poured himself another. Oliver followed suit, and they headed out the front door.

"Doesn't she need a leash?"

"Oddly, no. She never goes far from me. I think she must have been so grateful to be rescued that she attached to us really quickly." He grinned. "She knows a good thing when she sees one."

So do I.

Desmond laughed softly as they sauntered down the front walk, the black and white dog scampering happily ahead of them, but stopping to make sure they were close behind. They walked through the twilight streets, the breeze rustling the leaves on the old trees, Katrina zigzagging back and forth in a busy inspection of everything that dogs find so fascinating outdoors. Desmond could smell much of what she scented, although less sharply. He breathed in the cool fragrance of the air; the freshness of the plants and shrubs; the pots of chrysanthemums on front steps with their distinctive spicy aroma. Most of all, he could smell Oliver. The salty sweetness of his skin, clean, but with a day's patina of sweat. And, of course, his blood, warm and full, surging beneath that pale skin.

"Would you tell me about Asa?"

Oliver looked over at him, his face serious, then quirked his mouth. "Of course. So few people have ever asked."

"Why is that?"

"Asa was pretty closeted. He was twenty years older than I was. A school teacher. He would never come to museum events with me, too embarrassed at the idea of being publicly identified as my 'boyfriend.' Not that my being gay was a secret at work." Oliver rolled his eyes and looked back at Desmond.

"Surely he wasn't ashamed of you."

"Of me, no. Of himself, I'm not sure. Me–he was always wonderful to me."

"May I ask how long you were together?"

"Just over fifteen years. I was twenty-one when we met. I was still an undergraduate at Yale. He was forty, and so handsome. We met at a local bar in New Haven where the gay students all hung out. He was great fun to talk to. So much more mature than the college boys, less full of himself. He was a grown-up. He had a real life, and I was so anxious to have one of my own." Oliver hesitated and looked into Desmond's steady gaze. "This can't be interesting for you."

"It is, really. Go on."

"Well, I went to grad school at NYU, and we did a

semi-long-distance thing for those two years, but when I got my job here back in 1997, he found a teaching position in a suburban school and we bought this house together." He stopped, and they walked on in silence for a while, sipping their wine as Katrina continued her prowling.

"What happened?" Desmond asked quietly.

"It was stupid, so senseless. He loved living here, loved our house, our life together. But he seemed almost paranoid about people knowing about us. Oh, I made him visit my family with me, and they were always welcoming to him – but he was never totally comfortable, even there, even with me. Ultimately that was what got him."

"I don't understand."

Oliver's eyes were dark in the growing shadows, but Desmond could see them shimmer in the occasional streetlight. "He wouldn't go to a doctor. Simple as that. I have a great doctor, who knows I'm gay, even knows about–knew about – Asa. But the idea of going to any doctor and talking about anything intimate just freaked him out. We'd both been tested for HIV years before, and we were faithful to each other, so I guess he felt there was nothing to worry about."

"And?" The question was almost a whisper.

"And he started having trouble urinating, sometime after he turned 52. I finally forced him to go see my doctor. Turned out to be stage four prostate cancer. Beyond treatment." His voice shook with frustration. "Something so treatable when found early, and he just wouldn't think about it until it was too late because he was *embarrassed*. So suddenly our lives were full of radiation and then chemotherapy. Asa just withered in front of me. He was fifty-five when he died."

"Oliver, I'm so sorry. I didn't mean to pry," Desmond faltered. He found himself wanting to hold Oliver in his arms, to comfort him. He was startled by the sudden strength of his feeling.

But suddenly Oliver turned to him and gently placed

Vampire in Suburbia

his free hand on his shoulder, stopping him. Then he pulled him into a kiss.

Desmond was so startled he clenched up completely as that lovely, rosy mouth pressed against his own. After a few seconds—seconds that seemed like minutes—he relaxed, and allowed himself to respond to what couldn't possibly be happening. He let his own mouth soften against Oliver's, let his lips part. Oliver's tongue brushed tentatively across his lower lip and he replied in kind. All at once his tongue was in Desmond's mouth and his hand had moved to grip Desmond's wavy black hair and he was kissing him fiercely, his beard rough and soft at the same time.

What the hell?

Desmond pulled back, breaking the kiss, and looked into Oliver's hazel eyes, which were wide with some emotion he couldn't quite read.

"Oliver," he panted softly, "I don't get it."

"I'm lonely. You're beautiful. What's to get?"

Desmond thought he was going to hyperventilate, but Oliver dropped his empty wine glass onto the grass and wrapped his strong arms around the younger man and kissed him again. This time Desmond just leaned into him, let him hold him, went with it. He was hungry, almost desperate. He could feel Oliver's lean, muscular belly pressing against his, smell the richness of the blood pounding under the soft skin. He felt dizzy, and his knees started to buckle, but Oliver held him tight and helped him steady himself without breaking the kiss.

After a few minutes of this, Oliver pulled his mouth away, but didn't loosen his grip. He put his head on Desmond's shoulder and just held him, as they both struggled to catch their breath. At this point, bored with their inaction, Katrina lay down heavily against Desmond's feet, groaning contentedly, and drifted into a snuffling sleep.

I know what he needs. But I can't give him that now. And I know what I need.

Desmond let his glass fall onto the grass as well and

wrapped his other arm around Oliver's back. Then he turned his head slightly, his lips just brushing the smooth ivory-pink skin, under which the blood coursed. He lowered his canines and pressed them into the flesh, gripping Oliver's torso in his arms as he drank deeply. The blood filled him, made him tingle from head to toe. He could feel his cock grow as the taste of Oliver filled his senses. As his heart found the rhythm of Oliver's, he had a strange vision of the images he'd seen on the mantelpiece, but as in a film – a pony-tailed Oliver and a handsome, muscular Asa, walking down a crowded street together, arm-in-arm; Asa lying in bed close to him, dark eyes full of love and tenderness, locked onto his gaze. Warmth flooded through Desmond, increasing his arousal and giving him a sense of peace that he couldn't recall encountering before during his nocturnal feeding.

Not tonight.

A short time later, holding a somnolent Oliver with one arm, and bending awkwardly to pick up the fallen goblets, Desmond made his stumbling way back to the house. Katrina followed along obediently, unperturbed by what had happened. He maneuvered his burden through the front door and managed to set the glasses on the coffee table before laying Oliver out on the sofa in the living room. Then he went into the kitchen, poured the rest of the red wine down the sink, and brought the empty bottle to the living room, where he placed it next to the glasses on the coffee table.

He crouched down to rub Katrina's head and let her lick his nose.

"This'll be our little secret, eh?" The dog just wagged her tail cooperatively.

Kneeling, he placed a lingering kiss on Oliver's lips, feeling the prickle of the beard and the softness of his mouth.

Some other time, maybe.

Making sure the door was locked, Desmond slipped out into the darkness and headed the Volvo back into Newark to catch his train home.

Vampire in Suburbia

Chapter Nine

As he pushed through the glass doors into the Beckwith offices the next morning, Desmond could hear raised voices filtering down the long corridor. Approaching Jane's desk with some hesitation, he found her seated at her computer, looking up at a huge hulk of a man who was gesticulating aggressively as they argued.

"I don't care, Dane, we need the money!"

"How the fuck am I supposed to pay you if I can't …" Seeing Jane's eyes move, the man glanced in Desmond's direction and broke off.

"Oh, uh …" He seemed to deflate, becoming suddenly smaller as his anger was replaced by embarrassment, his arms limp at his sides.

"Desmond Beckwith." He extended a hand as if he hadn't walked in on something. Hesitantly, the man took it, not meeting his gaze.

"Uh, Dane Ashmun." He was taller than Desmond, with dirty blond hair, badly in need of cutting, and a broad muscular body that, if it hadn't run to fat yet, was showing the first signs of it. His face had probably been handsome, but the flabby skin and the red-rimmed eyes with their bruise-colored circles beneath them offered mute testimony to dissipation and lack of sleep.

"Dane is my ex-husband, Desmond," said Jane, her voice a monotone.

"Is there something *I* can help you with, Mr. Ashmun?" He was wary, having met Jane's ex in the past – but not since his regeneration.

"I, uh, guess I met your dad a couple a times."

"Oh, really?"

"Yeah. Look, Mr. Beckwith. Sorry to make a fuss. Jane's badgering me for support money, for the kids, and I just got laid off again, and I don't have … "

"I think I understand, Mr. Ashmun. But I think discussing it somewhere else than at Jane's workplace would be best." He fixed his eyes on Dane's, seeing that once they'd been clear and blue, but were now bloodshot, the whites yellowed.

"Yeah, right. Okay, I guess I'd better go, then." He looked back at Jane, whose face remained stony. "I'll call you later." She didn't respond, and he turned and moved down the hallway, head unconvincingly held high, as if defying his mortification.

Desmond turned his look to Jane, who said nothing, but raised her eyebrows in a question.

"Jane and Dane? Mind filling me in?" He knew the story, but figured he better make sure she repeated it to him so his younger self wouldn't end up seeming to know things he shouldn't.

"It was cute. Back then. We've been divorced for six years. Longer than we were together. We met at Rutgers in Newark and married right out of school." She continued, and repeated the story as he had heard it when he first hired her to be his assistant. Now, at least, they'd be on the same page – again.

"He's been paying child support all along?"

'When he can. It's been pretty on-and-off. He does try. I haven't pushed too hard since I met Dotty."

"Dotty?" Even though Desmond knew about her, he still had never met her. Jane kept her private life private.

"Dorothy Brown, my partner. We met at a bar in Newark. Jake's."

This he hadn't heard. "That restaurant over by the museum?"

Jane smiled at his tone of surprise. "That's the one. Restaurant by day, hot lesbian bar by night. In Newark you do what you need to make a profit. We still drop by when we can afford a babysitter." When Desmond only grinned at her, she went on. "But Dot's had job troubles of her own. You may not have noticed that the economy sucks."

There was no resentment in her tone, but Desmond found himself blushing, thinking of the huge house he'd just purchased without worrying about the cost.

"Do you need a raise?" His voice was gentle, not sure if this was the right thing to ask.

But Jane gave him a small smile. "I probably wouldn't say no, but that's not really the point. You pay me well, Desmond."

"But…?"

"Dotty's salary was a big help. It'll be tough to fill that gap, so I was trying to put a little pressure on Dane. I didn't realize he'd gotten fired again. He's drinking more heavily it seems, and probably went to work drunk. If that's true, he'll have a hard time finding work."

"I'm sorry."

"Yeah, me too." Turning away from him, apparently to bring an end to the conversation, she added, "You should check your calendar. I'm not sure you've been tracking."

Thus dismissed by his assistant, Desmond meekly

went into his office and opened up his computer. He had been a little distracted of late, and was still not entirely focused, an unexpected notion suddenly churning around in his brain. Even that nascent idea was pushed aside when he noticed two things on his electronic calendar that he'd entirely forgotten. There was a meeting set up for the next day with a Denis Schroeder, representing a Swiss investment firm called Chillon Investments. He vaguely remembered speaking to someone over the phone about that and had agreed to the meeting without giving it much thought. People were always asking for meetings, and usually listening to their ideas was at the very least educational. But the other aspect of the meeting was something he would normally not have let slip his mind: Roger was coming East.

In the meantime there were calls to make. He dialed Oliver's number at the museum across town, and was surprised at the relief he felt when he heard the familiar voice sounding perfectly normal.

"Oliver? It's Desmond."

"Oh, hi." Not unfriendly, but there was definite hesitation there.

"Everything okay?"

"Yes. Yes, sure. I'm fine."

"You seemed a little, shall we say under the weather last night. I was half afraid to leave you alone."

Silence. Then, "Look, Desmond, I'm sorry if I acted out of line."

"Stop right there, Oliver. There was nothing out of line. Nothing for you to be sorry for. At least I hope you don't think so."

"Well, I guess that's good, then."

"It was lovely, Oliver. All of it."

"I appreciate that."

"Look, could I see you tomorrow evening?"

"Oh. I … "

"I was thinking just for drinks. I need to get into the city tonight, but I'd like to see you. Just to talk some more. Get to know each other better. Get any lingering awkwardness out of the way."

There was a brief silence. "Yes, Desmond, I'd like that."

Was that a note of regret in his voice?

"Good. I'll come by your house around six?"

"Six it is."

"'Bye."

Next Desmond had Jane call Alex Duquesne's design firm. As he was reading emails, Jane called from the outer office. "I have David Parker on the line, Desmond."

"There's an intercom, Jane, no need to shout."

"Whatever. He's holding."

Sighing, Desmond picked up the phone. "Mr. Parker?"

"Mr. Beckwith, this is David Parker?" His inflection made it sound like a question. "Alex told me a little about this project. I was really hoping you'd call." His voice was not at all high-pitched, but to Desmond's ear something about the intonation made it clear that he was gay. In any case, Parker's enthusiasm was palpable, even over the phone. "I really would love to work with you. This would be such a huge win for me!"

A huge win? What is he, sixteen?

"Well, then, why don't we plan to meet at the house. Say, day after tomorrow?"

"I'll put that on my calendar. What time?"

"Let's make it early."

They set a time, and Desmond put down the receiver. He wanted the house project to move quickly, and wondered what it would cost to make that happen. The owners were ready for a quick closing date, which would let him begin the renovation and decoration. Maybe in time for Christmas.

His work drew him away from these pleasant thoughts, and the day flickered by. As the sun began to settle towards the horizon out his southern windows, Desmond looked up from his desk, and through the glass wall could see a tall slim figure in a tan gabardine suit striding purposefully down the carpeted corridor. Roger.

He moved quickly from behind the desk and flung open the door, crossing Jane's workspace in time to wrap his arms around his oldest friend in the world.

"Roger. So good to see you. I've missed you," he said quietly as the other man returned the embrace. Then he released him and held him at arm's length, looking closely at him, as if memorizing his features. Then, to avoid Jane's curious stare, he ushered Roger into his office and shut the door. He perched on the edge of his desk and smiled at his friend.

"You look great," he said softly, and this was only the truth. Even at sixty-five, Roger Deland had commanded attention when he walked into a room. His red hair had become heavily shot with gray, turning it the color of russet straw. Prone to ponytails in his younger years, as Roger aged, he wore his hair progressively shorter. Roger had regenerated back to twenty-one a few months before Desmond himself did, and now his lustrous hair was deep auburn again, swept back from the high forehead, still barely touching the tops of his ears. His prominent cheekbones and strong chin had kept the pale freckled skin taut as he aged, but gone now were the crepe-paper texture, the faint jowls that had softened the sculpted jawline, and the crow's feet that had crinkled the corners of his eyes, The delicious arc of his full lips was unlined once again, and Desmond wished, as he had for over two centuries, that he could kiss that mouth without restraint. Roger's dark green eyes, however, never ceased to sparkle with the same intelligence and affection they had since the two men had first met.

Vampires age with particular grace, but our eyes never age at all.

"And you, my friend, look wonderful." Roger remained standing, crossing his arms across his chest. Desmond bridled at the compliment. "I keep forgetting how beautiful you are at twenty-one. Good thing I'm immune to your charms."

The warmth of his smile mitigated the pain this truth

never ceased to cause Desmond. Roger Deland was the love of his life. Had been from virtually the day they met. But Roger was straight. Kinsey 0 straight. He had never once crossed the line of friendship with Desmond, even though with their kind the line was drawn in a somewhat different place.

"There are a few things we need to do to finalize the transfer of my estate to my new self." This go-round, Roger had taken a new name and a new identity. Re-establishing him as part of Desmond's world was a custom they had grown used to.

"You want to sit in on the meeting with the guy from Chillon?"

"Yes. That might be a good idea. Have you done any research on them, Desmond?"

Desmond found himself blushing under his friend's scrutiny. "Well, no. But we've been through these meetings before."

"I've been looking into them. It's a solid little firm, not unlike ours. Very low profile, so it took some digging. They also seem to be tied into various liberal charities, mostly linked to civil rights in various troubled areas. That's unusual, and once again rather similar to us. This Denis Schroeder who's coming to see us appears to be somewhere just below the top."

"That's interesting."

"It is indeed. And it suggests to me that they're more serious than just another group of hotshot moneymakers fishing for some extra capital." Roger settled himself into one of the leather armchairs that Desmond had facing his desk. "What's even more interesting is that I couldn't find out who the top *is*."

"What?"

"The ultimate ownership of the firm, which seems to be part of a larger network of small companies, is hard to determine. I couldn't put a name to their owner."

"That's rather like you, isn't it? My name is associated with the business. You're more of a shadow. I've Googled you, Roger, and although you aren't exactly invisible, with your, um, *public* lifestyle, there are no links to Beckwith Investments, at least not that most people would be able to find. In your new guise, you'll become even more difficult to track."

"I will remain, as always, a man of mystery." Roger beamed.

"So we'll ask Schroeder tomorrow."

"I'm not sure it matters, but I just found it curious."

"As regards all the paperwork about my estate, I haven't looked at it recently, but I'm sure it's all in order."

"My, Des, you're almost casual about all this. It's not like you to be this laid back. Usually you're fussing about like an anxious mother, fretting over the legal details, obsessing about every clause and signature."

They locked eyes for a moment.

"I've been feeling different this time around. Since the regeneration, I mean."

"Different? How?"

"It's hard to say precisely. I'm having the oddest sort of nesting instincts."

Roger simply cocked one of his eyebrows and said nothing.

"You should know, I've bought a house."

"Really?" Roger's tone had a sardonic edge that was not lost on his old friend.

"Yes. Rather a large one. It's from the 1920's, but it's Georgian, with lovely grounds."

"Made you nostalgic for England, did it?" Roger teased gently. "After all this time?"

"I guess that's it." Desmond hesitated, then gave Roger a small smile. "I've picked out the best guest room for you. It overlooks the pool."

"And staffing this estate of yours?"

Desmond looked down, abashed. "I'm still deciding what to do about that."

Roger only laughed, his brilliant smile like sunshine on Desmond's soul as he stood and dragged his friend up into another hug.

"You are the strangest man, my dear friend. But you go right ahead and do whatever you want. It's your money. If it makes you happy, then I won't trouble you over it. I just don't want you inhabiting a falling-down wreck because you haven't thought through maintenance issues properly."

"Thanks, Roger." Desmond felt as if he'd been given permission.

It startled him how much Roger's approval meant to him. Always had. And he'd been the one to save Roger's life all those years ago. At the start of their friendship he had called the shots; he had laid out the path for Roger's life as a vampire and a banker. On the other hand, as their shared lifetimes had progressed, Roger had always been the capricious one, living life on the surface, reinventing himself when the time came and slipping into each new cycle as easily as if he were putting on a new suit. Roger had never stayed in the same house or apartment for more than a decade, while Desmond had clung to the house on 4th Street through four lifetimes.

"That reminds me," he said suddenly, pulling back and letting Roger's arms release him. "I need you to introduce me to Vivian."

"You haven't seen her since…?"

"No. I've been feeling badly about that. She apparently took my supposed father's death harder than I would have thought."

"That's the downside of making friends, isn't it? Well, since she's met 'Robert Delacourt'— I rather like that name – with your *father*, I'll be glad to start you two off afresh. She wasn't nearly as cut up about Roger's passing as she was about yours."

"How do you mean?"

"When I went to visit her, I introduced myself, and explained that I'd replaced Roger Deland as your West Coast lieutenant. She was very sympathetic, and said she'd enjoyed meeting him – me – over the years. But when I broke the news about you, she just crumpled.

Obviously you meant a great deal to her."

Roger – who was always Roger to Desmond, and now to Bill – tended to have lots of acquaintances, but no real friendships. So had Desmond, until this last cycle. Fortunately he'd been able to bring Bill Lawrence with him, so to speak, into his latest life. Everyone else would have to be reintegrated into the new Desmond's world one way or another.

"I'll call Vivian now and see if she can see us later. We'll take her to dinner. You really need to reestablish ties with her, Des. Make sure she feels secure about the foundation and the support of Beckwith House." Then he stopped and tilted his head to one side.

"How did you know she was grieving, especially? I should have told you, I suppose, but I was trying to spare you any more trauma for the moment."

"Ah. Through a mutual acquaintance. A curator at the museum here in town. His name's Oliver Cameron." At Roger's beady look, Desmond couldn't avoid another blush, but he fixed his own hazel eyes on Roger's and offered a sly grin.

"And he's a redhead just like you."

Chapter Ten

The two men came up out of the subway by Washington Square, and walked east on 4th Street, pushed along by a chilly autumnal breeze that scattered paper and leaves around them. They paused in front of the gray marble steps of a four-story brick house, three bays wide with a columned marble entrance and dark green shutters. This was Beckwith House, although it had only taken on that name after Desmond had given it to the city as a museum, and installed his friend Vivian Lake as its director. Up until that time, it had simply been home. He had built the house in 1820, when 4th Street was far uptown, and he had remained there for over 170 years.

It was there he had collected his library. In those high-ceilinged rooms he had accumulated several lifetimes of things, the style of what he bought gradually adjusting with the changing world around him. From those windows he had watched Manhattan grow and change. He had seen this neighborhood slide from glamorous to seedy, and then watched it rise back up again.

It was to his bedroom here that he had brought a mortal man into his sanctum for the first time and made love to him – and taken his blood. For a short sweet moment this house had been theirs, his and Tony Chapman's. Tony had been only the second man who had ever truly known Desmond Beckwith, and had loved him anyway. But then that moment had ended, and Desmond had left the house behind, his sorrow along with his treasures.

Vivian Lake, trim and austere, with a shoulder-length gray pageboy haircut and nondescript wool suit, greeted them warmly in the marble-floored vestibule. As she shook Desmond's hand she seemed to be studying his face.

"You look very much as I always imagined your father would have when he was your age. It's quite remarkable."

"I keep hearing that the family resemblance is very strong," he answered vaguely. Then, to divert her attention from his looks, he continued, "We apparently have a mutual acquaintance."

"Oh?"

"Oliver Cameron, the curator over in Newark. I met him in the Ballantine House when I went to visit the museum."

"Yes, sure. Oliver. I've known him for years. He does a great job."

"I'm ashamed to say that he asked me if I'd been here, and I had to tell him I hadn't. He thinks very highly of you as well."

"Oliver is a fascinating man," said Vivian as she ushered them into the long shadowy hall. "I really enjoy it whenever I spend any time with him. I've never seen anyone – even in our fairly peculiar profession – who has such an intense connection to objects."

"How's that?" Desmond was curious to hear what this was about.

"He's been here before, of course, and I've never seen such a tactile curator. I remember how he kept running his hands over things – without gloves, which is breaking protocol of course – but it was almost a compulsion. It was like the feel of an object helped him understand it better somehow. I suppose to some degree we all do that, but I've never seen anyone else quite like him."

"You know, when I showed him the house I'm buying out in the suburbs, he did the same thing to the stuff that had been left behind by the last owners. It rather unnerved me at the time."

"So you've had firsthand experience. But, I must say, he's good. We have a little silver-collectors group that meets here in New York now and then, and we like to bring things for show-and-tell during dinner. He has the most amazing insights. Nothing seems to stump him."

Vivian proceeded to give Desmond a tour of the house, Roger/Robert tagging along patiently, as if he, too, hadn't been there hundreds of times before. Her presumption of ignorance on Desmond's part would have been comical if it hadn't been so painful. She spoke with curatorial reverence of the furniture, the fabrics, the ceramics that filled the rooms, of the remarkable historical documents regarding the house that his father had kept safely locked away. Desmond remembered purchasing nearly every single object. He vividly recalled visiting the cabinet shops and the fancy-goods stores in the 1820s and 30s. He remembered putting classical styles aside in the 1850s for the new French taste, and how proud he'd been of all that ornate carved rosewood in the parlor. Most poignantly of all, he remembered the gothic library on the second floor, where he and Roger had spent countless quiet evenings over the decades; where Tony, for a much briefer period, had worked on his inventories of the house, earnestly picking Desmond's brain for historical details that no one else could have known.

As had always been true, Desmond found the master bedroom the most uncomfortable room to see in its neutered museum state. Plainer than the other rooms in the house, in spite of the massive four-poster bed, it had always been comfortable rather than opulent. White dimity curtains, simple flat-woven strip carpeting in greens and tans, and a plain gray marble mantelpiece. It had been the place where he retreated for the six daily hours of deathlike sleep he needed. Here in this room he had prayed over Tony's shroud-wrapped corpse, and here he had confessed his great secret to Bill Lawrence. Bill, his closest mortal friend, who had opened his mind and accepted the unbelievable, and then had willingly offered his own blood to relieve the suffering of a grieving friend. He exchanged a look with Roger, who had been in California when Tony died, and hadn't experienced his anguish firsthand.

The tour ended, the two men accompanied Vivian to a favored uptown restaurant, where they plied her with excellent food as they both enjoyed cocktails and wine. Desmond had discovered the pleasure of gin martinis in the past nineteen years, relishing the quick buzz they afforded when his emotions were particularly raw-edged. The effects of alcohol didn't linger in a vampire's system, but even his high-powered metabolism was not immune to the potency of distilled spirits. The drinks softened the ache that visiting Beckwith House had triggered, and Desmond could see that Roger was watching him with affectionate concern.

Vivian, for her part, was uncharacteristically chatty. It startled Desmond to see her so informal. She had always treated the elder Beckwith with a certain distance, undoubtedly because of his money and the influence it had made in her career. He was amused to note that she almost flirted with his younger self, in spite of the husband and grown children he knew she had.

"You know, Desmond – it's so odd to say that, I have to confess – your father spoke of you only a few times to me. I wasn't sure he really intended to bring you here at all."

"He did keep me pretty well sequestered in London," Desmond replied with a thin smile. He had never liked the prevarication that accompanied the transfer from one life to the next, and this particular deception pained him especially. Vivian had been a good friend, to him and to Tony. Lying to her was distasteful, however necessary. "He spoke of you, and your work, during his visits to me and, um, my mother."

"Forgive me for my nosiness – blame it on this lovely wine – but I take it your mother and father were never married?"

Desmond paused, slightly taken aback at the question, before answering. "No, they were perfectly friendly, but their relationship was purely, uh, contractual."

"And of course, there was Tony."

He felt himself blushing unaccountably at the way Vivian said this, and stammered a response. "I never got to meet Tony. I regret that."

"Tony was a lovely man. He had such huge potential. I worked closely with him for a while, and grew very fond of him." She quaffed her wine, and Desmond could see unshed tears gathering in her dark eyes. "I was so shocked by your father's death. I'd never have suspected any sort of physical frailty in him. He seemed so much younger than his age always."

Touched by her emotion, moved by a depth of feeling he'd never seen Vivian display, Desmond reached out and clasped her hand. "I hope I can be a friend as my father was, Vivian. I have a lot to learn, but I seem to have inherited his interests. I know it won't be easy to fill his shoes, but I'll try my best."

He felt Roger place a comforting hand on his shoulder.

"Well," continued Vivian, straightening her shoulders as if she was consciously putting her sentiments in check, "you've made at least one friend in your new home town."

At his quizzical look, she smiled. "Oliver Cameron. I wasn't going to mention it, since you brought him up first, but he called me last week. He wanted to make sure I made a point of getting you here to see the house. Seems you made quite an impression."

Laughing softly, Desmond said "We had a nice time when I met him at the Ballantine House. He's very nice."

"That he is. He's also very lonely. You know about…?"

"Yes. We talked about Asa. I've been to his house."

He couldn't help notice the slightly amused expression that flickered over Vivian's face.

"Good then. Sounds like you've made a good start."

Desmond made sure to build on that good start the next evening over glasses of red wine at the little suburban trattoria with Oliver. He was aware of bashfulness on the curator's part that hadn't been there on their first date.

"I'm sorry I abandoned you the other night," he said, taking a mouthful of the wine, savoring its richness even as he inhaled Oliver's increasingly familiar scent from across the table.

Oliver gave a muffled snort. "I'll accept your apology if you'll forgive me for throwing myself at you like some horny fanboy." He sipped his own wine nervously.

"Horny fanboy?" Desmond laughed. "I'm not even sure what that means. But I hardly tried to fend you off, you know. And I sort of have a thing about red hair. You didn't find me – unwilling?"

"No. Not at all. You were … " he paused as if searching for the word. "Delicious."

Desmond raised his brows at that, and took another healthy swig from his glass.

Dropping his eyes, before looking up and holding Desmond's gaze, Oliver spoke rapidly, rushing to get it out before his courage failed. "It's just that you're so much younger than Asa was – so much younger than I am. I – I don't really know quite what came over me to be that forward. I think I was just panicking because I was so far out of my league." He gulped his wine, as if it was a reward for bravery.

Like everyone else, he finds my youth and beauty rather too irresistible.

A wave of regret swept through Desmond, cooling him in spite of the wine. Oliver was still grieving. Facing middle age alone. Desmond understood that, certainly. But was it Desmond with whom he was infatuated, or just a rich pretty boy who happened to have wandered into his museum unexpectedly?

When he spoke, his voice was reassuring. "Me, out of your league? Surely you don't doubt your own attractiveness?"

A blush stole up Oliver's fair neck, suffusing his cheeks under the coppery beard.

"Look, Desmond, I'm thirty-eight. I'm old enough to be … "

"My big brother," Desmond finished. "Although that would be incest, which isn't quite the direction I meant to go in." He reached across the small table, placing his hand palm up on the white paper tablecloth. Oliver let a moment pass before placing his own large, strong hand onto Desmond's slender one.

"You're very handsome, Oliver." He squeezed Oliver's hand, releasing it. "The point is, you shouldn't worry about the age difference. Your age means nothing to me."

Because I'm about two centuries older than you are.

Your age isn't the problem.

His thoughts tripped unpleasantly over an unwelcome idea that popped into his head.

But maybe mine is.

Oliver blew out a small sigh of relief, smiling and shaking his head. "I'm flattered, Desmond, really I am." He looked up, his blue eyes bright in the dim restaurant. "Can we start over, if I promise to behave myself?"

Desmond nodded, his smile filling the space between them with silent warmth. "Let's begin with friendship, and let things sort themselves out," he asked.

The double doors to the bar swung inward, and Desmond stepped from the late-night traffic noise of East 58th Street to the genteel hush of the Townhouse. It was still barely nine o'clock, and most of the clientele at this particular bar were still wearing the suits and blazers that made up their work attire. Desmond fit right in, with his pinstriped charcoal gray suit and his perfectly knotted silk tie. He wagered he was probably fifteen years younger than anyone there other than the cute piano player singing in one corner of the crowded room. He hoped his reclaimed youth would once again work to his advantage. The meeting with Oliver was still on his mind. He was thirsty as well as hungry, and he wasn't in the mood to waste time.

As an investment banker in his sixties, Desmond had found a ready welcome in this Upper East Side watering hole. This was not a dance club. It was a business-mans' lounge in the manner of the 1960s, except for the fact that all of the men were eyeing each other over their cocktails in a way that was distinctly post-Stonewall. Many of those eyes turned in his direction as he paused by the entrance, running a hand carelessly through his wavy hair. It was, he knew, an effect that worked.

For his older self, the Townhouse had been more social than sexual in its appeal. While it was one of the few places in Manhattan where an older man could readily find a night's companionship without the risk of having to supplement it with a generous tip, it was also one of the few places where manners and well-tailored clothes still mattered. He had spent plenty of pleasant evenings here; sometimes just drinking and talking, other times slipping discreetly away with a new acquaintance of similar inclination. It was but a short walk to the Four Seasons Hotel where, as was true this night, there would be a room waiting.

When he had first discovered the Townhouse, Bill Lawrence had been a sometime companion, and they had both been relieved that, for all its hauteur, the Townhouse was equally welcoming to everyone – provided they were dressed properly and behaved like gentlemen. Alex Duquesne, however, was not a night owl, and Desmond's visits in recent years had been mostly solitary.

This was only his second visit to the Townhouse since his regeneration, and Desmond had been sent two drinks within minutes of seating himself at the bar, in spite of the v-shaped goblet of gin sitting on the polished mahogany in front of him. He quickly focused on one particular man. Mid-forties, taller than Desmond, navy suit, brown hair carefully styled, deep brown eyes behind fashionably academic horn rim glasses. He offered his name as Peter, and Desmond was inclined to believe him. This was a man just beginning to feel the panic of increasing age. Desmond's attention would seduce him effortlessly.

"I'm Tony," he said, suppressing his English accent and smiling his best smile. He had used this as his hunting name for years, the reasons for which he never considered too closely.

They chatted for perhaps a quarter of an hour, finding it unnecessary to raise their voices over the muted susurrations of the conversation around them. Finally, Desmond sat back on his bar stool and looked directly into his companion's eyes.

"It's awfully crowded here. What say we go somewhere else? I'm staying nearby at the Four

Seasons." This was not the moment for subtlety.

Peter's smile sent a message of mixed lust and relief as he stood up and buttoned his jacket.

Note to self: pay more attention to middle-aged men. They're not going to turn twenty-one again.

Once inside the subdued elegance of the Four Seasons hotel room, Peter's gentlemanly behavior quickly dissolved into eagerness and an almost teenaged intensity. Although Desmond's mind kept wandering back to his conversation with Oliver, he gave himself up to the moment, and focused on giving and receiving pleasure with his partner. Before long the couple found themselves spent and panting on the cool linen sheets.

"I hope you don't have to rush off," Desmond said in a low voice, running his fingers down Peter's lightly furred belly, watching the skin shiver at his touch. It was more than an idle question; if Peter had to leave soon, Desmond would have to act quickly.

"I do need to get home at some point," said Peter, gladly snuggling into the younger man's side. "But I wouldn't mind a bit of cuddling, if you're up for it."

"I'd be happy to." This was what Desmond had hoped to hear; but the words made him feel oddly warm inside. The offer of a few more minutes of closeness was such a small thing to make, and yet it was accepted by both of them as something precious. Such intimacy didn't really banish loneliness, but it helped remind one of the tenderness of human contact.

As Peter began to doze, nestled in his arms, his head against his shoulder, Desmond began to very softly caress his cheek, ruffling the chestnut hair. He noted how the crow's feet at the corners of Peter's eyes had faded as he edged toward sleep. Age seemed to lift from his face, and Desmond could easily see what a pretty boy this man had once been. He had been through this himself; but there had always been the promise of regeneration in his futures.

Why was a man like this alone? Did he prefer

bachelorhood? Was he closeted in some way that made a relationship difficult? Had he lost someone, as Desmond had?

Or–and the thought sent a twinge through Desmond's heart – was there someone waiting for him somewhere; someone who assumed he was at a business dinner with colleagues or a client?

The emotional chill this idea brought on made it easier for Desmond to steel himself for what he needed to do. Oliver was off limits for the time being. But that didn't change his nature. Love and friendship were luxuries, perhaps; but blood was essential. Lowering his lips to Peter's neck, Desmond released his canines and pressed them home, taking the nourishment he needed to get through the days ahead.

But even as Peter's warm blood filled him with its power; even as his strong heartbeat pounded out its life-giving rhythm through Desmond's body, it was Oliver's image that gave him comfort.

Chapter Eleven

Both Desmond and Roger were in Newark, ready for their meeting with the representative of Chillon Investments. Roger was in his private, seldom-used workspace going over emails from the San Francisco office, when Jane – for once using the intercom – announced that the guest had arrived and she would bring him in. Desmond watched as her retreating figure headed to the reception area, but forced himself to keep his gaze down until he heard the door to his office open. It wouldn't do to stare at the newcomer as he approached.

He rose to greet his visitor, extending his hand. "I'm Desmond Beckwith."

"Denis Schroeder. Pleased to meet you, Mr. Beckwith."

"Jane, would you tell Mr. Delacourt that Mr. Schroeder is here?"

Jane bustled out with professional efficiency, leaving Desmond staring at the young man who stood smiling neutrally at him across his desk.

Denis Schroeder was absurdly beautiful. Appearing close to Desmond in age, he was tall and athletic. His white-blond hair was worn short, in a way that was both youthful and businesslike. The smooth skin of his fine-boned face was rosy, and the teeth revealed by the deep rose lips were toothpaste-ad white. His clothes were impeccable. A conservative dark blue suit, beautifully cut, emphasized his lithe elegant body, and a crisp white shirt made his skin seem tawny in comparison. A colorful patterned silk tie completed the look. He could have been an Armani model, but Desmond suspected the suit was custom made. Not even the best off-the-rack looked *that* good.

He shook Schroeder's slender hand, noting the coolness of the firm grip and the velvety strength in the long fingers. The scent of his cologne, muted and herbal, barely masked the underlying fragrance of his blood, which filled Desmond's senses like a crisp autumn breeze. A frisson shivered up his arm like a tiny electric charge.

Schroeder's ice-blue eyes held Desmond's a beat longer than they should have, and it was only Roger's entrance into the office that broke the gaze. Roger, never one to miss much, greeted the stranger, giving his name as they shook hands, before sliding a quick questioning glance at Desmond.

Schroeder's behavior throughout their meeting was capable and professional. He spoke with precision, just the faintest of accents coloring his fluent English. He had brought documents outlining Chillon's performance over the preceding few years, as well as long-term growth and profit charts. Both Desmond and Roger studied the paperwork with trained eyes.

"You've managed the economic downturn very ably, it seems," noted Roger, a look of restrained admiration in his deep green eyes. "It doesn't appear you're in any particular need of our collaboration."

"That was my thought as well," added Desmond, who was still finding it difficult to keep his eyes from Schroeder's handsome face. Roger's evident awareness of this was embarrassing.

The blond man smiled with charming modesty. "We have been both lucky and astute in the midst of the economic volatility of the past two years. It did not escape our attention that Beckwith Investments has followed a similar pattern. Unlike you, however, we have never branched out beyond our Geneva and Zurich offices. It occurred to us that an alliance between Beckwith and Chillon would be mutually advantageous. We have no major liabilities, and I must emphasize that we are not presenting you with any significant risk."

"You say, 'we,' Mr. Schroeder?" Desmond asked.

At this, Schroeder reached into his jacket and pulled out two white cards, of the typically larger size used by European business people. He handed one to both Roger and Desmond. In elegant black type was his name and title: *Denis Schroeder, Directeur Général*.

"So you are the managing director of the firm?" asked Desmond.

"I represent the wishes and intentions of our chairman, *messieurs*."

"And he is...?" began Roger.

"Partially in retirement, but still very active in advising me," finished Schroeder.

Desmond and Roger exchanged a quick look at this coyness. It was Roger who asked the unspoken question in both their minds.

"You seem – forgive me the impertinence, Mr. Schroeder, very young."

The breathtaking smile that spread across the blond's features was genuine and unselfconscious. He had heard this before. "I am older than I appear, Mr. Delacourt. I confess that it confuses people, but I am used to it. I assure you, I have earned my position through experience."

As the meeting ended, they all stood shaking hands, Jane waiting at the door to escort Schroeder out. Schroeder made a point of clasping Desmond's hand in both of his in farewell.

"You have a flat in New York, Mr. Beckwith?"

"Ah, yes," he replied, registering the fact that Schroeder must have done some research himself.

"Perhaps I could give you a call some evening? I am here for quite a while now, and I haven't many acquaintances in the city."

"Why, um, of course. Yes. That would be very nice." Slightly rattled, Desmond took one of his own cards, and hastily writing down his cell number, handed it to Schroeder.

Schroeder took the card with a small smile and put it in his inner pocket without looking at it. Then he nodded, almost formally, at both Desmond and Roger, and let Jane lead him away.

There was a brief silence in the office. Desmond couldn't look Roger in the eye. Roger broke the silence first.

"My my, I think he almost clicked his heels together. Our *Schweitzer Jungen* is rather a forward little trollop isn't he?"

Desmond choked on a laugh, but managed to get out, "I guess I was a little obvious wasn't I? I couldn't take my eyes off him."

"He certainly is attractive. You two seemed to have … *something*."

"Well, we'll see. I set no great store by his invitation."

"And your ginger-bearded curator?"

Desmond felt himself flush. "Oh, I like Oliver very much. We've become good friends."

"Just friends, then?" There was an expression of

fraternal concern on Roger's face, and his deep green eyes bored into Desmond's.

"Yes, I'm afraid. I'm not saying there might not have been more, eventually, but I felt it best to retreat from that particular path. I suspect I rather frighten him."

"Oh, well then, Desmond, I think you could use a little fun in the meantime. You still sound too much like your father. A fling with a hot Swiss boy might bring your behavior into the twenty-first century. I worry that you still act like a sexagenarian."

Desmond just snorted derisively at his old friend. Then, his look softening, he asked, "By the way, Rog, anyone in your life these days, now that you're back to your old young self?"

A wistful look settled into Roger's handsome features as he gave his oldest friend a frank look. "No. Not for now."

"Are you all right? I'm so wrapped up in my own petty concerns, I don't ask as much as I ought."

"I'm fine, my friend. And if circumstances change, you'll be the first to know."

Roger, too, was no stranger to sadness. For all of his social superficiality, there had been a woman. Not a wife – that wasn't Roger's way – but a longtime companion. It had never happened previously in all their years, but sometime shortly after Tony's death, Roger had met Wendy while on vacation. She had been slightly older than Roger; beautiful and accomplished, wealthy and divorced. She had also been patient with Roger's wandering eye and restless ways. Over the years Roger had become increasingly devoted – and faithful – to her, rather than the opposite. As if the gods somehow couldn't accept Roger as a doting spouse, Wendy had developed leukemia in her mid-sixties. She had fought bravely, but had died just a year ago, after Roger's sixty-fourth birthday. It seemed ironic, the consort of a vampire dying of a blood disease. There had never been a question of her knowing his true nature, and Roger had been as helpless as any mortal lover. It was as close to being part of a couple as Roger had ever come, and Wendy's death had left a shadow on his eternally sunny disposition.

Impulsively, Desmond reached out to hug his friend, and felt the warmth of his embrace. Then they parted, each to his own workspace, each to his own piece of the business they shared.

Chapter Twelve

The next morning, Desmond collected David Parker from Newark's Penn Station and together they drove against the commuter traffic out to Llewellyn Park. There was a distinct nip in the air, although the foliage was in its full summer green still. As he steered the Volvo out Route 280 to the exit for The Oranges, he smiled at Parker's combination of sharp observation and almost child-like chatter. His frosted blond hair was short and spiky, his slender frame loose and willowy. Large doe-like brown eyes and a small pouty mouth added to his boyish look. He had a pleasant voice, but spoke with an oddly teenage cadence, increasing the impression of youthfulness. Although in his mid-twenties, David Parker seemed like he was from a different world. He nattered on excitedly about the project and how anxious he was to see the house. In between looking at emails on his iPhone, which Desmond found mildly irritating, he talked with complete ingenuousness about his boyfriend, with whom he had been living for six months; about his family, who lived in Massachusetts and barely talked to him; and about his employer, Alex Duquesne, who was a great boss and trusted him and mentored him.

As they pulled off at the exit for West Orange, David asked why the towns were called The Oranges, in that random way small children ask things. Most people hadn't a clue why these suburban Essex towns were named as they were, so Desmond explained that the name came from the House of Orange – a Dutch royal house linked to both the Netherlands and England. As Desmond recalled, his own father had actually once laid eyes on William of Orange, the Dutch-born king of England who died shortly before Sir Charles Beckwith had made his fortune and gained his knighthood. This information he kept to himself.

As they pulled up to the gravel sweep by the carved front doors of Oakwood, David clambered out of the car, almost squealing with excitement.

"Oh my gosh, this is just spectacular, Mr. Beckwith. I can't wait to get inside."

Before Desmond could even answer, his attention was diverted to the little castellated stone playhouse at the end of the drive. The decorator made a beeline for it and peered in the windows.

"This is amazing. What a neat building. Do you know what it was for?"

"The son of the original owners built it for his son to use as a playhouse. I think they had an English Gothic folly in mind – sort of a garden pavilion – but fitted out for play."

"I could do something really fun with this. It's too bad you don't have children." Then, catching himself, he looked over at Desmond, an abashed expression in those large innocent eyes.

Desmond was quietly delighted with the evident discomfort that sobered up his companion. Before his eyes, Parker seemed to mature several years. His shoulders straightened, his fluttering hands grew quiet. A half smile lingered on his pretty mouth, his look now professional and intelligent.

"Let's go have a look inside."

Jointly they explored the house as Desmond had with Oliver and on his own. This time, however, he was barraged with ideas of what could be done, what shouldn't be done, and what absolutely had to be done. Keeping Oliver's admonition in mind, Desmond gently interposed his own thoughts when he felt that Parker was going overboard. The great surprise was how much he enjoyed himself. For all his fey mannerisms and boyish giddiness, Parker was smart and knowledgeable. He was also receptive to Desmond's input, and was clearly thinking in terms of a budget, consistently mentioning ways to save costs and get better prices for materials. Desmond had never named any figures, and he was pleased to see that Alex's designer wasn't simply trying to bring in a lot of cash for the firm. He realized that his own excitement over redecorating the house grew by leaps and bounds as he listened to David's ideas, and he found himself in agreement with most of what Parker suggested. The young man had a surprisingly refined sense of period, and seemed to understand the house as well as Oliver had.

Desmond was particularly happy with Parker's reaction to the renovation idea for the servant's wing.

"This would make a great apartment. It would give a housekeeper, even a couple or a small family, wonderful privacy – and yet keep them right on the premises. A house this big really needs someone here living-in full time."

"It's gratifying to hear you say that," commented Desmond, feeling a growing affection for Alex's protégé.

"And that sort of servants' hall that faces the swimming pool, but off the kitchen area? That was probably placed there so that the cook or butler could see the family outside, and be ready to jump if they were needed. But I see it as a sort of downstairs sitting room for the housekeeper. Whoever takes on this job would need an office as a sort of control center, but the space could double as a living space. It has a nice view. One of the pantry areas could be converted into a small private kitchen – again, for when you're not in residence. The back stairs would connect right to the apartment on the second floor. That whole section of the house could be heated separately, so that when you were away, whoever lived in could be comfortable without having to cool or heat the entire building. That would save energy and money."

"You amaze me," said Desmond, bowing like a Georgian courtier. Parker giggled happily at the praise, and they continued their exploration.

Desmond had not looked around much in the house's cavernous and complicated cellars. The furnace was modern, but would need to be added to if the house were to be zoned as Parker had suggested. There was a large workroom, complete with old tools hanging on the walls and a massive pine workbench. A refrigerated wine cellar and a walk-in silver safe –both of them near the service stairs up to the kitchen – raised much curiosity.

Desmond began to consider the collecting he'd be able to do to properly furnish and equip this place as it had been lived in before the Great Depression. He had never acquired objects from the period of his own mortal youth. He had sold Beckwith House in England with everything in it, bringing nothing but a single painting of the house with him to the United States. Everything he'd bought for the 4th Street house had been modern when he'd bought it. Only for the Dakota flat had he purchased "antiques," and these had all been late nineteenth-century – representing the moment when his old house had ceased to evolve and had begun to entrap him in its layers of memory. A house like this would be the perfect setting for an entirely *new* collection of old things. It would help him pass a lifetime – this lifetime.

It would be, he realized with a start, just as it had been after the death of his father, without his beloved manservant, Jeffrey, all by himself in that big brick country house. Still in his twenties, eternally transformed, yet never changing. A wave of sadness chilled his heart at the thought of the years ahead of him, alone in this enormous place.

"What are all these doors?" asked Parker, bringing Desmond back to the present. A corridor lined with a series of storage rooms yielded nothing but some old trunks and a few pieces of broken lawn furniture. As the light bulbs were burned out, Desmond and David used their cell phones to cast faint blue glows into the murky corners. One storeroom had several large crate-like cabinets, longer than they were high, built up against the walls. Opening one of them, they found faded damask window curtains, carefully laid out, layered uselessly with ancient crumbling newspaper, apparently to prevent creasing.

Desmond stood peering over David's shoulder at the discolored draperies, and was suddenly aware of the strong sweet odor of the young man's body, and the powerful fragrance of his blood. An unexpected undercurrent of fear gave his scent a sharp edge.

"It's so creepy," commented David with a nervous laugh, bending over the case as he shoved the drawer closed. "It's like we're in one of those horror movies, doing just what we're not supposed to do, and we've stumbled on a whole bunch of ancient coffins just as the sun sets and the vampires are going to leap out and get us."

"*What?*" Desmond's startled exclamation jumped out of his mouth at the unexpected use of the word that defined him. His cry in turn startled David, who straightened up and stepped back, treading directly on Desmond's foot and throwing himself off balance. He grabbed at Desmond's wrist as he stumbled, but only succeeded in pulling them both down onto one of the wooden cases. Their cell phones clattered out of their hands and skittered across the dusty floor, leaving them tumbling in the gloom.

"Owww," he heard David groan, and in the dimness Desmond's sharp eyes could see that he'd clapped a hand to his forehead.

"David, what's wrong?" The only response was another groan and Desmond rolled over and knelt down next to the supine blond. A third groan, still fainter, was followed by silence, and Desmond was aware of the sharp tang of blood – blood from a wound, not safely coursing through the body's enclosed circulatory system. He drew close to David's face, and saw the dark wetness of blood trickling down his forehead and onto his left cheek. There was a gash, and it was bleeding the way head wounds were wont to – profusely.

Without thinking, Desmond bent forward and ran his tongue gently over the open wound. Immediately the taste of David's blood, as sweet and tangy as it had smelled earlier, filled Desmond's senses. His thirst surged powerfully. Unconsciously his canines lowered into position, and with only the slightest hesitation, Desmond moved his lips down to David's exposed throat and followed the instinct of his race.

His arms enfolded David in a tender embrace, lifting his torso off the cold floor. He pressed his chest to Parker's as he drank, feeling the blond's heartbeat fall into sync with his own. The warm blood pulsed into his mouth, and he felt its strength fill him up, calm his anxieties, bring him a sensation of peace and completion. Once finished, he laved the other man's throat with his tongue. Then, retrieving both of their phones, he pulled Parker into a sitting position, and then hoisted him to his feet.

Out in the corridor, Desmond could see that the wound on Parker's forehead had already stopped bleeding due to his ministrations. He decided to leave it as it was. He could make the scar disappear entirely at this stage, but its presence would explain away any aftereffects of his actions. It was a shallow wound and would fade on its own in time. He half carried and half walked Parker upstairs, and laid him on a frayed Louis XVI settee in the living room.

By the time he had driven a slightly confused and very embarrassed David Parker back into Newark, the young decorator assured Desmond that he was perfectly fine and able to take the train back into New York. Ever the gentleman, Desmond insisted on staying with him until they parted at David's subway stop.

As Parker moved to leave the car, he impulsively leaned forward and planted a kiss on Desmond's cheek.

"Thanks, Desmond. We're going to be great together on this project. We'll make your house drop-dead gorgeous." Then he paused, and batted his eyelashes comically. "My boyfriend is going to be so jealous!" And with that he disappeared into the evening crowd on the platform.

So it seems I've made another friend for my new life.

Desmond smiled as the doors hissed shut and the subway lurched forward, taking him home to the Dakota and the security of the nineteenth century.

Chapter Thirteen

"You look stressed, Jane." As soon as he'd gotten to the office, Desmond had noticed his normally cool and professional assistant looking slightly off center. It was nothing obvious, not as if her hair was askew or her tailored suit was rumpled; but something about the way she greeted him didn't seem to be – usual.

She looked up at her boss from behind her computer, and Desmond could tell she was weighing how much to say. He saw her eyes soften as he held her gaze.

"I'm okay. It's just Dane. He came over to our place again. He'd been drinking, which is no surprise, but last night it seemed like he was more out of control than usual. We were arguing over the whole child support issue. He's still really freaked about losing his job, and unfortunately his response is to increase the bad habits rather than ratchet them down." Jane sighed deeply and went silent a moment, glancing at her computer screen, as if she'd find some solution to her problems there. She looked back at Desmond.

"Sometimes I'm a little scared of him."

"He's a big guy. Has he ever been violent?"

"Not to me. Not to Janay or to Speck." She hesitated again. "I don't usually pressure him, but with Dot out of work, it just seems to me that he owes it to his kids to help."

"That would make sense."

"Right, but he was acting all paranoid about it, as if we were ganging up on him on purpose. I've never seen him so worked up."

"How did things end?"

"He left. Nothing got resolved."

"Jane?"

"Yes?"

"You'll let me know if there's anything I can do, won't you?"

"Sure."

Desmond went into his office and logged onto his computer. He read through correspondence on his desk, all carefully organized by Jane in order of importance. There was more paperwork from Chillon Investments about the pending partnership, and an invoice from Alex Duquesne's firm for David Parker's hours and materials. Desmond was pleased to see that David wasn't padding his bills, and although it was pretty clear the house in Llewellyn Park was going to cost a bundle to decorate, it would be worth what he paid. He liked the idea of supporting David's budding career; and Alex's relationship with Bill made everything feel pleasantly familial.

The dozens of emails that he sifted through were mostly business-related, but one caught his eye. It was from Denis Schroeder, proposing that they have dinner together in the city. Desmond emailed him back, suggesting that they meet for a drink later and then go to a club. He figured it would be easier to start off with Schroeder without having to go through his elaborate sleight-of-hand sitting in a restaurant over plates of food.

Just as he hit the send button to Schroeder's reply, Jane tapped on his door and pushed it open, holding a porcelain mug full of black coffee.

"I thought you might like this about now." She smiled at him, still looking slightly off kilter, but also with a warmth that made it clear that his concerns were appreciated.

He took the proffered mug and sipped at the coffee. It was strong and dark, as she knew he liked it. Coffee, like red wine and any drink of a similar physical composition, passed harmlessly through his system.

As Jane turned to leave, he stopped her.

"Jane, wait a minute, would you?"

She turned, and aimed a quizzical look at him without saying anything.

Desmond suddenly found himself tongue-tied in the face of this strong woman who had been such a constant help to him over the past years, and who had become so quickly a loyal friend to the new Desmond.

He finally forced himself to speak.

"Jane, you know I've been working on this house out in West Orange. I'm having it all redecorated and I'm updating the kitchen and bathrooms."

She didn't speak, but nodded slightly as if to give him permission to continue.

"Well, one of the things that David – David Parker, my decorator – suggested is that I renovate the old servants' wing into an apartment. The house is big, and it has a lot of grounds around it, and I've never really learned – I mean, at my age – anything about taking care of a house, much less a big property like this one."

Desmond paused. Jane's expression didn't alter at all. She clearly wasn't going to help him on this. He sighed and forged ahead.

"I was hoping I could convince you and Dotty to come see the house with me – and bring the girls. I've realized that I'm going to need someone to manage Oakwood for me."

A faint look of dawning understanding was beginning to light up Jane's large dark eyes, giving Desmond the push he needed.

"I've been thinking that Dot might be the perfect person to do that. You've said how organized she is, how hard she works. And I've been thinking about the two of you and the girls, and how great this place would be for a family. I'm just a bachelor, and I think I'm crazy taking on a huge place like this all by myself."

"Desmond, I can't accept an offer like this."

"I'm not asking you to accept anything. I just want you and your family to come see the place, and talk it over with me. Can't you think of it as doing a favor for a friend, not just for your boss?"

That last question seemed to break her mental logjam, and suddenly Jane smiled, her old familiar wise smile.

"I'll talk to Dotty about it. You know I can't really say anything without discussing the whole idea with her."

"I know."

Then her face softened again. "I'm just sort of stunned at this offer, Desmond. This is so much more than just taking a polite interest in my life. Do you understand how big this is, what you're proposing?"

He nodded, taking a swallow of his coffee, but saying nothing further.

A stiff breeze scattered fallen leaves from Sheridan Square across Christopher Street as Desmond made his way through the sparse traffic. Tiny silhouettes danced and whirled in front of the oncoming headlights, and Desmond thought back to a similar fall evening two decades earlier. It had been colder that night, and a different bar, and he hadn't expected to meet anyone. But Tony Chapman had been there and had thrown Desmond's carefully controlled world into a tailspin. He anticipated this rendezvous with a faint sense of dread mixed with a vague longing.

It was well past dark when Desmond walked into the Stonewall Inn on Sheridan Square. He'd decided it would be fun to start Denis' evening at the place where his own experience as a modern gay man had begun in the 1960s. Desmond hadn't been present at the Stonewall riots in 1969, but he'd been four years into a new life and had begun to make a tentative circle of gay friends. In recent years the dingy old bar had been renovated and had become, once again, a sort of gay tourist attraction. For young gay men, to whom Stonewall was historically akin to Bunker Hill, the newly trendy bar was the perfect place to start an evening's revelry.

No longer smoke-filled, now that smoking had been banned from all of New York's bars, the Stonewall was still loud, crowded and replete with the comingled scents of beer, cologne and sweat as it had always been. Desmond had to fight back a smile at the sudden and unconcealed attention his arrival drew. Gay men were far less subtle than the general public in this regard. His post-regeneration beauty always took some getting used to in the months immediately following his return to twenty-one. He dropped his jacket at the coat check, and made his way into the crowd. Lithe and dark-haired, tall enough to be noticed, Desmond moved with a sinuous grace through the packed rooms, his keen night vision scanning for a familiar face, a wry smile on his lips.

Well, if I misread his signals and he's not gay, this will certainly scare him off.

"There you are," came a soft but distinct voice very close to his ear, making him jump in spite of himself.

Desmond turned to find himself just inches from Denis Schroeder's perfectly sculpted features. Schroeder leaned in and gave him a chaste kiss on the lips. Startled by this forwardness, and simultaneously embarrassed at his old-maidish reaction, Desmond found his eyes locked onto Denis's, which looked grey in the bar's twilight.

"Worried I wouldn't show up?" he asked, trying to sound arch and, he suspected, failing.

"No, not at all." Denis smirked charmingly and took a sip of something colorless in a martini glass. "I've only been here a little bit. I spotted you the moment you walked in."

"Good eyesight, then, I've been prowling for a while and didn't see you."

"Well, everyone saw *you*. I watched you work your way back here, and it was as if Adam Levine had suddenly shown up shirtless and sweaty with all his lovely tattoos."

"You like tattoos?" gulped Desmond, again annoyed at himself for reacting like a teenager.

"I like a lot of things." Denis smirked and sipped again. "Can I get you a drink?"

"What've you got?" Desmond asked, slanting his eyes to the glass in Denis's hand.

"Hendricks, very dry."

"One of those then." He attempted a smile, and thought he'd gotten it right. At least Denis stopped smirking and flashed him a dazzling grin in return.

As Denis went to fetch the drink, Desmond collected himself. His heart was pounding weirdly fast for him, and while he didn't sweat, he could feel a hot flush working its way through his body, moving from his groin to his neck like a slow wave of tingling heat.

Denis returned, deftly handling the two glasses, both full now, without spilling a drop. Even in the dimness, his pale blond hair shone as if lit from inside, and he moved like a dancer, never knocking into anyone or taking his eyes off Desmond. Desmond let out a sigh.

They chatted for a while, sipping their drinks. Denis reported on how he was enjoying his first visit to New York, and how he was settling in to a rented corporate flat in a bland high-rise on the Upper East Side.

"Geneva is so tidy, so pretty, but very small-town," said Denis, pitching his voice perfectly so Desmond could hear it over the ambient noise. "New York is so vast and full of contrasts, from glittering elegance to gritty hipness. It's fascinating. I love feeling completely lost and unknown here."

Desmond had to think before he spoke. He'd theoretically only been here for a few months himself, although he'd seen New York grow from a cobbled port city down by Battery Park to the teeming metropolis it was now. "It is. I find it endlessly intriguing. Frustrating, but exhilarating."

"And yet you're bought a whopping great house in the suburbs." Denis raised his golden eyebrows, succeeding in looking arch where Desmond had not.

"How did you know that?" He wracked his brain to figure out how Denis could have learned this. He certainly hadn't told him. Jane? But she would never reveal anything personal in a business context.

"I could say something mysterious like 'I have my sources,' but the fact it, it showed up in one of the reports filed with us over the collaboration."

At Desmond's puzzled look he continued, "When you drop that kind of money all at once, it usually registers with a bean counter somewhere." He smiled again, a gentle, affectionate smile this time. Desmond's heart fluttered.

"One of our accountants here caught a sudden discrepancy in your assets, and figured out why. Must be a nice house."

"Yes. It is. But I'm keeping my flat at the Dakota. At least for the time being."

"Why the need for suburbia for one so young? The view from Central Park West not green enough for you?"

Struck by the insight of this offhand remark, Desmond tried to answer the question he'd been struggling to answer for himself.

"Something like that. It's been so long since I've had real green space around me. City parks, even

Central Park, are all fine, but I've, um, never owned any *land*. There are seven acres around this house, and it feels like I'm a million miles away, even though it's probably only twenty miles from where we're standing."

"Sounds beautiful. I'd like to see it sometime." Denis sounded completely sincere. No irony in his tone, no veiled sarcasm. His lovely face was open and candid as he gazed at Desmond.

"When it's finished, I'll have a party."

"I'll look forward to it." He turned and put his empty glass down on a nearby table. "Dance?"

With Denis holding Desmond by the hand, the two young men made their way to the crowded dance floor. There seemed to be an infinite number of bodies packed onto the parquet, but they seemed to have no problem finding space. Desmond marveled; it was as if people magically made room for them.

Desmond and Denis were dressed alike, with light-colored dress shirts fitting close to their lean frames, tails out, over dark jeans. Skinny jeans they were called, Desmond remembered with a wry smile. Tony had forced him to buy some blue jeans in the late 1980s, but even something as basic as jeans had gotten remarkably complicated in the early twenty-first century. Desmond also couldn't fathom the sneakers that so many young gay men wore. He noticed that Denis, too, wore elegant dark leather slip-ons, similar in quality and style to his own.

Denis danced beautifully, which was no surprise to Desmond. His body swayed with the music, following the tempo and rhythms as if he'd rehearsed the entire playlist. He stayed very close to Desmond, sometimes scant inches away from him, but didn't touch him; seeming to match him move for move without effort. Desmond could feel the heat radiating off the other man's body, and every once in a while his gaze would catch Desmond's, and those pale eyes would lock onto his. For all the exertion, Denis remained cool and unruffled. No sweat stains on his shirt, no sheen on his high forehead. He smiled, this time with obvious seductiveness. Then he leaned forward and gave Desmond a kiss, moving his hand around to the small of Desmond's back, pulling him in so that they finally touched, chest-to-chest. No chaste peck on the lips this time, but a full-on liplock. Denis's tongue brushed against his lower lip, and Desmond found himself opening up, welcoming the intruder with a rush of hunger. His senses filled with Denis's scent, and Desmond could feel the blood throbbing through his arteries, crisp and alpine, bracing. He felt his cock stir, bound up in his briefs beneath the tight jeans.

He pulled out of the kiss, putting his cheek against Denis's. "Let's get out of here," he whispered hoarsely in his ear.

They were silent in the dark taxi as they headed uptown from Greenwich Village. Desmond reached over and tentatively took Denis's hand, and they sat that way throughout the ride, exchanging an occasional slightly sheepish glance. Desmond had to keep reminding himself that while they seemed to be the same age, Denis was truly a young man, and this must all feel much different to him than it did to Desmond. Denis had given the driver an address on the West Side, but that detail didn't register until the cab pulled up in front of Therapy, a hot gay club on West 52nd Street.

At Desmond's puzzled look, Denis just grinned at him. "I thought we could have some fun here. Do you know the place?"

"Sure. Been here a couple of times, but ... " Desmond had been expecting to go to Denis's apartment. Had actually been yearning to move on to the next step with this handsome near-stranger, even as he tried not to think about his friendship with Oliver.

"Don't worry, my friend." He kissed Desmond quickly but hard on the lips as he handed some bills to the completely blasé cabbie. "I have something in mind. You'll see."

Newer and sleeker than the Stonewall, Therapy was

expansive and lofty, carefully lit and perfectly ventilated. It was full of people, mostly men, mostly under forty, but its ample spaces allowed for more elbow room, and large walls of windows offered glamorous city views for anyone who cared to look.

Denis pulled Desmond over to the long bar and got them two seats, ordering two more martinis before Desmond had a chance to react. The gin was making him light-headed. It was hard to get a vampire drunk, but Desmond was accustomed to red wine, and the gin was having a distinct, and not unpleasant, effect.

As they sat and drank, Denis carried Desmond along with idle conversation. A little bit of work, some conversation about Jane, a little more detail about the house in Llewellyn Park. In return, Desmond learned a few details about Denis's childhood in Geneva, about getting the job with Chillon Investments right out of university, about feeling forever under scrutiny in Switzerland.

And they danced some more, out on Therapy's much larger dance floor. Once more Denis's astonishing grace dazzled the young vampire. This time Denis touched him as they danced, held him now and then to bring their bodies closer. Together they seemed to be apart from everyone else, and the rest of the noise and the crowd faded into secondary importance. Desmond inhaled Denis's clear fragrance, the alluring tang of his blood mixed with that of a subtle cologne that made him think of mountain rivers and pine forests. His cock stirred again, still trapped in its nest of knitted cotton under the thick black denim.

As they swayed and flexed to the beat of the music, Denis abruptly took Desmond's hand and pulled it down to his own groin, where his excitement was evident. At Desmond's look of surprise, Denis brushed his lips across Desmond's and hissed, "Come with me."

He led a willing Desmond through the noise-filled spaces and through a swinging door into a smaller, dimmer space, but where the music continued its pulsing beat. Desmond looked around.

"This is the men's room."

Denis grinned at him naughtily. "Indeed. And a very notorious men's room it is."

Without any further ceremony, he took Desmond by the shoulders and gently shoved him into the nearest stall, stepped in and locked the door behind him.

"Not lots of privacy, but then that's probably the point, isn't it?"

Flustered, Desmond managed to stammer out, "But I thought ... your apartment ... "

"Not tonight, love. But I couldn't let this opportunity slip by. You're too beautiful."

The blond dropped to his knees and expertly unfastened Desmond's jeans, pulling them and his briefs down to his ankles in one surprisingly smooth movement. Freed from its fabric prison, Desmond's cock swung out as Denis leered at it greedily. He ran his long slender fingers up under Desmond's shirt, caressing his ribs, and took Desmond's entire length into his mouth as gracefully as if it were another dance move.

Giddy from the gin, Desmond couldn't move at first, pressed up against the stall divider. As Denis worked his tongue along his shaft, Desmond finally gave in to the dizzying sensation and began to run his hands through the silky blond hair.

It didn't take long, and Desmond was too off balance to try and take any control. He felt his balls tighten and gripped Denis's head in both hands as he hit a shuddering climax, banging his own head against the metal partition as he stifled a groan.

Suddenly horrified that he hadn't pulled out, he looked down, wide eyed, to see Denis, his big blue eyes fixed on Desmond's face, beaming like a child with a popsicle as he continued to suck on Desmond's softening cock, clearly enjoying every last drop.

Denis quickly stood up, his own clothes undisturbed. He gave Desmond a deep, long kiss, letting him taste himself on the other man's tongue. Then he pulled back and smiled a sleepy sort of smile.

"That was wonderful, dear friend. Every bit as nice as I'd hoped. But I have to go."

"What? You can't ... " Desmond started.

"But I must. I hope you'll see me again after this. I had a great time." And with another quick peck on the lips, like the one that had begun the evening, he vanished, leaving Desmond standing alone in the stall with his pants around his ankles.

Chapter Fourteen

Desmond peered out through the dust-streaked glass of the kitchen window at the gravel driveway. It was a nasty November day, typical of early New Jersey winters – cold enough to be unpleasant, but not cold enough for snow. Bone-chilling, damp and gray. Never had the half-finished house seemed less appealing. The air inside was clammy and smelled of plaster dust and paint. The new furnace was installed and had been turned on, but Desmond feared it wouldn't take the tomblike cold out of the rooms quickly enough, and he fretted that it would make the place a hard sell. He turned and surveyed the space behind him. At least the kitchen renovation was far enough along that you could see how great it would be. If his plan was going to work, he needed Jane and her family to see this as someplace they would want to spend time.

The sound of a car approaching turned him back to the window, and he saw the little red Toyota wagon making its way hesitantly under the dripping, leafless oak trees along the drive. His keen eyes could make out the expressions of disbelief on Jane and Dotty's faces as they peered up through the windshield at the enormous stone pile that was Oakwood.

Uh oh, they're overwhelmed already.

He almost ran to the front door, throwing the heavy oak panels open just as Jane was climbing out of the passenger door. Before he could even offer a greeting, the squeals of ten-year-old Janay and her eight-year-old sister Cassandra filled the chilly air.

"Holy crap, Mom, look at this place!"

"Janay, watch your mouth," came a sharp voice, as the scowling features of Dorothy Brown appeared over the car's roof on the driver's side. She was beautiful, just as Jane had told him; but there was a fierceness in her face that made it clear to Desmond that he was in for a rough time.

The two girls burbled up to him as he stood there on the front steps. He solemnly shook their hands and introduced himself, which made them giggle and bat their big hazel eyes at him flirtatiously. They were gorgeous, just as Jane had said. They looked like smaller versions of her, but with lighter complexions, gold highlights to their tawny curls, and those luminous eyes that Desmond recognized as their father's.

"Can we go in and look?" asked Janay, her coyness evaporating, replaced with a clear-eyed sense of purpose.

"I think we'd better ask your mother." Jane just nodded mutely, and Desmond waved them inside, calling after Janay as she grabbed her sister's hand and dragged her into the shadowy interior, "Watch out for your sister! There's paint and stuff lying around that your mom won't want her to get into."

Desmond listened for further squeals – either of fear or delight – but heard nothing. The big rooms seemed to have swallowed them up.

A clearing of the throat brought his attention back to the problem at hand, and he found himself confronted by Jane, looking wide-eyed and apprehensive, standing at the foot of the steps with Dotty at her side, hands on her hips. Clearly Ms. Brown was ready to take on this spoiled rich boy with his noblesse oblige assumption that her family needed his help. He realized his heart was beating a little faster than usual.

He defused the initial standoff by going down the steps and pulling Jane into a big hug and kissing her on the cheek.

"Thank you so much for coming, Jane," he said softly.

Then he turned to Dotty, who, undoubtedly fearing the same treatment, put out her hand for him to shake. "Dorothy, I'm so pleased to meet you at last."

"You can call me Dotty."

And before she had a chance to continue, he jumped right in. "You know, Dotty, I love Jane. She's been my rock since I got here this summer. I was totally at sea, and she became my friend and helped me through things."

Dotty merely looked bemused. "Yeah. I know. She's said," she replied somewhat grudgingly.

"Let's go in, so I can show you the place – and

explain what I have in mind."

He gave the women a quick tour of the main part of the house. All of the furniture was under dust sheets, and there were ladders and hanging wires and raw spackle visible in almost every room. In spite of that, Desmond could see his guests wide-eyed at the scale of the place as he nervously took them up the winding staircase, pointing out the various bedrooms and talking about his small group of friends who would, he hoped, stay in them once the house was finished.

All the time they were walking from room to room, the girls could be heard in the distance, calling occasionally to each other as if they were on a treasure hunt, their footsteps drumming on the bare floors.

Eventually, Desmond got to the servants' wing, which had been gutted and rearranged into a snug apartment with three cozy bedrooms, a playroom and two bathrooms. He was careful not to point out that David had designed it with them specifically in mind, but it was clear from their expressions – and from Janay and Speck's overt enthusiasm – that they all recognized a space tailor-made for their family.

They made their way down the back staircase, and immediately the girls spotted the huge flat-screen TV installed in the office/family room. Dotty and Jane wandered around the kitchen, not speaking, but quietly inspecting every detail, every appliance, every drawer. Without comment they looked in at the small second kitchen, designed for their personal use. It was everything any suburban housewife could have wanted. Or so Desmond hoped.

Just when Desmond was afraid he'd explode with the silence, Dotty turned to him, hands on her hips again. Her face was not hostile, but there was no questioning the challenge in her expression. Jane hovered to one side, a hand protectively on Dotty's shoulder.

"So what's this Jane's been telling me about some crazy-ass idea of me working for you?"

Desmond gulped, and then forged ahead. "I'm

talking about someone to really manage this place. Not do housework, but to arrange for that to be done – and for everything that needs to be done – the gardens, the lawn, the pool. I need someone here to do for me the kind of essential things Jane has always done for me at the office." He halted. "And for my father before me," he finished awkwardly.

He took a breath and plunged on before they could raise objections. "Look, Dotty, I've been blessed – obscenely blessed – with money and education and everything people think they want and need."

"Right about that," Dotty muttered, but softly, assessing him with an odd puzzled look in her eyes.

"But I've been alone too much in my life. I wouldn't be doing this just for you and Jane –although that's important to me, don't get me wrong. I'm doing this for me. I need you guys there. I've been crazy enough to buy this place, and I love it already because it's amazing and beautiful – but it just makes me too sad to think of being there all alone." He could hear the girls delightedly chattering about the cartoons they'd discovered on one of the endless cable channels his digital package provided. "Think of what this place could be for Janay and Cassandra."

Dotty had lowered her eyes at this, and sort of chuckled resignedly. "Shit, Desmond, how can I say no to something so damn pathetic? You'd probably start crying if I said no."

Desmond had smiled at her, "I might at that."

I really need this, Dotty. You don't know how much.

Then she grinned at him, her solemn expression broken by the dazzle of what he suspected was an all-too-rare smile.

"Okay. Let's say we'll try it out. When would I start?"

"Well, the house will be ready by mid-December, and I'm going to throw a weekend party for a few friends to launch it. I'd love to have you take care of some of the preparation for that, 'cause I hear you're such a fabulous cook. But you don't have to move in by then, not until you're ready. I'd love to make it in time for Christmas."

He could see some hesitation in her face.

"You see, Dotty, I've never had a family Christmas. I haven't had a family in a long time." Then he amended it, remembering that he was only twenty-one. "My father was always here, and I rarely saw him. My mother was busy and never as focused on me as I would have liked. I have no other relatives. I love the idea of your family here, with me, for Christmas. Then I wouldn't have to be alone."

"You make it sound like we'd be doing *you* the favor."

"You would. You really would." And, Desmond realized, it was nothing more than the truth.

"Damn, Desmond, you're good." Dotty shook her head, trying to keep a grin off her face. "You want to try the big puppy dog eyes on me?"

He widened his eyes and let his lower lip tremble a little, cocking his head slightly to one side. Dotty just let out a belly laugh, leaned over and smacked him on the shoulder.

"Now stop that, you crazy homo." And she yanked him into a crushing embrace, sealing the deal.

Chapter Fifteen

Three weeks till Christmas, and the first snow of a surprisingly mild New Jersey autumn had finally fallen. It was only a couple of inches, but the temperature had dropped suddenly, and in the outside lights the thin frosting glittered like crushed diamonds on every surface in the crystalline air.

Desmond stood at the tall living room window, holding back the jade-green curtains by the fringe as he stared out over the front lawn. He turned and looked back into the enormous room, softly lit with a dozen lamps and fixtures. David had done an extraordinary job. The tall carved stone fireplace on the end wall was austere and elegant against the deep bottle-green Genoa velvet that David had located to cover the walls. Just what the architect would have envisioned in the 1920's. The complex *parquet de Versailles* floor shone a rich deep brown, contrasting with the pale Aubusson carpets that David had bought at auction. They weren't eighteenth-century – Desmond had balked at walking on carpets that old – but they were Second Empire copies from a French country house, and they looked incredible here. Not since his childhood, centuries ago, had he lived in a room this large. Even the lofty spaces at the Dakota looked domestic and cozy in comparison. And yet it wasn't a forbidding room, but a room for nights like this, full of friends and conversation.

He moved away from the window and walked back through the series of hallways, past the library, where a fire already burned brightly, and through the dining room to the kitchen. Platters of room-temperature hors d'oeuvres and pans of dinner entrees ready to be popped into one of the large commercial-size ovens were waiting, ready to go in when the time came. Desmond knew there was champagne and beer and wine in the large fridge.

He mused at the extravagance of the kitchen. He'd never cook here, except for parties like this, but somehow his kitchens had always been important to him, or at least at certain moments in his life. He remembered watching while Tony wolfed down bacon and eggs that Desmond had cooked in the little 1930s kitchen on 4th Street in New York. He remembered small dinners he had pulled together in the kitchen at the Dakota flat for Bill and Alex and Vivian and her husband, Luke. He smiled, recalling what a good sport Luke was at the little parties, surrounded by middle-aged gay men and their gossip. Luke Lake was an accountant, and nothing seemed to unnerve him. Desmond, for all that he couldn't eat, loved the smells of food, and his heightened senses made cooking almost a sexual gratification for him. Almost. He'd had to learn not to lick his fingers; not to accidently take a little taste of something, lest it trigger a strong reaction from his vampire body. His love for Tony had motivated him to learn to cook, and even Tony's death hadn't killed that pleasure for him.

He walked from the kitchen down the back hall to the media room – the room David had designed to be a combination television room for Desmond and family room for Jane and her family. He had gotten a selection of current videos of in case anyone wanted to be a couch potato over the weekend.

As Desmond climbed the back stairs, he thought through the plans for the near future. Jane and Dotty and Janay and Cassandra would move in at the end of the following week.

He'd be on his own for the weekend, but he wouldn't be alone and the house was all clean and ready. They'd already been in to see the place several times during the renovations, the girls running about, fighting over which of the cheery little bedrooms they'd have as their own. He glanced into the trim apartment in the old servants' wing as he moved into the long upstairs corridor, mentally ticking off the room assignments.

He had put Vivian and Luke Lake in the chintz guest room at the end of the house nearest the kitchen wing. Bill Lawrence and Alex Duquesne had gotten the best guest room – the large bow-fronted one above the library, overlooking the now-covered pool. Oliver Cameron was to be in the little room over the front door, and he would have to share a bathroom with David Parker and his boyfriend Jeffrey, who had the blue guest room.

Desmond had put Denis Schroder in the sitting room adjacent to his own bedroom. They had seen each other several more times since that first unnerving evening together. They had danced, they had kissed, but nothing like the first night had been repeated, somewhat to Desmond's relief. Taking a little blood in a crowded bar was nothing new to him, but blowjobs in bathroom stalls were something he'd probably never get used to. He was sincerely hoping that Denis wouldn't actually be staying in his assigned room, but he didn't want to seem presumptuous, so he had dutifully set up a camp bed with the same good linens he had bought for all of the beds.

Roger hadn't been able to make it for this, but he had promised to come for Christmas. Desmond felt a vague relief, since he wouldn't have known where to put Roger anyway.

The Lakes and Bill and Alex had not yet seen the house at all; nor had David's boyfriend. But David and Oliver had gone through the place with Desmond a couple of times as the work had moved forward. At first the decorator and the curator had eyed each other suspiciously, especially as Oliver had performed his odd curatorial ritual of running his hands over the things David had gotten Desmond to buy at auction.

As his well-formed fingers caressed the carving on a Regency center table in the entrance hall, Oliver's eyes had lit up. "You know this is older than you thought it was."

To David's confused look, Oliver had replied, "It's not a turn-of-the-century copy. It's really from the 1820s."

"Looks like the auction house really messed up on this. Score!" David had crowed, high-fiving Oliver as they laughed in shared triumph.

With reassurance like this, gradually David's anxiety had melted, and they'd warmed to one another as the curator had whole-heartedly approved of David's skill. On the last visit, just a few days earlier, Oliver had impulsively hugged Desmond and David and declared that the house was amazing.

"You have totally honored this place. It's ravishing," he'd said, a broad smile shining in his ginger whiskers, his blue eyes sparkling.

David had merely given him a modest 'thank you' and a kiss on the cheek, but Desmond had been touched at the enthusiasm.

"This means a lot to me, Oliver – your approval, I mean."

"Well, I'm pleased that my opinion matters to you, but I never really had any doubt that you'd pull it off." He had taken Desmond's hands and looked deeply into his eyes for a long moment. Desmond saw a hint of something unexpected; something that didn't make him entirely comfortable.

The sound of a car on the gravel drive brought Desmond out of his daydream. He all but ran down the curving staircase and across the hall to the vestibule. He threw open the big oak front doors and struck a camp pose just as a rented Nissan pulled up in front of the playhouse, disgorging Bill and Alex and David and Jeffrey. They all hailed him as "Aunty Mame" as they made their way across the drive, suitcases in tow, their tracks tearing up the new-fallen snow.

"Good grief, look at this palace," exclaimed Bill in his rich baritone, arms outstretched in mock horror. Alex just rolled his eyes and gave Desmond a warm buss on the cheek. David kissed Desmond too, and introduced him to Jeffrey, who was tall and quiet and muscular in a dim jock way, a distinct contrast to his boyfriend.

"Alex didn't believe it was so close," reported David.

"It only took forty minutes from midtown!" added Alex, as David gave him a smug smile.

"Well you lucked out with the traffic coming against the flow," said Desmond. "It can take a lot longer if the traffic is bad."

The lights of a second car started up the long drive, and this turned out to be Vivian and Luke Lake, who joined the crowd on the front steps, exchanging greetings and introductions. Vivian's husband was, as she herself was, trim and self-consciously nondescript, as if his profession would be compromised by anything too noticeable. He had always struck Desmond as a good sort, quietly supportive of his wife and ready for anything in terms of social life. From his cheerful greeting, Desmond could see no apparent dismay at the thought of spending the weekend in a houseful of gay men. Vivian was lucky in her spouse.

They all moved into the entrance hall, stamping the snow off their shoes, the newcomers oohing and aahing appropriately as they took in their surroundings.

"David, would you get everybody up into their rooms? Here's a list of who goes where." He handed a little scribbled note to David.

"I've put you and Jeffrey in the blue room – you'll have to share a bath with Oliver, but I figured the old folks would need their privacy more."

Alex and Vivian both objected to that with comic loudness but happily followed David off down the hall and up the stairs, their chatter receding and leaving Desmond alone in the silent hall.

The sound of the heavy knocker on the front door drew him back into the vestibule, and he opened it to find Oliver, bag in hand, grinning at him from the stoop. Oliver gave him a hug and a quick kiss and let himself be ushered inside.

"Excited?" he asked, his eyes twinkling.

"Very. I've been on pins and needles all week. I'm so glad you're here, Oliver."

They were interrupted by the sound of yet another car, and they both turned as a black limousine – a Maybach, Desmond was startled to see – pulled up right in front of the steps. No chauffeur appeared from the driver's seat, but Denis Schroeder let himself out, unfolding his long legs from the dark interior, then leaned back into the car to get his overnight bag and speak to the driver. The car quietly backed up, reversed into the entrance to the garage court, and went on its way back down the drive and into the winter night.

"Hello, Des," said Denis, his hair shining gold in the porch lights, his beautiful face dramatic in the evening shadows. He walked up the steps and, leaning in, gave Desmond a full, slightly longer-than-casual kiss on the mouth. Then he turned his gaze on Oliver, who was looking slightly stunned.

"You must be Oliver Cameron. Desmond's told me

so much about you."

Desmond suddenly felt something slightly territorial in the way Denis had done all this, but there was nothing but open friendliness on his face as he smiled down at the shorter redhead. Oliver for his part, managed a slightly faltering smile but, Desmond noted, did not offer his hand.

"I'm afraid you have me at a disadvantage, then. Desmond hasn't told me anything about you at all." His eyes cut to Desmond quickly, but returned to Denis's smiling face.

"Oh, I'm sorry. I'm Denis Schroder."

Is he putting on a stronger accent than usual?

"Desmond and I are working on a business partnership between his company and mine."

"Ah, I see," replied Oliver, clearly seeing more than Denis's words suggested.

He turned his attention to his host.

"Well, I guess I should go in. Where've you put me, *Des*?" he asked, emphasizing his use of the diminutive.

"Um, the little room over the front door – you know where it is, right?" Desmond was nonplussed at the chill in Oliver's voice.

"Yes, I know. I'll go catch up with the others. They're probably all poking around in each other's rooms already." He smiled, a trifle wanly, Desmond thought, and headed off into the interior of the house.

"He's adorable," said Denis.

"He is." Desmond hesitated, sensing something dismissive in Denis's tone, but unable to pinpoint it. "He's a good friend."

"I like redheads, do you?"

Startled by the question, Desmond stammered, "Uh, yes, as it happens, I do."

"Indeed. Mmmm … all that lovely pale skin contrasting with the wonderful color of the hair – everywhere. So, Des, have you ever…?" Denis raised his eyebrows with the unfinished question.

"No, no. Never," answered Desmond too quickly,

guiltily remembering that night in Oliver's house earlier in the fall. He and Oliver had lunched together with some regularity over the past few months, and Desmond had been to visit Oliver at the Museum several times as well. While their friendship had ripened, they had never again approached the intimacy that had seemed to be in the air that night at the trattoria. At the same time, he couldn't deny that his attraction to the curator, both physical and emotional, was still very much there.

Denis stroked Desmond's cheek softly with an ungloved hand and stepped past him into the house. "So where am I for the weekend?"

"I'm rather full up, even for a house this big. I've put you on a camp bed in my sitting room." He faltered, suddenly aware of the obviousness of this ploy. "Hope you don't mind."

Denis gave him a naughty smirk. "Not at all. Very convenient I'd say." He picked up his bag effortlessly and headed off into the house.

"Wait, let me show you," Desmond called after him, and hurried to catch up.

They climbed the stairs in silence, Desmond noticing every glance that Denis gave as he ascended in front of him. Pausing at the top of the stairs, Denis turned and gave Desmond a questioning look.

"To the right, then straight ahead."

They moved down the hall into the master suite, Denis looking quickly into the large master bedroom, where a four-poster with a silk-draped canopy had been set up. He continued into the spacious sitting room, where his own modest bed had been made up in front of the fireplace.

"This is nice. I must say, Desmond, this is all pretty splendid. I am floored."

He opened his arms and enfolded Desmond in a warm embrace, kissing him with an urgency that stirred him up. As their tongues fluttered together, Desmond felt his discomfort fade away, giving in to the pleasure of the beautiful blond's closeness, the feel of his body against him, the smell of his blood.

This is good. This is what I want.

The sound of a door shutting in the corridor behind them brought them apart. Together they stared down the long hall, but no one was visible. Desmond pulled back from Denis reluctantly.

"I guess we can continue this later on?"

"Absolutely. I'm sort of guessing that my nice little boy bed in there isn't going to get mussed up."

"I guess I'll just have to cope."

"Let me freshen up a bit and I'll join you downstairs?"

"Of course. Right in there. There are 'his' and 'hers' bathrooms in this suite. You get 'hers' for tonight."

Denis just waggled his eyebrows comically before slipping into the bathroom and leaving Desmond to tend to his other houseguests.

Desmond silently thanked David's foresight in installing gas logs that could be switched on and off at the flick of a lever in all of the fireplaces. The three main rooms had cheerful fires going when the company began to filter downstairs, and Desmond realized that even with Dotty in residence he could hardly have wanted to deal with lugging all of that wood. No maids, no footmen, no butler; and the very idea of asking Dotty to make up nine log fires was unimaginable. This way his guests would be able to have fires in their rooms if they wished when they went to bed.

He was waiting for them, somewhat lost in thought, in one of the big green velvet sofas by the fireplace in the living room. There were four large sofas in this room, each of them scattered with bright silk brocade cushions. They delineated four seating areas, accompanied by pairs of antique English and French armchairs. Aside from the lamps, the tabletops were as yet bare of ornaments, as was the chimneypiece. Desmond wanted to take his time to collect, as he had with the apartment in New York, and before that in his little house on 4th Street. David and he had decided to purchase enough furniture to make the place seem finished, but not to go too far.

Very little art hung on the walls as yet anywhere in the house, with the single exception of this room. David had talked Desmond into three large paintings, two of which had been shockingly expensive. On the western wall, over one of the sofas, was a large-scale full-length portrait of an Elizabethan woman. David had spotted this in a New York gallery, and had convinced Desmond to buy it. The anonymous sitter was resplendent in a stiff lace ruff, an ornately slashed red velvet and gold brocade gown, and dripping in heavy ropes of pearls. Gold badges set with diamonds and emeralds were sewn onto her gown, and she looked out into the room from her carved gold frame with a smug assurance that always made Desmond laugh inwardly. The period was too early for the style of his house, but the lady's unabashed glory in her opulence was irresistible.

Opposite this lady was another one, but of a very different type. Another full-length portrait, this was more appropriate to the pretensions of the architect who had designed Desmond's house. By the English painter John Hoppner, this picture also featured a lady, but here she was dressed in the voluminous white muslin of the late eighteenth century, her pink sash coordinated with the ribbons in her long curled hair. Like her Elizabethan counterpart, she looked out of her frame at the viewer with an expression of frank appraisal; but there was a warmth in her eyes, a casual elegance to her pose, that somehow put Desmond in mind of his own mother. Lady Anne Desmond had married Sir Charles Beckwith in the early 1700s, but she had died shortly after giving birth to her only child in 1724. Desmond had never known his mother, and hadn't had the heart to take the portrait of her with him when he and Roger Deland had moved to America in the 1810s. Even this Hoppner, by an artist whom Desmond had actually met in London during his second lifetime, was two generations later than his mother's portrait, but it still warmed his heart to see it.

"Holy mother of pearl!" The exclamation came from the walnut double doors that opened into the room. Desmond turned, and laughed out loud at the expression of shock on his friend Bill's face. It was not the room that had elicited such a response from this elegant elderly black man, his reaction at odds with his general demeanor of propriety and self-control. No, Bill had seen Desmond's overstuffed Victorian flat in New York. He knew what Desmond's money could accomplish. Desmond turned in his seat and looked up at the third portrait in the room, hanging over the English Palladian chimneypiece.

"Where the hell did that come from?" asked Bill, his tone softened considerably as he approached the picture.

"David found it. Online if you can believe it. He was so proud of it. Sort of an eerie coincidence, its turning up that way."

This find of David's had, at first, shaken Desmond to the core. When the portrait had turned up in a London antique shop's website, the dealer had not been particularly enthusiastic about it. But he had been far more excited about taking Desmond's money, and readily shipped the darkened and dirty portrait at no extra cost off to the crazy American who wanted it. It was not by an especially important artist, Jonathan Richardson Sr., who had been a portraitist in London. Well known in his day, his name had never inspired the collecting lust of American millionaires in the early twentieth century. But in 1745, the year he had died, the artist had traveled down to Berkshire to paint the portrait of the young Desmond Beckwith.

And there he was, full length, newly restored, in a carved and gilded frame, glinting against the green velvet of the living room walls. He wore a velvet frock coat and breeches of dark red, trimmed with gold buttons, over a white silk waistcoat sprigged with gold florets. A simple white linen stock wrapped his slender neck and fell down into the opening of his waistcoat. Shoulder-length dark hair curled around his ears and collar. His large hazel eyes stared out into the room, and a faint smile played across his full lips.

"Good Lord, Desmond, it looks just like you."

"It is me, Bill." He looked up at his oldest mortal friend. "Me as I was when I had just become what I am today."

"You? You were a vampire in that portrait?"

"Yes. I'd just returned from my trip abroad. Jeffrey was dead, and Baron Tsolnay had transformed me. My father commissioned it to celebrate my return from my long journey. He didn't understand the depth of my grief, nor could I fully explain it to him. He surely wouldn't have been able to grasp what had happened to me. I would barely sit for my portrait, and the poor artist was on his last legs."

He paused, and looked up at the picture again.

"I refused to let them powder my hair. It upset my father terribly. He was so very conscious of propriety, being a self-made man. I assured him it was all the thing in Europe to be painted with my hair like that, no wig, no powder. And that look on my face. I knew they didn't know what I was, and that alone kept me from despair. That new life I'd been given was all that kept me together, the knowledge that I couldn't die the way Jeffrey had."

"Which Jeffrey died?" asked Alex Duquesne, walking into the room and across the expanse of elegant carpet. He stopped next to Bill, and put a hand on his partner's shoulder as he gazed up at the portrait. "What an astonishing likeness, Desmond."

"It is, isn't it? We were speaking of another Jeffrey, Alex. A Jeffrey who you never knew."

"AIDS?" Alex asked. Together the three of them had lost many friends to the plague, attended too many funerals. But Alex didn't know that; the Desmond he had cared about had died, too.

"No, an accident. Jeffrey was someone I knew as a boy."

Well, that's the truth anyway.

"Sorry, Desmond, I didn't mean to barge into your conversation. Tell me about the picture. There must be a story."

If you only knew, Alex.

And so the first part of the evening unrolled. As each guest entered the room, the portrait stopped them in their tracks, and Desmond had to retell his version of the story each time, adding praise for David for coming across it.

After a while, he let David take over the storytelling, and began to get drinks for everyone from a marble-topped table at the side of the room. Denis was the last to come down, looking sexy and casual in jeans and a dark form-fitting silk shirt. He took a proffered martini from Desmond, locking eyes with him as he sipped from the glass.

"The portrait is astonishing, Des," he said softly.

Desmond just smiled, and raised his own glass of champagne.

It was easy to let everybody else do the talking as they moved from the living room, to the sunroom, with its tinkling fountain and brightly-colored tiles, and finally to the dining room, where the sideboard was loaded with the heated-up food that Dotty had left for the meal. People helped themselves and sat where they wished. Bill, ever the journalist, even in retirement, sat next to Denis, quizzing him about business and the economy. Vivian sat with David, delighted by his fey animation, pumping him for stories about adventures in decorating, and trying to find out if Desmond was a difficult client.

Oliver sat with Alex, and they compared notes over the antiques market and exhibitions they'd seen and museums they'd visited. Desmond marveled at how naturally the two men got along. It reminded him of Oliver's uncanny skill at making people feel at ease. Oliver liked people immediately, and they tended to like him back just as readily.

Luke, somewhat to Desmond's surprise, settled in with Jeffrey and apparently had a long involved conversation about sports, even evaluating Jeffrey's opinions as to who the cutest baseball players were. He had to smile, both at Jeffrey's obliviousness to any notion that a straight man might not entirely enjoy comparing pro-ball players' relative hotness; and at Luke's open-hearted acceptance of the young man's uncomplicated approach to his own sexuality.

Desmond, as host, added a comment here and there, joining in a conversation when it felt right; but mostly he sat happily, not eating his dinner, and watching these people enjoy themselves. More champagne was drunk, followed by other wines, as the gathered friends grew looser and more voluble with each other, and blessed Desmond's new home with their fellowship.

As everyone was clearing away the dessert dishes, while Desmond and Vivian stacked them in one of the two new dishwashers, Desmond realized that Oliver had slipped away. He signaled Vivian that he'd be right back and quietly walked down the service hall and into the entry. The library was empty, ready for cognac and liqueur, the fire reflecting off the polished walnut paneling. The house was quiet but for the ticking of a clock in the hall, and the faint background noise of dishes in the far-off kitchen. Desmond quietly peeked into the living room, and there found Oliver, standing on a Queen Anne armchair in his socks, one of his beautiful hands raised as he ran his fingers gently over the surface of the portrait above the fireplace.

Desmond saw Oliver start and heard a soft gasp of surprise. Then he retreated a few steps into the hall before making a more obvious entrance, his heels ringing on the parquet floor. Oliver was still on the chair when Desmond walked in, but he had turned to face the doorway.

"Everything okay, Oliver?" he asked, making his tone light. "Something wrong with the picture? I hope it's not a fake. It wasn't as expensive as the other two, but it wasn't cheap."

"No, no, Des. Not at all." Oliver hesitated, climbing down from the chair with as much grace as possible, and sitting to put his shoes back on. He looked up at Desmond, a sort of quenched wonder in his eyes.

"It's quite good. I, um, thought I saw a repair and was just checking to see if I was right." He looked down at his hands, now clasped in his lap. "I was wrong. It's perfect. The conservator did a great job."

"You recommended her, after all, Ollie."

The redhead looked up at this use of his nickname.

"You've never called me that before."

"Sorry, I won't do it again."

"No, I didn't mean that. I like it. Not many people call me that. Only my mom. And Asa."

"Oh, Oliver, I'm sorry. I didn't know … "

"Please, call me Ollie. Please, Desmond. I'd like it if you did."

Oliver stood and put the chair back in its position, then, slipping on his shoes, moved over to Desmond's side.

"Very bad form, that, standing on an antique chair. Not very curatorial of me, was it?" He smiled at his friend, the warmth of his look filling Desmond with an unexpected thrill of happiness.

Desmond took Oliver's arm in his, turning toward the door. "I imagine curators stand on chairs quite a lot when no one's looking. Let's go to the library. Everyone's going to settle in for a nightcap."

The evening wore down pleasantly. Jeffrey and David took Desmond up on his offer to watch *Milk* on the media room's huge flat-screen television, and Luke again surprised his host by venturing to join them. Vivian looked at her watch and decided she'd turn in and read a while in bed. Taking her cue, Bill and Alex both yawned and made their excuses, following Vivian upstairs into the silent upper region of the big house.

With the lull in conversation, Desmond found himself standing by the fire, staring into the oddly regular gas flames, watching as their reflections flickered and danced on the curved moldings of the dark green marble mantelpiece. Without looking, he knew that Oliver was in an overstuffed armchair by the bow window, where he'd been talking to Luke. Denis was at one end of the long sofa under the wall of bookshelves, pretending to study an antique volume of poetry he and David had pulled off the shelf earlier. He felt himself frozen, awkwardly unable to break the silence that had fallen on the three of them.

All at once Denis shattered the quiet, addressing Oliver, who started and looked over at him.

"So Desmond tells me you consulted with the work on the house."

"Uh, yes. Consulted sounds a little formal. This is a period I know and love, and Desmond asked me to give him some pointers. As a friend. It really wasn't much. David did all the work. I was just sort of, well … " he trailed off, looking over at Desmond as if for assistance.

"Making sure the decorator didn't go overboard?" finished Denis.

Oliver chortled softly. "Yeah, I guess that was it. But David sure proved himself, I think." He smiled – that same wan curve of his pretty mouth Desmond had seen earlier – and added, "Desmond really didn't need me, I think. He was just being nice."

Desmond started to speak, but Denis interrupted him by standing and walking over to him. He put his hands on Desmond's shoulders and gave him a quick, but clearly intimate, kiss.

"I think I'll turn in and … read, too," he said. With a nod to Oliver, who was still in his chair by the windows, he slipped out of the room.

Desmond looked helplessly over at Oliver, feeling that he'd managed something very badly, but unsure exactly of what it was. Oliver rose and started over to him, but Desmond left his spot by the fire and met him halfway across the room. He reached out as if to touch the redheaded man, but instead Oliver clasped the extended hand in both of his own and held it, looking searchingly into Desmond's eyes.

"Desmond, you know how much I appreciate your friendship. And your support of the museum. Thanks for inviting me tonight. It's been really lovely. Alex and Bill are great, and clearly important to you."

"They were close friends of my father's, and I've quickly grown fond of them."

"So, I guess I'll see you in the morning." He held onto Desmond's hand, his eyes glistening oddly, a quizzical expression flickering over his handsome features. Then he broke contact and went out the double doors into the darkened hall.

Desmond listened to his steps receding up the staircase. He went around the room, switching off the lamps, and finally, as he was bending down to turn off the gas fire, he let himself slump down into a chair.

He sat staring into the flames, cradling his head in his hands. When he heard the clock in the hall strike the hour, he roused himself to switch off the fire. He straightened up, and making his way through the house, turning off all the lights as he went, he headed upstairs in the dark.

He gently closed the door into the suite behind him, and going down the short passage, turned into his bedroom. The lights were off, and the fire played in the grate, making the whole room shift and flutter in its light. As he moved into the room, Desmond realized the bed's silk cover had been pulled back and folded at the foot against the tall carved bedposts. Denis, naked, was lying on the white blanket on his right side, one long leg hiked up slightly, his face turned away from the door. The pale bed curtains framed the scene like a theatrical vignette.

Desmond's stomach jumped at the sight of the firelight playing along those willowy ivory-gold legs and across the blond's flawless pale backside. He wanted to go over and run his hands along that smooth flesh, to feel the give of those muscles under his fingers. But he decided to have a quick wash-up and not wake Denis quite so quickly.

The 'his' bathroom in the master suite had a large shower lined with tawny polished limestone with a matte finish that was like satin to the touch. Desmond loved modern plumbing, thinking it equal in importance for the development of the world as airplanes or even computers. He turned on the powerful jets and stepped under the hot spray, letting the water pummel his knotted shoulders and the back of his head. He released his bladder and a stream of red wine, virtually unaltered, spiraled down the drain set in the stone floor. It was always the same with those liquids Desmond had learned his body could tolerate. Whatever chemical effect was possible, whether caffeine or alcohol, did its job, but the rest just kept on going.

Turning off the shower, Desmond grabbed a large bath towel from a rack and dried himself off quickly. Dropping it on the bathroom floor, he moved silently into the bedroom and across the carpet to the bed, where he hesitated, watching Denis' unmoving form, before slipping onto the blanket and spooning up to him.

There was no response. Denis' motionless form was cool as Desmond skimmed his fingers down one of the long lean flanks, giving the muscles the gentlest of squeezes, just to feel their firmness beneath his touch. When he reached over to run his hand down Denis' belly, he felt his cock, rigid and ready. Suddenly Denis raised his head, and that beautiful face turned back over his shoulder to catch Desmond's eyes. The bright blue of his irises glittered in the dancing firelight.

"What took you so long?" he whispered with a smirk on his lips. And in a move so quick Desmond couldn't follow it, Denis had him pinned against the mattress, his prick digging into Desmond's abdomen as he ground his hips against him. Clasping Desmond's head, he kissed him fiercely, his tongue forcing its way into Desmond's mouth. He sighed out a moan.

Overwhelmed by the suddenness of the blond's passion, Desmond let himself lie there, enjoying the kiss,

Vampire in Suburbia

tasting the faint bitter aftertaste of the evening's wine, inhaling the dizzying alpine rush of Denis's blood just below the surface of that alabaster skin.

A rare thing it was for Desmond to fully abandon himself to a physical encounter. In the years since Tony's death he had restricted himself to relatively anonymous hook-ups, often – but not always– accompanied by the taking of blood. He had never brought anyone back to the Dakota flat, but had fallen into his pre-Tony custom of going home with the other man, getting a hotel room, or doing without. His lingering grief had been assuaged – enough at least – by the immediate physical connection and by the blood, if that was part of the picture. His solitary life and even his loneliness had become almost sacred to him. But Denis had awakened something long dormant. The fact that he was here in Desmond's bed was proof of that.

Surfacing from his torpor, Desmond reached down with both hands and cupped Denis's buttocks, kneading the gluteus muscles with increasing roughness as his own arousal grew. His erection jutted upward between Denis's legs, rubbing against the other man's scrotum as Denis continued to grind into him. The soft rasp against the top side of his cock made Desmond tremble with frustration.

Their lovemaking grew more intense as they explored each other's bodies; each discovery for one a sensual revelation for the other. Denis's hunger seemed to match Desmond's; something the vampire had difficulty crediting. How could such a beautiful creature feel so desperately needy? How could he possibly share the sort of isolation that had been Desmond's lot for so long a time? The idea that he had sparked this passion in the blond man was flattering and exciting, and every one of Desmond's heightened senses hummed with yearning.

They came to a brief pause when, both of them panting slightly, they lay side by side, facing each other. Denis again trained his eyes on Desmond's for a long moment, and it seemed that an internal lock had clicked.

Once more in a move that seemed both uncannily fast and unnaturally graceful, Denis was suddenly on his knees between Desmond's legs, his strong, slim hands grasping the darker man's ankles. He raised one of Desmond's feet to his lips and kissed the high arch, then ran his tongue from the heel to the great toe. Resting Desmond's foot on his shoulder, Denis reached over to the nightstand and pulled a small tube and a condom from the drawer. Then with his other hand he leaned in and stroked the opening between Desmond's legs. As he increased the pressure, Desmond's eyes went wide.

"Oh. Oh," he managed breathlessly. "I don't usually … It's been a long time…." The sensation of Denis's fingers on that tender spot made it hard to form words.

Not since Tony. Oh, Lord, never since Tony.

"Don't worry, Desmond. I guessed you'd be used to topping." His eyes lingered flirtatiously, the long honey-color lashes lowering as he looked down at Desmond's lithe form spread out beneath him on the white blanket.

"Grant me this one wish. Please?" The lust in his voice belied the odd courtliness of the question.

Desmond lasered into Denis's eyes, trying to see inside that intelligent mind, to understand what he was doing–beyond the obvious. Then, wordlessly, he nodded his assent.

There was no significant pain; Desmond had no fear of that in any case. There had been no real need for the condom. He was immortal. But he respected that Denis was safe, and the pleasure that Desmond soon felt flowed in waves through him, making him shudder over and over. He banished all thoughts of the past and let himself fall into the sensation, riding each of the blond's thrusts with increasing bliss until he felt himself rushing with dangerous speed toward the edge. He realized, slightly startled, that he hadn't even touched himself.

All at once, as their mutual frenzy began to peak, Denis lifted his other ankle up onto his shoulder, and pressed forward, rocking into Desmond's body with all his force, bringing his chest to Desmond's chest, his face closing in as if for a kiss. But instead, he spoke softly, urgently, into Desmond's mouth as his lips fluttered over Desmond's.

"Bite me."

Confused, Desmond focused on Denis's mouth, and felt a jolt scissor through him. Behind those lush lips, bruised and moist from kissing, were the sharp ivory points of his extended upper canines.

He has fangs. He's a vampire.

"Bite me, Desmond," repeated Denis with a frantic urgency, turning his head to bare his most vulnerable place. "Now."

Desmond's own canines extended, his instinctive thirst driving him into the moment. He lifted his head and clamped his mouth onto Denis's offered throat, feeling the smoothness and tasting the salt of his skin before pressing home his vampire's fangs and letting flow the blood – the heavenly, life-giving, overwhelmingly delicious liquid that had been his sole nourishment for over two and a half centuries.

Denis cried out in ecstasy as Desmond's fangs bit into him, but continued thrusting into Desmond's body as his blood was taken. In just a few seconds he all but screamed once more as his climax overwhelmed him, and Desmond could feel him spending himself in waves of heat.

Desmond's mind seemed to unhinge, and every feeling in his body exploded as if his system was short-circuiting from sensory overload. His mouth still affixed tightly to Denis's neck, Desmond let out a muffled roar as he followed his lover over the edge, the blood flowing into him as his seed shot up his own chest.

He forced himself to withdraw his canines, and lingered on the wounds only long enough to clean them with his tongue. Even as he did this he felt the tiny openings close up as if they had never been. He pulled away, and Denis withdrew from him, letting Desmond's legs fall, and collapsed on top of him, their chests heaving together, their hearts pounding in unison.

Desmond rolled them over so that they clung to each other face to face, legs intertwined, sweaty and sticky and reeking of semen and blood. He reached up to stroke Denis's cheek.

"How did you know?" he murmured.

"Surprise," answered Denis, more a breath than a word. "I suspected from the moment I first shook your hand. The way your blood smells, the strength that radiates from you." He raised his head slightly and looked quizzically at Desmond. "Didn't you notice anything unusual about me?"

Desmond considered this a moment. "Well, you *were* different. But, then, everyone's different." His eyes widened as the recollection dawned on him. "Your scent was always – I don't know – cool. Most people smell warm. The significance didn't register." He ran his fingers over Denis's smiling mouth. "I guess I had nothing to compare you to. It's been centuries since I've met another vampire."

He wondered why he didn't mention Roger.

I'm so used to Roger's scent; I never thought how it differs from a mortal's scent.

"You know," he said lazily, "I've never had sex with another of our kind."

Denis's eyebrows shot up in surprise. Then he smiled a tiny coy smile. "Was it good?"

Desmond let his lips widen into a boyish grin.

"I think I died. Again."

Denis giggled quietly, and nestled in closer, his lips against Desmond's, his long-lashed eyes closed.

Together they lay, arm-in-arm, and breathed in time with one another. Gradually, unthinkingly, each of them let go of consciousness and slipped into the dreamless deathlike sleep that was unique to their kind.

His eyes popped open. Above him the sunburst pleating of the canopy liner glowed in early morning light. He turned his head to the right, and saw the still form of Denis Schroeder, eyes closed, no breath coming from his nostrils, no rise and fall of his body. Still out. Dead to the world as it were. He reached his hand over to rub Denis's side, feeling the slender ribs beneath the cold skin.

I should have seen. I should have guessed. How could I have been so obtuse?

And there were Denis's eyes, looking into his. He heard the intake of breath as consciousness returned to the other vampire. Their six hours of immortal sleep were done. Desmond had never shared sleep this way with anyone before. Tony and he had shared a bed, but Tony slept a mortal's slumber. Roger, aware of Desmond's feelings, had never allowed them this sort of intimacy. It was like nothing he had ever known in all his long life.

"Hey, lover."

"Good morning."

They smiled shyly, stroking each other languorously for a few minutes before exchanging a kiss and climbing reluctantly out of bed to shower.

Wearing jeans and a v-neck sweater, his hair hanging in damp curls, Desmond padded barefoot down the stairs and across the rug-strewn parquet to the kitchen. Pale sunshine suffused the high-ceilinged rooms, and Desmond marveled at how beautiful this new place was. How much joy Davey would have seeing it like this. How proud he would be at the success of his work.

He entered the kitchen, and found Vivian and Bill talking quietly over mugs of coffee at the marble-topped table. He helped himself to a third mug – black, the only way he could drink it – and sat with his new old friends. He had to keep reminding himself that Vivian barely knew him – or thought she barely knew him. Bill smiled his old smile, full of understanding and familiar affection.

"Well, well, well, if it isn't the night-calling lovebird out of his nest."

Desmond blanched as Vivian snorted into her

coffee, trying unsuccessfully to stifle a laugh.

"I beg your pardon?"

Good grief. What did they hear?

"Poor Luke and poor Alex." Bill rolled his eyes dramatically upward, indicating the bedroom floor. "Our men could hardly sleep a wink last night from all the ruckus coming from the master suite."

Desmond just looked at them in mortification, and Vivian finally guffawed, hiding her mouth behind her hand.

"Oops," came a voice from behind them, and they all turned to see Denis, dressed identically to Desmond, leaning on the doorjamb. "Guess we got a little carried away, Desi."

Ignoring Bill's look of surprise at hearing his least favorite nickname, Desmond got up from the table and moved over to the refrigerator, where he began pulling out juice and milk and breakfast fixings. He figured he could hide his embarrassment by keeping busy. Good thing he'd learned to cook for Tony. It was a useful distraction.

Denis, with no visible discomfiture, poured himself a cup of coffee from the carafe and joined the others at the table. They chatted among themselves, tactfully ignoring Desmond as he puttered and avoided making eye contact.

It wasn't long before Alex and Luke both surfaced, neither of them, Desmond noted pointedly to the shared glee of his small audience, looking remotely like they'd had trouble sleeping. Luke had in fact already been out for a run, and extolled the virtues of Llewellyn Park's winding roads and natural beauty. Alex just cuffed Bill on the shoulder and told him to stop being mean.

Things were going smoothly, and Desmond was finally subduing his emotions when David and Jeffrey came bouncing down the hall, holding hands like high school sweethearts. David said nothing, but, with a cheery greeting to the assembled company, helped himself to the bacon and eggs and toast Desmond had laid out and sat with everyone at the table. Jeffrey followed him to the food, but took his coffee and set it down as he ate his breakfast standing up, leaning against the granite countertop. He was tall and muscular, and his handsome frat boy face bore an oddly sheepish expression, a fact that Desmond noted with increasing anxiety.

All at once, during a lull in the general conversation, Jeffrey blurted out, "Gosh, Desmond, what were you two doing in there last night? It sounded like there was a WWE match going on."

The kitchen exploded in laughter – Denis included – as Desmond fled, his pale face flushed with Denis's blood, into the blessed quiet of the main house.

Over the last forty-four years, since his regeneration in 1965, Desmond had begun to live what was almost a normal mortal life. He had gradually grown accustomed to having friends; to having other people – mortals – play a part in his life. It had been a radical departure for him at the time. For most of his two and a half centuries on this earth he had been a loner, living in elegant solitude on the margins of society, interacting only superficially, as business and its adjacencies had required. He had, after all, two secrets that could get him killed if not kept hidden. Maintaining a low profile, people would say today.

Roger had been his only friend, his only companion, his only love. Since 1921 they had lived apart, on separate coasts. Roger had blossomed in San Francisco, but Desmond had fossilized in his little townhouse on 4th Street, his few attempts at a social life – Corbin Fletcher chief among them – leaving him alone and forlorn. With the coming of air travel, the distance between him and Roger had lessened, but Roger could only do so much, and that particular lifetime had been Desmond's loneliest. Things had started to change in the 1960s, when Desmond had, with Roger's insistence, sought out friendship in the gay subculture of Manhattan, and not just anonymous sex or the needful slaking of his thirst for blood. It was in the post-Stonewall years of the early 1970s that Desmond, with his best friend Bill Lawrence – his first *new* best friend since the eighteenth century – threw themselves into causes surrounding gay rights and later, in the 1980s, AIDS.

And even that had changed, seismically, after Tony's death in 1990, when Bill had stumbled upon the truth and become the first mortal to know Desmond for what he really was. It had only made their friendship deeper, much to their mutual surprise and gratification.

But now that Desmond had regenerated yet again, and had still another new life to build, he found himself suddenly fearful once more. Afraid of being alone when Bill, as he inevitably would, passed on. Afraid of having no one but Roger for the long haul. The Desmond of the 1960s was dead, and this new, beautiful twenty-first-century Desmond was terrified at the prospect. Denis Schroeder was his light at the end of this dark tunnel, and there they all were in the kitchen, laughing at him. Teasing him.

The way friends did.

His *friends*.

Vivian and Bill and Alex and Luke from his last life. Friends of his father's and now friends of his. David and Jeffrey and Denis from his new one. And Denis could be much, much more, if last night was any indication. Denis could be what Roger could not.

Desmond sat heavily in an armchair by the front window in the living room, looking out across the frosted lawn. His whirling thoughts gradually wound themselves down, and his mind settled.

He heard his name called from the other end of the house. Clearly the ungrateful crew was realizing what they'd done. Desmond laughed to himself. Silly man that he was. They were there for him, weren't they? He'd better get back to them.

As his bare feet moved lightly down the hall, he saw Denis approaching, looking terribly sexy, from the other direction. Just as they were about to meet by the marble-topped table in the entrance hall, Desmond noticed an envelope showing bright against the dark grey surface. He stopped and picked it up as Denis came to his side and slid a comforting arm around his waist.

The note in the envelope read:

Dear Desmond,
Please forgive my slipping out this way, without saying thanks or expressing my congratulations. Something came up and I have to be at the museum this morning. Wretched timing, but there you are.
The house is a dream. It is more beautiful than it probably was when the Fletchers built it, and you can be proud of that.
Be happy in your house. I will always be your friend, and I hope I'll be welcome there.
Yours,
Ollie

"What is it?" asked Denis, nuzzling Desmond's neck.

"Oh, um, just a note from Oliver."

Denis looked up, hearing the tone of distress in Desmond's voice.

"What's wrong?"

"Here, read it." He handed the sheet of paper to Denis, who read it slowly, then looked up.

"I guess he heard us last night, too," he said gently. "Sounds like he went away with his tail between his legs."

"You saw that, did you? I was afraid so. I feel so badly. Oliver's a friend."

"And friends forgive each other little mistakes, Desmond," said Denis, putting his arm around Desmond's shoulder in a hug, and steering him back toward the kitchen, where cheery conversation could be heard and the smell of coffee wafted into the grand silent rooms beyond.

"I know," sighed Desmond, letting Denis lead him back to his guests. "I know."

He was surprised to find that his eyes smarted unaccountably, and he blinked to keep the tears from escaping.

Chapter Sixteen

Janay ran screaming through the glittering powder on the driveway, headed full speed toward the castle playhouse with her little sister in her wake.

"Hey, Desmond, can we go inside?" she called.

"Inside! Inside!" echoed Cassandra.

Desmond turned from where he was hanging a

second wreath on the double front doors.

"Hold on a minute!"

He finished adjusting the red velvet bows, and stepped down into the snow-covered gravel to make sure the wreaths were even. A little late for the start of Advent, but then they'd barely gotten settled in and he had only just cooked up a scheme to make their first Christmas at

Oakwood memorable.

He turned and jogged down the driveway to the turn-around, where the girls were jumping up and down on the playhouse's tiny front porch. Desmond pulled out his keys and fitted the shiny new brass one into the door, which opened inward with a satisfying creaking of rusty hinges.

The girls pushed inside and proceeded to inspect every visible corner of the place, from the stairway to the little tower, to the neat fireplace with its carved stone mantelpiece, to the miniature galley kitchen, complete with a microwave oven, working sink and under-counter fridge. There were no furnishings in here. Desmond had decided to wait till spring and let the girls help redecorate. Even at ten and eight, Janay and Speck had missed a lot of the carefree fun of childhood. Their delight in their new rooms, and their surprising lack of awe at the scale of this house that had suddenly become their home, pleased him deeply.

He shooed them out of the playhouse and headed them back inside, following slowly as their high-pitched voices faded in the crisp morning air. Passing through the front doors, Desmond looked back at the stone playhouse. It hadn't been here when he had first visited Oakwood with Corbin Fletcher. The sight of it made him think about Fletch's son, the only child of that well-calculated marriage; the little boy who had been the one to enjoy this product of his parents' indulgence....

It had been a brilliant early November day when Desmond stood in the drive in front of Oakwood's entrance, having just concluded a walk around the grounds. Seven acres was a lot of land, especially in the densely packed New Jersey suburbs. Although there were houses on large lots on all four sides of his property, it still felt as if the lawn and gardens, edged with old trees and wooded thickets, were far more expansive than they in fact were. Not the hundreds of acres that Beckwith House had encompassed, perhaps, but still far more than Desmond had ever imagined owning again.

Typically late for New Jersey, the trees throughout the Park had only just reached their colorful peak, and were beginning to drop their leaves in earnest, carpeting the borders of the huge lawn with speckled mats of red, gold, orange and brown. The air was exhilarating in its clarity, with strong fragrant undertones of dying grass, mold, and small woodland creatures busy preparing for the winter to come.

One of the crew of electricians David had hired to work on the kitchen and bathrooms wandered out the main entrance to ask Desmond a question. As he finished with the wiring consultation, Desmond had followed the man inside and had started poking around, wandering through the mostly empty rooms testing light switches and making sure no switch plates were missing. A house like this seemed to have an endless number of faceplates for all the electrical outlets. For all its Georgian pretentions, Oakwood had been built as a completely modern building, with conveniences unimagined in the worlds of Desmond's childhood.

He climbed to the third floor, a place he'd almost never visited during the renovation project. With the staff quarters over the kitchen wing, the attic at Oakwood had been built purely for storage. The only finished rooms were at the top of the service stairs, and had been intended for trunks and suitcases, a few moldering examples of which lingered in their shadowy spaces. The rest of the long low attic under the slate roof was open to the rafters, entirely dark but for two tiny dormers. Desmond had made sure that all the wiring up here, minimal as it needed to be, was up-to-date and safe. Few things were more terrifying to a vampire than the idea of a house fire while they were helpless in sleep.

As he stepped carefully through the attic, mindful of the rough floorboards, his sharp eyes could peer into the dimmest recesses. With all of his attention focused on the lower floors, Desmond had never really explored these largely disregarded spaces. He noticed a slightly darker shadow tucked into one corner, a shadow that turned out to be a small mahogany desk.

He ran his hands over the dusty surface. Showing clear signs of use, it looked like it was some manufacturer's notion of a Chippendale piece. He recognized it as matching the suite of furniture that had been left behind in the small bedroom over the front entrance. But it was oddly undersized, and it dawned on Desmond that this desk had been intended for a child. That little room, where Desmond himself had stayed as a guest, had been furnished differently when he had visited. It must have been fitted out as Corbin Fletcher's son's room later in the 1930s.

Curiously, Desmond opened the various drawers, finding them empty save for random paper clips and pencil shavings, along with a few yellowed index cards from a long forgotten homework assignment. As he was about to close the shallow center drawer after a cursory look inside, Desmond noticed a white corner sticking out from under the divider that split the drawer into front and back sections. He pulled the drawer all the way out, and tugged at what turned out to be an envelope. It was not empty, and he noted that it hadn't been sealed. As he turned it over in his hands, the hair stood up on the back of his neck.

On the front of the envelope, in peacock-blue ink, written in a strong, still-familiar hand, was the single word: *Desmond.*

Trembling, Desmond shut the drawer and moved quickly across the attic to the landing. He descended the stairs to the first floor and went to the library, where he threw back the dustcover from a newly upholstered Queen Anne love seat and sank down into the cushions. He gingerly pulled out the single folded sheet of heavy white letter-paper, its smooth surface covered on both sides with the same deep turquoise script.

> *November, 1960*
> *My dear Desmond,*
> Your mother has gone to bed, complaining (as is her wont) of a headache. I wanted to take a few moments to write this, although I find the words do not come easily. We need not talk about this, if it makes you uncomfortable, but I felt I could not let this moment pass without some confidence between us.
> First off, you must know that we both find Henry Burton to be a very nice young man. His lovely manners and his charming smile surely make him an ornament to any social gathering. He is able to be pleasing without being obsequious; a skill far too underrated these days. He is just the sort of friend your mother and I hoped you would find at Yale. I am glad you wanted him to meet us, and only regret that you waited so long to bring him to Oakwood.
> But there is something more to this, I think, than meets the eye. I could not help but observe, over the course of cocktails and dinner, the way you and Henry look at each other. It is discreet, but I was quite aware of it. And I also saw the various little ways you contrive to touch each other – a hand on the arm, a pat on the shoulder – that are not strictly necessary. It led me to suspect – indeed to believe – that there is something more to your friendship with Henry than just friendship.
> If I am wrong, please forgive my presumption; but if I am correct, I want you to know that I understand, more than you know. I never thought I would have cause to confess this to you, but it seems to me that I must. When I was your age, I, too had a special friend. He was British, very handsome and had me completely

captivated. Sadly, our friendship did not stand the test of time. I fear it was more my fault than his, but we parted amicably, and within a few years I had met and married your mother.

His name was Desmond, and of course you will realize that it was after him that you were named. Your mother was puzzled, but ultimately gave in to my whim, because she thought it was a distinguished name. She met Desmond only once, at our wedding, and after that he and I lost sight of each other. But I never forgot him. Every time I called your name when you were a child, I thought of him and of that time in my life when things might have gone very differently for me, had I only had the courage to face facts.

In closing, my darling son, I wish to ask only one thing of you – if you are serious about him, as I think you are, hold on to Henry. Do not let him slip away from you as I let Desmond do. The world will undoubtedly look askance at you, but the world is not all that matters. Happiness is not so commonplace that we can dismiss the opportunity to grasp it when it is offered to us.

Know that we love you, and that you and Henry will always be welcome at Oakwood.

Your affectionate father,

Corbin Fletcher

Desmond had sat for a long time in the library that day, the letter clutched in his hand, his mind reeling, his heart filled with a dull ache as he tried to imagine what might have been.

Chapter Seventeen

As he made his way to the back of the house Desmond thought of that letter, now carefully tucked away in the desk in his sitting room. After the initial shock wore off, this unforeseen link between his ill-fated liaison with Corbin Fletcher and the long-forgotten benediction offered by a loving father to his gay son had given Desmond a sense of rightness that warmed him weeks later.

He found Dotty in the kitchen in a frenzy of Christmas Eve preparation, and she ordered him out of her way to let her work in peace. Jane was in the dining room, muttering under her breath as she searched in cupboards and drawers.

"What's up?" Desmond ventured, walking into the dining room.

"I'm trying to find the right dishes. And I have no idea where you stashed the flatware." She looked up at him in exasperation, which changed into a laugh when she saw him making puppy-dog eyes at her.

"Actually, I think I left the silver in the basement for safe-keeping. I'll go get it. Which dishes did you have in mind?"

"David said something about red and gold. I assume you know what that means?"

"Of course I do. It's the Minton bone china with a deep red brim and gold decoration." He moved over to a built-in cupboard in the wall and popped the door open.

"And there's Bohemian ruby glassware to go with it. Festive don't you think?"

"Oh, Desmond, how can the rest of the gay world keep up with you?" Jane shook her head in mock concern. "Now go get that silver before I kick your ass down the cellar stairs."

Desmond and Jane set the table together, placing pieces for the main course, for soup and for a salad at each setting, then adding flatware for each course as well as dessert. Desmond had chosen an antique set of Tiffany's English King, thinking it suited the house. He had brought almost nothing from the Dakota flat, where the style was so completely different than at Oakwood. It struck him as funny, for someone who didn't eat, to own so much tableware. But, if he was going to entertain mortals, what choice did he have?

A week or so after his abrupt departure, Desmond had called Oliver. No apologies had been made, no personal pain had been discussed; but their friendship had been reaffirmed, tentatively and with mutual relief. Desmond had asked Oliver to Christmas Eve dinner. To his surprise, Oliver had agreed readily, saying he didn't need to be at his brother's house in Connecticut until midday on Christmas. He was even more surprised when Oliver said he'd stay the night in the same little room he'd occupied at the housewarming. Desmond suspected it was because Denis was out of the country, having made vague excuses about visiting friends in Switzerland.

David and Jeffrey had also been recruited without much trouble. David's family lived far away, and Jeffrey's had not been pleased with the news that their athletic handsome boy was in love with another man. Desmond's invitation was a welcome diversion from an awkward family situation. He also needed them to pull off his Christmas surprise for the girls.

And of course, Roger was there, as promised, comfortably ensconced in the chintz guest room. He had been gratifyingly and sincerely impressed by Desmond's latest adventure in domesticity, and had already made himself popular with Janay and Cassandra. For someone who had never expressed any interest in children, Roger had a ready ease with them that Desmond found quite moving. It was important to him that Jane's family get along with Roger – who was, after all, as close to a family as he had. Aside from a mild uneasiness over the fact that Jane was eyeing them both with bemused detachment, as if trying to work something out in her own mind, Desmond couldn't remember feeling more content at Christmas in many years.

David and Jeffrey had driven a rented car out from the city, stopping at a place recommended by Oliver in Maplewood to pick up a massive Douglas fir, which was expertly hogtied to their roof. Desmond made them park on the road that ran behind Oakwood, hidden in the shadows, where the children wouldn't see it.

Dotty's dinner was delicious – or at least Desmond assumed it was from the way his guests wolfed down the turkey with oyster dressing, creamed pearl onions, garlic mashed potatoes, candied sweet potatoes, a green salad and a variety of homemade pies. It smelled heavenly. Ironically, it probably smelled better to the one person who couldn't eat it than it did to those who were packing it down their gullets with all speed. Desmond presided at the head, with Dotty at the other end by the fireplace. The girls were in the middle of each side of the long linen-draped table, partly to put them in the middle of things, partly to keep them from getting at each other as sisters will do. Roger sat on his left, and David on his right; Jeffrey and Jane on either side of Dorothy.

Oliver was happily seated next to Janay, with whom he maintained a steady patter throughout the meal. The curator was as at ease with children as he was with adults. He kept the conversation simple, but talked to ten-year-old Janay as if she were a colleague. Desmond bridled with pleasure to see her rise to the occasion and even flirt with Oliver a bit in her girlish way. Like everyone else who knew Oliver, it seemed, Janay had fallen for him.

A little shiver of sadness flickered through Desmond's heart, making him frown slightly in confusion.

As salads were being finished, he raised his glass of deep red claret, one of many he had consumed that evening, leaving him feeling pleasantly buzzed and somewhat emotional.

"To dear friends, well met. May the love of the season fill you all."

They all raised their glasses and drank, and responded with their own toasts. Desmond looked around the small gathering, in this beautiful setting, their varied voices blurring together in a cacophonous harmony of good cheer. Tears burned at the back of his eyes, but he blinked them away.

If only Tony Chapman were here.

"But Desmond, where's the *tree*?" piped up Cassandra, breaking his train of thought. "We don't have a *tree*!"

"Desmond told me that Santa Claus will bring the tree tonight, because it's our first Christmas here in this house. So you shut up, Speck!"

"Language, Janay!" snapped Jane, her sharp tone belied by the smile on her face.

"Sorry, Mom," answered Janay in her best compliant-daughter voice. Then she turned her flashing hazel eyes on Desmond. "Ain't I right, Des?"

"*Aren't* I right, and yes you are," he replied, taking another swallow of the claret.

"See, told you so, Speck." She stuck her tongue out at her little sister, who promptly started to whine.

"Cassandra," Desmond said, his voice raised to stop any escalation in the moment.

"Yes?"

"Janay is correct. I know you always had trees in your house before Christmas Eve, and I promise we'll do that in future. But tonight is a special Christmas Eve. This is the first Christmas in this house in a long time – I spoke to the gentlemen who used to live here, they were always in Florida at Christmas time. It seems that Santa wants to make it extra special. So we'll just have to go to sleep and wait and see what he brings us." Desmond used his calculated father-knows-best voice, which he found didn't do much for Janay, but still struck awe into Cassandra's little heart. He was gratified to see the little girl, her curly hair glinting in the candlelight, look wide-eyed and then break into an ear-to-ear grin.

After dinner, Dotty and Jane corralled the girls and dragged them off to their apartment to get them bathed and into bed. David organized the clean-up with Desmond, while Roger and Oliver helped Jeffrey wrestle the ten-foot-tall tree in through the garden doors under cover of darkness and set it up in the center of the huge living room. Desmond had made sure the vendor trimmed the trunk to fit into an extra large stand he'd purchased, to insure that there was no awkward struggle once they got it into the house. He'd instructed the boys to lock the living room doors, to prevent any peeping.

They made quick work of the kitchen, started both of the dishwashers, and hearing that things seemed quiet upstairs in Jane and Dotty's apartment, crept down to the basement. There, in one of the storerooms, David had stockpiled a rainbow assortment of Christmas ornaments and tinsel, colored lights and a huge gold-foil star.

"Desmond, this is such fun!" gushed David, wrapping the young vampire in a surprisingly strong bear hug. Desmond hugged him back, and then loaded him up with boxes to carry up the stairs.

Three short knocks gained admittance to the living room, where the tree towered over them as Jeffrey filled the stand with water from the sunroom fountain.

"I got some extension cords, so we can plug the lights in over there under the Elizabethan portrait. Does that seem about right, Des?" asked Jeffrey.

"Perfect, then you won't see the cord when you walk in."

"I found a ladder in the garden shed," announced Oliver proudly, "so we'll be able to reach the top."

The five men worked in happy collaboration, stringing the lights, placing the ornaments evenly all over the green expanse of the tree, scattering tinsel with increasing abandon as the evening wore on. Somewhere in the middle, Jane quietly joined them, reporting that the girls were asleep, or at least quiet in their rooms, and Dotty was keeping watch to make sure there were no security breaches.

When it was all but finished, Desmond pulled out the enormous gold foil star, which had a wire coil at the bottom so it would sit on the topmost spike.

"This is spectacular, David. Where did you find it?"

"I was in one of the Christmas shops in the Toy District, and it just looked right."

"It's beautiful. Jane?" He held out the star to his assistant.

"It's your tree, Desmond, really ... " she stammered.

"It's *your* tree, Jane," Desmond corrected her gently. "It's your home, too. This is for your family. I just get to enjoy it."

Jane blinked, gave him a wry smile, and took the proffered star. Climbing the ladder, she leaned over and carefully placed the star onto an upright needle-covered branch that pointed up toward the high ceiling. As she did so, Jeffrey turned on the lights, and the tree was suddenly a blaze of color and reflection that filled the large space with radiance.

The assembled company just stared silently at the tree for a moment, and then spontaneously they all reached out and took each other's hands, standing there in the glow, basking in the warmth of friendship, good food, and a plenitude of wine.

Dispersing quickly, the guests went up to their rooms and returned shortly, each holding elegantly wrapped packages. Jane appeared with two shopping bags full of bright parcels for the girls, and a small gold-wrapped box.

"For Dotty," she said shyly, at Desmond's questioning look. "Something she's been wanting. I went and got it the day she accepted the job here, 'cause I knew I'd be able to afford it then." She placed the shimmering box carefully on top of the pile growing under the tree.

When the tall clock in the entrance hall chimed the hour, it was only ten o'clock, but everyone began to stretch and yawn and make their excuses. David preceded Jeffrey, who stayed to help Desmond carry the now-empty boxes back to the cellar. Oliver and Roger, assured that they were not needed, both kissed Desmond on the cheek before slipping up to their respective rooms. Jane hugged him tightly and disappeared into the servant's wing to join her family.

Desmond and Jeffrey made two trips to the cellar, taking care to be quiet and not waken the girls. As they stacked the boxes in what had been an old larder for canned goods, Jeffrey chatted quietly about himself and David. Desmond stayed mostly silent, letting the sweet jock have his say.

"I really appreciate your asking me and Davey to come here. My folks are still pretty messed up about my being with him, you know? I guess I sort of surprised them. I was varsity at Caldwell College. Football. They had, like no idea. So when I showed up last Fourth of

July with Davey, they just didn't know how to handle it. We'd been dating for like six months already, and it just felt like it was time for me."

"Did you meet David in the city?"

"Yeah, at Posh Bar."

"I know the place."

Found some lovely blood there, now and then.

"So what about Robert, Desmond? He's gorgeous – but he's straight, right?"

Desmond, caught off guard by this sudden shift in topic, didn't answer right away. All evening he'd been very careful to call Roger by his new name, but had nearly slipped up at least once. It was so difficult to suppress the past they shared.

"Robert, alas, is very straight. You know he runs our San Francisco office?"

"Yeah, Davey told me that. But he acts like he's known you all your life. All those little asides he makes – I'm not the sharpest knife in the drawer, but even I noticed. How's that work?"

Desmond shivered a little over the treacherous path this conversation was taking. His mind raced to find some adequate explanation.

"Well, I guess Robert and I bonded pretty quickly when he came East after my father died. I guess I sort of fell for him, and he had to put the kibosh on that pretty fast – to keep from hurting my feelings. As a result he got to know me really well in a very short time." He glanced over at Jeffrey, who was reaching up to stack an empty box on a high shelf, and decided he needed to take control of things.

"So did you and David hit it off right away?"

"Pretty quickly, actually. It sort of surprised me at the time."

"How so?"

"I mean Davey wasn't at all what I thought I'd fall for."

"What, not your type?"

"Yeah, well no. I don't know. He's so pretty and

everything, but he wasn't like I expected ... " Jeffrey went silent.

"You mean that he's a little gayer than some guys?" Desmond gave Jeffrey a reassuring smile. "Is that a problem for you?"

"No. But it didn't dawn on me that it might be a problem for my family. It got really awkward when I took him home to meet them. They couldn't even talk to him." His voice hitched, and Desmond looked closely in the dim light of a single low-watt bulb.

"Ouch. Did it cause problems for you afterwards?"

"Nah, Davey's a great guy. He totally understood." Desmond watched as Jeffrey's face began to crumple.

"Aw, Des, I just love him so much. And I want to protect him. I don't need him to be all butch and jocky like I am. I'm just so afraid that my family won't ever accept us...."

His voice hitched again, and without thinking about it, Desmond moved over and pulled Jeffrey into a consoling hug.

"Don't worry, Jeffrey. You know they'll come around. Being away at Christmas like this will remind them what they might lose if they can't accept who you love."

Jeffrey just sniffled a little and hugged Desmond back, his big head on Desmond's shoulder.

As they stood there, Desmond was suddenly aware of the powerful fragrance of Jeffrey's blood, mixed in among the scents of dust and old wood and stone that mingled in the gloomy storeroom. He could feel the pulse under Jeffrey's shirt, almost hear the teeming life as it pumped its way from that big heart, through those muscular arms, up that strong, smooth neck.

Desmond hesitated. This was David's lover. This man loved David. How could he...?

But then, this wasn't about love or sex or cheating or fidelity: this was about life. About taking what vampires needed to take to survive. He'd had no dinner, only wine. He hadn't fed in days, and his newly-young body was craving blood. And Jeffrey was full of what Desmond needed.

He began to talk to Jeffrey in his low, mesmeric voice, speaking words of comfort that were calculated to lull the big man into a gentle torpor. As he felt Jeffrey relax in his arms, Desmond let down his canines and brought his mouth to the thrumming pulse in Jeffrey's exposed neck. As the blood filled his mouth and poured down his throat, Desmond felt a sense of peace and contentment fill him. His heart began to beat in unison with the athlete's strong rhythm, and he allowed himself to luxuriate in the savor, the wine-dark taste.

Jeffrey was strong. As Desmond pulled away, he barely staggered, and only looked with mild confusion into Desmond's eyes.

"I think you've had a little too much holiday cheer, Jeffrey, my boy. Here, let me help you back upstairs."

The two made their way up the cellar stairs, then down the service hall to the entrance hall, and from there up the winding stairs and down the corridor to the chintz bedroom. David answered Desmond's soft knock, his face showing a look of worry when he saw Desmond standing there holding Jeffrey up, his arm around the other man's waist.

"We were just getting the last of the boxes put away, David. Jeffrey got all woozy. I think the wine finally hit him."

David tut-tutted and pulled Jeffrey into the room. He handled the bigger man with surprising ease. David was stronger than he looked.

Desmond spoke softly. "We talked about his family a bit. Seems like they're a little difficult right now."

David, having lain Jeffrey down on the chintz bedspread, turned to Desmond with a dismissive flick of his slender wrist. He rolled his big childlike eyes.

"Oh, they'll be fine. I'm just a little more to get used to than they expected. That's all."

"You sure you're okay?"

David smirked at Desmond. "Oh, please, Des. I've

been a sissy all my life. Eventually everybody loves me. You did, right?" He batted his eyes flirtatiously with comic timing.

"They'll come 'round, eh?"

"Well, we hope they'll come 'round." David came over, gave Desmond a kiss, and gently shoved him out the door. "Now go to bed. Those girls'll be up at the crack of dawn. Get some sleep."

The door closed, and Desmond went back down the long dark hallway to his own room, feeling sated and strangely happy, in spite of missing Denis, and Tony.

Six hours of dreamless, unmoving sleep. No heartbeat, no discernable brain activity. The body cooled. But he woke quickly, his body recharged, his senses fully active. On this particular morning he woke, but didn't open his eyes right away. He felt like he was floating, and the happy memory of the evening before came back to him, making him flush with pleasure as his blood began to circulate.

And then he smelled it. A familiar, enticing scent. Close by.

He opened his eyes to find Oliver, fully dressed, sitting at the end of the bed, looking at him. A smile appeared at the corners of his ginger beard, and his eyes shimmered in the faint morning light that filled the room with its blue glow. Desmond noted that Oliver's eyes looked a little red. From last night's wine? From crying?

But it doesn't make him any less beautiful, does it?

"Good morning, sleepyhead." Oliver reached out and stroked the back of Desmond's hand. "I thought I'd wake you, so we could go make coffee before the girls get up. Frankly, I'm astonished they're not downstairs already. I wonder if Dotty actually tied them into their beds." He beamed at Desmond, who looked over at the open door of the bedroom.

"Oh, didn't I lock my door?"

"You didn't even close it. That's why I figured I was safe to come in. I must say, you didn't want to wake up."

Desmond shuddered at this thought. How long had Oliver been there?

The idea that someone would find him in his vampire sleep and think he was dead .... He'd gotten careless because of Denis. He didn't have to worry about these things with Denis.

He looked up at Oliver and smiled thinly.

"Just let me take a quick shower and throw on a robe. Won't be five minutes."

By some miracle, Oliver and Desmond got to the living room before the girls did, and managed to plug in the towering tree and do a final arrangement of the pile of presents under it before they heard excited squeals in the distance. Desmond had just turned on the gas fire when Janay and Cassandra exploded into the room, expressing Christmas cheer at the top of their lungs.

"Look, Janay! Look at what Santa did!" yelled Cassandra, on the edge of hysteria.

"Pretty cool, Speck," answered her big sister, rolling an unsettlingly cynical look at the two men in the room. "Good job, guys." But her smile, for all the assumed worldliness of a ten-year-old, was wide and genuine.

At that moment, Roger appeared, looking serene and elegant, his dark red hair brushed back, a moss green cardigan bringing out the green of his eyes. Desmond went over to give him a hug and a brotherly kiss.

"You don't look like you just dragged yourself out of bed."

"I've been in the library for a couple of hours, actually."

"Working on Christmas Day?" Desmond asked archly.

"Just a little research on my laptop. So thoughtful of you to have Wi-Fi. There's something I think I should show you. But we can talk about it later." He reached up and ruffled Desmond's still-damp hair in a way that was meant to be comforting, but somehow triggered an alarm somewhere in the back of Desmond's mind.

They were interrupted by a beaming, sleepy-eyed Jane pulling an equally drowsy Dotty by the hand past the tall mahogany doors. Both were wrapped in terrycloth robes, and Dotty tried to assume an expression of superior amusement. But her eyes widened at the sight of the huge glowing tree with its pile of presents, and the packed Christmas stockings lying on the hearth in front of the ornate stone mantelpiece.

"Niiiice," she murmured in her low voice, her smile widening, her head nodding in appreciation.

"Stockings first, girls, then breakfast, then presents," Jane said, raising her voice to be heard over the excited prattle of her two daughters, who were already pawing through the pile of gifts to see what was for them. The general moan at this gross unfairness was replaced with renewed squealing as the girls spotted the stockings and rushed over to the fireplace. There were four – one for each of the Ashmun-Brown family. Desmond had taken particular pleasure in finding hand-knitted stockings and filling them with absurd little treasures calculated to please them.

"No stocking for you, Des?" asked Oliver quietly.

"Having them here is gift enough for me," answered Desmond.

As the girls were tearing through the many little tissue-wrapped packages in their stockings, their mothers following suit more slowly, a tousled and endearing David and Jeffrey appeared in the doorway, yawning and holding onto each other for support.

"Good work keeping the kids in bed until daylight!" burbled David. "How did you manage it?"

"Threats of bodily harm," intoned Dotty, deadpanning. The men all cackled at the joke, while Jane just rolled her eyes and punched Dotty gently in the shoulder.

Coffee helped wake up the adults and sweet rolls with hot chocolate kept the girls from declaring mutiny. The happy crew settled once again on the velvet sofas in the living room. Dotty and Jane gave each other practical gifts, other than the slim gold bracelet Dotty received with uncharacteristic girlish enthusiasm. They also bought the girls practical things, knowing that Desmond would provide the more indulgent presents. This he did, swelling with happiness at the joy Janay and Speck expressed as they opened each hideous plastic doll or irritating noisy game. Jane and Dotty shot him an occasional dirty look, softened with gratitude.

For his male guests, Desmond had bought beautiful, handmade shirts from his preferred Manhattan tailor. He had decided that he wouldn't get too personal this year, not wishing to play favorites. Jane had been very efficient at finding out everybody's size, and the shirt maker had been eager to accommodate the son of a longtime client. He and Roger had always exchanged this sort of gift, unable to offer more than fond gestures after all this time.

David and Jeffrey presented him with a set of elegant luncheon linens – matching placemats and napkins, from a Madison Avenue boutique.

For all those elegant little luncheons I'll be hosting here.

But he was startled when Oliver handed him a small oblong box, beautifully wrapped in silver paper and tied with a red silk ribbon.

"Don't be too impressed, Desmond," he said self-deprecatingly, looking down in mild embarrassment at Desmond's expression of surprise. "Remember, I do this for a living, so I know where to look."

He opened the box, and found a silver tablespoon. Desmond knew the form immediately – the oval bowl with the pointed rib down the back, the upturned handle. This was the sort of silver his parents had used at Beckwith House when he was a child, when George I was king of England. His eyes widened when he turned it over and saw the engraved coat of arms on the back. Three stag's heads arranged above and below a chevron. The Beckwith coat of arms, created for his father after receiving his knighthood. He looked up sharply into

Oliver's blue eyes.

"Where did you find this?"

"Online." Oliver smiled a naughty smile. "A dealer in the silver vaults in London. I figured, if that painting had gotten out into the world, that your ancestral silver might be scattered to the winds too."

He took the spoon from Desmond's hand, his warm fingers brushing against Desmond's cool ones. He held it, looking into Desmond's eyes as he did so.

"It seemed just right for you, somehow." He lowered his eyes, as if suddenly embarrassed, and handed the spoon back to Desmond, shivering slightly as they touched.

"Thank you, Oliver," was all he could manage. He was surprised by the upwelling of emotion he felt, but chose not to dwell on what it might mean.

The doorbell rang, causing all the adults in the room to look at each other in surprise, as if none of them knew what had produced the noise. Desmond got up and went out to the hall, and unbolted the big double doors.

There, in the sparkling chill of Christmas morning, stood Dane Ashmun, a big red Macy's shopping bag full of presents in his left hand. He raised his right hand and offered it to Desmond, who automatically grasped it and shook it.

"Merry Christmas, Mr. Beckwith." He looked up at Desmond, who stood blinking uncertainly at him in the bright light. Then he added, "Um, could I come in?"

Ashmun looked groomed and sober. His hazel eyes were clear, and his dirty blond hair was washed and cut. He wore a down parka against the cold, but it was unzipped and Desmond could see that he had on a necktie and a button-down shirt with a pair of clean blue jeans.

"Who the hell is ringing the bell on Christmas morning?" Dotty's voice rang out in the vestibule behind Desmond.

He turned to her, a pleading look on his face.

"It's Dane. It seems that he's brought presents for

the girls."

A scowl darkened Dotty's face. It was clear she was on the verge of launching into a tirade against her partner's good-for-nothing ex-husband when Desmond cut her off.

"Dotty, would you please get some coffee and cinnamon rolls for Dane, and bring them to the living room?" His tone was gentle, but there was a sliver of ice in it that suggested he was not inclined to argue with a disgruntled employee over admitting this unexpected guest.

Dotty's defiant glare softened into a look of pained acquiescence, and she silently turned and went down the hall in the direction of the kitchen. Desmond gestured for Dane to enter.

"Please come in, Dane, and do call me Desmond."

Dane was wide-eyed with amazement as Desmond led him across the hall and down the passage past the staircase. He paused for only a moment when they entered the huge living room, taking in with a swift glance the luxurious décor, the great tree and the piles of ruined gift wrappings before quickly spotting his daughters in front of the fireplace.

Jane had risen from the sofa when he entered the room, and stood staring at him as he crossed toward where the group was seated.

When his ex-wife said nothing, Dane offered gamely, "Merry Christmas, Jane." He raised the bulging shopping bag. "I brought presents for Janay and Cassie."

Still she said nothing, but looked from Dane to Desmond, an expression of frustration and heartache shifting across her pretty features. At this point the girls spotted their father and leapt up from their loot to run to him as he moved toward them.

"Daddy's here!"

Desmond had moved over to Jane's side, where he spoke softly to her.

"I know this wasn't in your plans."

She turned to face him, the look on her face

hardening. "How could you let him in?" Her voice was a harsh whisper, almost a hiss.

"It's Christmas. How could I turn him away?" At her unrelenting glare, he added with emphasis, "Jane, he's their father."

"This was *our* Christmas."

"It is our Christmas, Jane. And that means my Christmas as well. Dane is my guest."

Her only response was to turn and walk out of the room, leaving Desmond standing in mute dismay. He turned to find Dane and the girls settled onto the Aubusson carpet, happily oblivious to the little drama that had just unfolded. From the velvet sofas, David, Jeffrey, Oliver and Roger looked at him expectantly, feeling the tension in the air, but not fully understanding its source or its depth.

Desmond pulled himself together and went over to tap Dane on the shoulder. He said with a cheery bravado he didn't quite feel, "Let the girls play a bit. I need to introduce you to my friends."

The next hour passed without incident. Dotty eventually stalked in with a tray of coffee and rolls and, having plunked it unceremoniously on a coffee table, stalked out again without saying a word or acknowledging Dane's presence.

Dane did not stay overlong. After the somewhat awkward introductions, Oliver, David and Jeffrey gradually slipped away to shower and dress, leaving Desmond and Roger alone with Dane and the children. There was very little conversation among the men. Dane talked quietly with his daughters, and their piping voices filled the room with bursts of laughter and occasional squeals of delight. Roger sat by Desmond's side on one of the sofas, maintaining a comfortable silence that helped soothe Desmond's rattled nerves. At one point he placed his hand on Desmond's and squeezed, without looking at him.

When Dane was finally able to tear himself away from Janay and Cassandra, he kissed them both and headed toward the front door, signaling for Desmond to follow him.

They reached the entrance, and Dane turned to Desmond. "Thank you for letting me in. I wasn't sure you would."

Desmond didn't know what to say, and just shook Dane's hand, hoping that his sincerity showed on his face.

"This is an awesome house, Mr., um, Desmond." Dane looked abashed and kept his eyes downcast as he struggled for words. "I just want to thank you for giving my family a home." He gestured vaguely. "I could never give them this in a million years. Even if I wasn't a total fuck-up." His broad shoulders sagged in defeat. "I know I've failed my girls. I lost Jane because I'm weak." He paused, his eyes, full of unspoken pain; locking with Desmond's fleetingly before dropping again. "Just – thanks." And with that he turned away and moved quickly down the steps, hurrying toward the battered little Toyota he'd parked down the driveway.

Chapter Eighteen

There had been little fallout from Dane Ashmun's unscheduled visit to Oakwood. Jane had, much to his surprise, hugged him and apologized. Dotty had been less forthcoming, but had given him no further grief over his pulling rank on her. In the end, they had just carried on as if nothing had happened, and Desmond's first Christmas in his new home had come off relatively unscathed.

Denis returned from Geneva after the turn of the New Year, and he and Desmond continued as before, their relationship progressing as it had begun prior to the holidays.

They dated, they hunted together, drank together, both booze and blood, and they had ferocious, dazzling sex together, always in Desmond's ornate ebony bed at the Dakota. Denis's reticence about letting Desmond see his corporate apartment hadn't given Desmond any undue pause; he much preferred to bring the beautiful blond man back to his haven, to the upholstered Victorian lair that had marked a new beginning in his long vampire lifetime in New York.

Roger had alerted him to some deeply buried irregularities in the background of Chillon Investments. His holiday research had unearthed a string of rather dubious land speculations in Eastern European countries, all of which had been complicated by ongoing political conflict and inter-ethnic disturbances in the wake of the break-up of the Soviet Union in the late 1980s and early 90s. There seemed to be a German real estate investor somewhere in the picture, a shadowy figure named Denis von Riesenfelder, although the name only appeared a few times in scattered documents related to one or two of the deals. Whatever von Riesenfelder's connections to the transactions were, the coincidence of his name was a source of nagging doubt in Desmond's thoughts.

He recognized that he had not probed Denis's past sufficiently, now that he knew he was a vampire and could well have lived any number of lifetimes under different names. He had never even pressed for more information about Denis's true age or his maker. He resisted, excusing his own reluctance by reassuring himself that Roger would have given him clear instructions had there been anything he was meant to do. Desmond chose not to raise the issue with Denis, and quietly acknowledged that he was afraid to upset what he hoped was evolving between them.

Hunting for blood together had turned into something of a game. Desmond had never before done this other than by himself and the novelty of having a vampire partner at his side added a heady rush to what had always been merely needful and pragmatic. They tended to go to gay bars together rather than more public cruising areas, both for the liquor and the dancing as well as the ultimate payoff. Desmond knew that no casual sexual encounter could match the intensity of what he experienced with Denis, and his cohort seemed to share that feeling. Thus there was never any spark of jealousy during their intricate nighttime choreography; they were both in it for the same things.

One unseasonably warm late winter evening found them at Ty's on Christopher Street in Greenwich Village. Desmond had known this bar in his last lifetime, when it had been one of the social centers of the Village. Although still pretty queer by general American standards, much of the Village's gay life had moved uptown to Chelsea, where a new generation of circuit boys and gym rats still filled the restaurants and bars and stylish condominiums. Ty's had settled into a comfortable existence as a neighborhood pub for the remaining gay population: small, crowded, genial, and more varied in its clientele than the trendier watering holes elsewhere in Manhattan. Denis and Desmond took special pleasure when they pushed open the door into the dim, funky warmth of the bar. Tall, clean-shaven and young, they stood out in this place, which tended toward the bear end of the gay spectrum. They knew that they'd be noted and watched, and this always made their little vampire *pas de deux* more exhilarating.

After ordering red wine at the bar, the two separated, each moving through the milling clientele, bodies synchronizing to the music, eyes peeled for their intended of the evening. Desmond always flinched inwardly when Denis referred to their target as the "victim," because, even after all this time, the predatory connotation of the word made him uncomfortable.

This evening's target turned out to be a man in his late thirties, seated at the far end of the bar, whose neatly groomed hair and beard, along with the tortoise-rimmed glasses he wore, gave the lie to the rumpled flannel shirt, jeans and cowboy boots he wore. No longer slim, his sturdy torso showed a healthy thatch of dark hair above the open collar of his shirt. Big dark brown eyes glinted behind the glasses.

Rather a professorial bear, isn't he?

Desmond started as his mind suddenly projected an image of Oliver, with his soft rusty beard. He shook his head slightly to clear the distracting image, and moved in to sit next to the man at the bar.

"Hi," said Desmond with a smile.

The professor turned, and with only the least rise of his brows, returned the greeting.

"I'm Tony," Desmond continued, putting out his hand.

"Tiger," answered the professor, taking it and shaking it with a firm grip.

"Tiger?" It was Desmond's turn to show surprise.

"Nickname. Goes way back." The older man smiled sheepishly. "Don't read too much into it." He laughed self-deprecatingly, which Desmond found charming.

"I had a thing for tigers as a kid, and the name just stuck with me." He lowered his gaze from Desmond's eyes as he said this, which charmed the vampire even further.

Desmond laughed softly, his voice penetrating the dull roar of the room, reaching its target's ears, drawing him closer.

They chatted quietly for a while, Desmond bringing all the effect of his voice into play, accompanied by an occasional casual touch on Tiger's arm. At some moment, Denis joined them noiselessly at the bar, placing himself on Tiger's other side.

"So, you come here often?" he asked, his voice silky and, Desmond noted, without accent. He might have rolled his eyes at the hackneyed pick-up line; but both Desmond and Denis knew that success and not style was what mattered.

Tiger looked around at Denis, visibly surprised. "Um, no, not really. I live uptown. But I like this place. Friendly."

Denis just smiled, a smile calculated to bemuse and lure. His eyes flicked up to Desmond's, then back to the bearded man's.

Tiger took a long pull at his beer, and beamed at each of the younger men in turn, clearly pleased with this unexpected turn of events. Desmond could see that it wasn't often that he got attention from men like them, and that understanding pained him a little.

Their teamwork was flawless. They chatted him up. Plied him with a second beer, and a third. Then, as he was showing signs of slowing down, they deftly moved him from the high visibility of the bar stool to the relative seclusion of a banquette at the back. There, they carried on as before, a few more beers for Tiger, some more wine for the two of them. The rest of the bar receded, their combined attention, and Tiger's as well, focused on the carefully modulated sexual electricity that crackled between them. The bearded man was flattered, increasingly tipsy, and fairly overwhelmed.

Desmond and Denis, on the other hand, were alert, attentive, and thirsty.

Desmond found himself making the first move. He put an arm across Tiger's chest and pulled him in, pressing his lips against the bearded fuzz, again shaking off the image of Oliver that popped into his head at the feel of his kiss. He concentrated on making the kiss memorable, and felt Tiger relax in his grasp.

Then Denis, taking Desmond completely by surprise, leaned down and purred into the bearded man's ear. "Let's get out of here, eh, Tiger?"

At Desmond's shocked expression, Denis merely raised an eyebrow, and proceeded to help a rather unsteady professor to his feet. Knowing that Desmond would hear him above the noise of the room, he said as he steered Tiger toward the front of the bar, "I've planned a little something different for us this evening."

Desmond stood, gobsmacked, watching Denis and his new friend disappear in the direction of the street door. Then, not knowing what else to do, he followed along in their wake.

Outside on the sidewalk, Tiger seemed to regain some lucidity in the cool evening air. He staggered slightly, leaning against Denis and shaking his head.

"Sorry, guys, I seem to be a little giddy," he said sheepishly, allowing Denis to keep him steady on his feet.

Denis merely grinned at him, all boyish charm. He casually pressed his palm against the professor's chest, splaying his long fingers as if feeling for a heartbeat under the leather bomber jacket. "No problem at all. Tony and I rather hoped we could convince you to come back to our place for a nightcap." His gaze lasered into Desmond's and stayed there as he continued. "We're staying uptown a few blocks at the Abingdon. It's awfully cozy."

"That'd be nice." He reached out and, placing an arm on Desmond's shoulder, pulled him closer. Thus sandwiched between the two vampires, Tiger allowed himself to be walked north along Hudson Street. The slightly unsteady trio drew little attention from the sparse late-night crowd on the Village streets.

Denis and Desmond exchanged looks across their companion's slightly bowed head. Desmond offered a weak smile, to let Denis know he'd go along with whatever it was he'd cooked up.

The Abingdon was a tiny hotel on Eighth Avenue, installed in a plain brick-fronted row house of a slightly later date than Desmond's old house on the east side of the Village. Denis managed to pull out a key that let them in the front door, while simultaneously nuzzling Tiger's ear. He guided them past a highly amused night clerk and up the narrow stairs to a room on the second floor at the back of the house.

"That's a little brazen, don't you think?" chided Desmond in a hushed tone, trying his best to get into the spirit of the thing.

"My dear, it's a gay hotel in Greenwich Village. I don't think it's the first time they've witnessed a drunken three-way about to take place."

Three-way?

"This obviously wasn't spur-of-the moment."

Denis eyed him, a smirk on his lips. "Don't be jealous, darling. I just thought it might be fun to try something new." He unlocked the door and pushed it open into the dark room.

It was furnished like a bedroom in a private home, without any of the standardized feel of even the most luxurious hotel room. An old four-poster bed piled high with pillows; a fireplace, a wardrobe instead of a closet. If not for the flat screen television and the automatic coffee maker neatly arranged on a side table, it might have been a guest room in Desmond's 4th Street house.

As Desmond surveyed the room, Tiger suddenly seemed to come to life, and tugged Denis into a rough kiss. Clearly he had hit the jackpot and wanted to enjoy his good fortune.

Denis pulled out of the kiss and turned his gaze toward Desmond. His eyes were heavy-lidded, their vampire alertness now mildly fogged with alcohol and – apparently – lust.

"Help me get our teddy bear undressed, *Tony*," he whispered, his voice rough.

Desmond did as he was asked, getting Tiger out of his coat and flannel shirt without ripping off the buttons as Denis might have. As he helped Tiger pull down his snug jeans, Denis stepped back, tossing his jacket on a chair, and began to undo his own shirt.

As promised, Tiger was wonderfully hairy–a soft pelt the color of dark honey. For all his resistance, Desmond couldn't help but notice Tiger's clean, savory fragrance. Soap and a very faint trace of some supposedly manly cologne mingled with the powerful lure of his blood.

Aroused in spite of himself, Desmond looked up at

Denis, who merely waggled his brows naughtily and stepped up to take Tiger in his arms and gently steer him to the soft white surface of the bed. Once their guest was supine, Denis, still half dressed but shoeless, joined him on the bed and began to kiss him hungrily.

Desmond pulled off Tiger's boots and socks, then slipped the jeans over his feet and let them fall to the floor. He climbed up onto the bed, watching the two intertwined figures with a sort of odd detachment. Having not been part of the arrangement, he felt strangely unconnected with what was going on. The only thing that disturbed him was the *lack* of any twinges of jealousy, or even envy.

What's wrong with me? I'm not that *emotionally stunted, am I?*

He began to idly stroke Tiger's naked form, enjoying the contrast between his hairless sides and the dense amber curls on his chest. The professor's arousal was all too apparent, and before long Denis noticed it too. He shifted his attention southward and soon had Tiger groaning with pleasure, his hands gripping the down coverlet.

Desmond took advantage of Tiger's exposed left side, leaning down to kiss him, feeling his gasps as Denis worked his oral magic. He gradually moved his kisses toward the bearded man's neck, nipping and teasing with his tongue along its length at first; then skillfully attaching himself firmly to the major blood vessel and starting to feed.

Eyes closed to better enjoy the rush of hot life into his mouth, Desmond felt only the faintest tremor from Tiger as his blood began to flow. He let himself go, sinking into the hypnotic pleasure of the moment. The coppery warmth filled his mouth and his throat, spreading its gentle fire through his body.

As he was finishing, he felt a more violent convulsion as Tiger reached his climax. Withdrawing his fangs, Desmond ran his tongue one last time over the wounds, then looked over into Denis's eyes. At this wordless exchange, they simply switched places. Desmond reclaimed Tiger's mouth, covering it with his own full pink lips, while Denis bent to his right side, quickly extending his canines and sinking them into the warm, pulsing flesh and drinking his fill. They had to be more careful feeding in tandem like this; too much taken would leave their host ill. It meant they had to feed more frequently, but the pleasure of hunting together made up for the inconvenience.

As Denis pulled away, licking the wounds so they would heal rapidly, Desmond pulled out of the kiss as well and gazed back into the blond's eyes. Between them Tiger lay, barely conscious in his post-orgasmic bliss, happily unaware that he had been a shared meal for two immortal creatures. A faint smile on his face indicated that they'd done well. In a little while, after a restful sleep, he'd wake up, perhaps with a mild headache, a little disoriented.

"This is a safe place," said Denis softly. "He can sleep it off here, or the night clerk will make sure he gets a cab home, none the worse for his adventure."

The two vampires leaned over the dozing bear and exchanged a lingering kiss, eyes locked, tasting the remnants of Tiger's blood in each other's mouths. Rising silently and quickly putting on their shirts, shoes and jackets, they slipped out of the room and into the sheltering gloom of the winter night.

"Your turn," Desmond gasped, his voice low and hoarse with passion, his mind overpowered by the sensation of being buried deep inside his lover. Denis lay beneath him, his perfect pale body glowing in the faint light that found its way in through the louvered shutters that covered the high windows. Thin bars of light striped the slender, muscled arms and flat belly sprinkled with the faintest suggestion of golden hair. His eyes were hooded, his beautiful mouth curved in a half smile as he looked lazily up into Desmond's hazel eyes.

"Hmmm?"

"Your turn. Drink from me. Now." Desmond held back, keeping his body still, fighting the urge to thrust, to satisfy his need. He leaned his torso down, forcing himself deeper still into Denis's body, bringing his own pale neck with reach of Denis's mouth. He could feel the man strain beneath him as he pushed the long ivory legs up and to the side to lessen the distance between their chests. Denis groaned, but not in pain.

Good thing vampires are flexible.

He nuzzled Denis's shoulder until he felt the other man's lips on his carotid artery; felt the twin pinpricks of his extended canines; felt at last the brief sharpness, followed by the dizzying sensation of his blood rushing into his lover's waiting throat. He began to move his hips, matching his movements to the rhythm of the suction on his neck. In this moment they were one, locked together in a cycle as charged and powerful as an electric circuit. Their heartbeats began to echo each other, in turn echoed by his pelvic thrusts and Denis's mouth pulling at his neck. The intensity of his vertigo began to peak, until a harsh, snarling moan was forced out of him as he climaxed, pounding into his lover's body, feeling his lover's teeth clamped onto him, before collapsing onto the cool velvet surface of the other man's skin. He could feel Denis's tongue on his neck, licking away the last traces of his feeding.

He let his softening cock slip out, then rolled to one side, cradling Denis's head against his chest, pulling him close. The loss of blood had cooled him and made him feel as if he were floating. He found himself craving the relative warmth of Denis's body, newly infused with his blood. He sat up partway and grabbed the comforter at the foot of the bed, lying back as he pulled it over their intertwined bodies.

They lay in comfortable lassitude for a while, the minutes passing insensibly, time having momentarily evaporated for them. Desmond finally let out a long satisfied sigh, snuggling into Denis's side.

"It's so ... astounding," he murmured, running a

hand across Denis's chest and belly.

"What?" The soft question was barely audible, would not have been to ears less acute.

"The whole feeling, that connection. When you're taking my blood and I'm inside you. I ... it's just unlike anything I've ever known."

Denis stirred and lifted his tousled blond head slightly, looking at Desmond.

"Oh come on, you must have felt this before. When you drank from Roger, or he drank from you." He nuzzled back into Desmond's shoulder.

Desmond just purred in response.

"Mmmmm ... but I never had sex with Roger. You know he's straight...when we took blood from each other it was only ..."

Desmond sat up suddenly, leaning on one elbow, and looked sharply at Denis.

"It was only when we regenerated that we took blood from each other."

Denis's eyes suddenly went wide as he looked up at Desmond's darkening features.

"How could you possibly know that?"

"Know what?" Denis's voice was small, hesitant.

"How did you even know Roger's name, much less that he's a vampire? I've never told you. I've never talked about Roger at all, and you've never asked. How could you possibly know our history? You've carefully avoided all discussion of your past, and I've followed suit so as not to crowd you."

Denis sat up, trying to put his arms around Desmond, who was suddenly distant and colder than his body temperature. But Desmond batted the caressing hands away. He got out of the ornate ebony bed and moved across the room, retrieving a figured silk dressing gown from a tall carved armoire. He shrugged into the ankle-length robe and quickly tied the sash into a loose knot at his waist. Then he turned back to Denis, facing him as he half sat–half lay on the bed.

"I need to understand this, Denis." His voice was

tight.

"You must have talked about him. After all, I met him at your office." Denis's voice was calm, but Desmond could tell that he knew he was on thin ice, that he had blundered fatally.

"You met Robert Delacourt, not Roger Deland," he declared tersely, pacing across the figured carpet. "Who is it you work for?" he asked, his voice quiet but steely.

"What?"

"I'm guessing that whoever you work for knew about me. Whoever that is must have briefed you about Beckwith Investments, and about a great deal more than just our current financial health. I'm guessing that whoever it is you work for knew everything about me. Knew about Roger. Our history."

He turned and glared at Denis as he lay wide-eyed on the bed. "I want to know how you knew."

Denis was silent, his gaze locked onto Desmond's icy stare. There was no fear in his face, but Desmond could see a change in his expression, a gradual sadness stealing into those big blue eyes. A shiver crept up Desmond's spine as he noted a liquid shimmer in the low light.

Tears?

His shoulders slumped beneath the silk robe. His tone softened as he asked again. "Who told you about me, Denis?" There was no anger in his words, only resignation.

Denis dropped his gaze for the first time, shifted in the bed so he was sitting cross-legged. It was incongruous to see him there, rumpled and naked and terribly sexy, his face vulnerable, almost despairing.

"Who?" Desmond repeated.

"My employer." Denis looked Desmond straight in the eye now. "My mentor."

"His name?" Seeing the beseeching look move across Denis's features, Desmond had a terrible premonition.

"His name, Denis."

"Gregory Charlon. He is the owner of Chillon Investments."

"Gregory Charlon?" asked Desmond stupidly, unable to absorb this revelation. He moved to an armchair by the fireplace and sat heavily in it, his hands gripping the armrests, his eyes staring blankly into the empty grate.

Gregory Charlon had brought Desmond Beckwith and Roger Deland together. He had changed Roger into a vampire. He had also tried to destroy Roger when he defied him, and only Desmond's desperate efforts had saved Roger's life. That rescue had cemented their lifelong love for each other. Platonic as it was, no love had been stronger in his many years. Not even Jeffrey's. Not even Tony's. He had not seen or heard Charlon's name since he and Roger had left France.

And all this had happened in Paris, during the French Revolution.

Without turning to look at Denis, Desmond spoke, his voice low and expressionless. "Tell me, Denis. There's no point in lying anymore."

"Charlon hired me when I was just out of university in Geneva. I did tell you a little about my family. I was something of a prodigy, the proverbial golden boy. My parents wanted me to go into banking. Charlon was there, successful, influential."

Desmond glanced over, and found Denis staring at him, eyes dry now, but the same sad expression on his beautiful face.

"Monsieur Charlon was good to me, Desmond. He encouraged me, he trusted me." His voice faltered. He dropped his eyes to the coverlet and took a deep breath.

"What?"

"He saved me, Desmond."

"How?"

"Perhaps a month into my job with Chillon Investments, I was arrested for solicitation in the Jardin Botanique." He looked up again.

"My family threw me out, and Charlon took me in.

He made the police back off, although I never knew how. He covered up the public scandal, but it was too late for my family. I was disowned, out on the street, and in desperation I went to Monsieur Charlon, and he gave me a place to stay. He allowed me to keep my job. He never judged me."

"He didn't mind that you were gay." It was a statement, not a question.

"No. And eventually I learned that this was because of you."

"What?" Desmond sat up in his chair, eyes riveted on Denis's still, naked form.

"We didn't discuss it at first. I was too shaken, too grief-stricken and shamed by my parents' disgust. I just worked in his office. I lived in his house. I never saw him at meals, which his servants prepared and brought to me in my rooms."

"What happened? How did my history enter into it?"

"My twenty-first birthday. July 5th, 1921."

"July 5th? But that's ... "

"Your birthday. I know."

"I don't understand."

"Charlon chose that day to reveal to me his secret, the secret of his long life, and the secret of his success."

"He told you he was a vampire?"

"The whole story, including the part about meeting a young foreign banker, an Englishman who shared my birthday, who had taught him a very important lesson. A lesson that had changed his perspective on life."

Denis shifted on the bed, folding one slim leg beneath him, stretching the other out in front of him, leaning back on his hands.

"He told me about Roger, how he brought him into their coven. He told me about the way you defied him openly when he invited you to his house in Paris, and how Roger followed your example and defended you. That's when he brought up the fact that you preferred men to women."

"And then what?"

"Then he began to talk to me about my own life; about my skill as a banker, my potential as an associate of his firm. It was all a little surreal, as you can imagine. But I was broken, alone. I had lost everything, and he was offering me eternity."

"I understand, Denis, truly I do." For Desmond also had been alone and broken, far from home, when he had chosen to become a vampire.

"He told me I reminded him of you, and that I could have a life like yours, if I would allow him to transform me."

"And you agreed?"

"More than that. I all but begged him to change me. To end my pain by ending my life and giving me a new, everlasting one."

He shrugged, looking suddenly like a teenager. "At least that's what I thought."

"Has it been less than you'd hoped?" Desmond asked softly.

"No, just – different. After all, I'm just a banker. I do what Monsieur Charlon tells me to do." There was a pause, and Desmond glanced over to see Denis's eyes focused, unseeing, on the bedcovers.

The blond chuckled softly and shook his head, letting out a deep sigh. "Whether I want to or not. It's not exactly the sort of adventure my rather romantic imagination had me living."

"And you were changed on your birthday?"

"Yes."

"Which means you just regenerated for the second time this past summer."

"Yes, starting on the fifth of July."

"The same day I did."

"Right."

"So our lives are perfectly aligned. Day for day. Year for year."

"So it would seem."

"And Charlon somehow thought he'd send you here to arrange this deal between our two firms because …?"

Vampire in Suburbia

A note of ice slipped back into Desmond's voice.

"Because he wants the legitimacy of your firm. He loves the idea of being permanently tied to another firm managed over centuries by a fellow vampire."

Denis hesitated, as if deciding whether to go on. Then he added, "He knew you'd like me, would connect with me. And once you found out I was also a vampire, he thought you'd …"

"Fall in love with you?"

Denis's golden head dropped. "Yes," he whispered.

Desmond sank back into the chair, his hands in his lap. He closed his eyes.

The silence built up in the room, as if the heavy draperies had absorbed all noise. Even the street traffic seemed to have vanished, leaving the two vampires alone in a thrumming void.

"Were you also Denis von Riesenfelder?" The question was soft as a caress, but it struck home like a tiny poisoned dart.

"Yes," came the answer, so soft that no mortal could have heard it.

"And you were in charge of Charlon's dirty dealings in Bosnia and Herzegovina. You helped him take advantage of the ethnic cleansing and the entire post-Soviet mess to reap enormous profits for your firm."

There was a pause. "I was his agent. He trusted me. Our transactions were entirely legal, Desmond, I swear to you. I owed him everything."

The silence dragged on for a full minute before Desmond spoke again.

"I think you'd better go."

Wordlessly, Denis rose from the bed, his body flickering through the slatted light as he moved over to the chair where his clothes had been tossed. He dressed in silence, then stood uncertainly, looking at Desmond across the big dark room.

"Desmond, I'm sorry."

Desmond didn't turn to look at him. He kept his eyes closed, but he knew Denis would see the track of a tear shining on his high cheekbones, even in this dim light.

"I'll call you, Denis."

"But, Desmond …"

"I'll call you."

The blond vampire slipped silently out of the bedroom and down the long corridor. Desmond waited until he heard the faraway click of the front door, and only then did he raise his hands to his face and let himself cry. Even as the tears wet his cheeks and his chest heaved with sobs at the all-too-mortal pain tearing at his heart; he couldn't help thinking of Oliver and how he had squandered his friendship.

Chapter Nineteen

Jane looked up from her desk as Desmond wearily walked the length of the carpeted corridor. Her expression was quizzical.

"What's up? You stayed in the city last night. You could have called."

In spite of his broken mood, Desmond had to smile at that. Jane had definitely taken on a more maternal, proprietary attitude since moving her family into Oakwood. Her subtle but distinct sense of *ownership* both irritated and comforted him.

"Yeah. Denis and I went out."

Jane said nothing more, understanding from his demeanor that it hadn't ended well. But her face expressed an unasked question.

"I want you to get some people working on more background research on Chillon Investments."

"Problem with the negotiations?"

"Possibly, but not for the reasons you might think. I'm interested in getting more historical information on what the firm does in terms of philanthropy. They've also got some unpleasant professional secrets that I need to be sure of before I'm comfortable."

Desmond turned to go into his office, but stopped and continued.

"Oh, and I've found out who the principal is behind the firm. A man named Gregory Charlon. I want as much background information on him as possible. It might be hard to dig up."

"Is there something special about this Charlon?"

Desmond offered her a weak smile. "Turns out he's someone I knew a long time ago."

"A long time ago, now that you're pushing twenty-two?" Jane's look was puzzled now, and Desmond winced inwardly at the slip.

"Let's just say I was a stupid kid and we didn't exactly see eye to eye."

He turned and went into his office, closing the door behind him, feeling Jane's eyes boring into his back the whole way.

"Robert Delacourt, please." Desmond sat, tapping a pen idly on his desk as he waited for Roger's assistant to notify him. Roger's assistants tended to come and go, although they were always rather voluptuous and tended to speak in a breathy Marilyn Monroe-sort of voice. During his years with his almost-wife Wendy, the assistants had become plainer and more efficient; but since her death the old pattern had slowly reasserted itself. Desmond had always thought of Roger as stronger and more self-sufficient than himself; but he was realizing that perhaps Roger was just as lost as he was. The difference was in how each of them covered their weakness. Desmond collected things; Roger collected people.

Until now, he realized.

I seem to have started collecting people, too.

"Des?" Roger's throaty tenor interrupted his thoughts.

"Hi." He couldn't seem to formulate the words.

"What's happened?" The note of concern that instantly colored Roger's words gave Desmond the focus he needed.

"Looks like we may have a hitch in the Chillon collaboration."

"What? How?"

And Desmond told him the whole story.

Roger gave a long, low whistle. "Charlon, after all these years. Jesus."

"He's intentionally hidden himself from us all this time. But why surface now and try to get to us?"

"He's a lot older than we are, remember. He was already two centuries into his life when I met him; perhaps he sees things with more distance. He watched you for forty years before he contacted you the first time, remember. Maybe time slips by faster for him because he doesn't regenerate."

"And maybe it all started up again when Denis Schroeder suddenly entered his life."

Desmond pondered this. "Sort of as if both you and I appeared in one person."

"Something like that." There was a momentary silence. "Is the deal dead?"

Desmond hesitated only slightly before answering.

"Not necessarily. Obviously I'm not happy about this turn of events. I am angry at myself for ignoring the information you turned up because of my relationship with Denis. I let myself be played, and that smarts. But I've been thinking about it a lot since last night, and I realize that I can't just throw this deal over because my feelings are hurt. Once my anger dissipated, I just wanted to know why, to understand what Charlon's up to. I want to know if he's hiding other ugly details that we need to know about. The whole Bosnian thing really sticks in my craw. But that's over with at least."

"And Denis?" Roger's voice had grown very soft.

Desmond sighed. "That's done, I'm afraid."

"Desmond, I'm sorry. You were so happy."

"Seemed like it, didn't it?" He paused, making sure that emotion wouldn't affect his voice. "Denis played me to get at the company. Charlon put him up to it – and I wish I knew why he had to do that."

Desmond cleared this throat before speaking again. "Roger, he wasn't just faking it the whole time, I'm sure of that. Even if he was calculating every step of the way, following Charlon's instructions, I can't believe what I felt between us was all false."

"You know what, Des?"

"Hmm?"

"I think we need to meet with Charlon and Schroeder face to face. If he's serious about this, he'll come to you. Don't you think?"

"That's sort of where I was heading, too. Thanks for confirming it. I'll call Denis and have him arrange it."

"Desmond?" Again Roger's voice was gentle, solicitous.

"Yes?"

"Are you going to be all right? Is it all right if I come East for a few days?"

A wave of emotion swept over Desmond.

Here, at least, I know where I stand..

"I'll be okay. Promise. But you know I'm always better when you're here."

"You know I love you."

"I do."

"Good. I'll be in touch as soon as I know my travel plans."

"Of course. Love you too."

Desmond put down the phone, and then paged Jane.

"Yes?"

"Get Denis Schroeder on the line for me, would you?"

"Right away, boss."

Chapter Twenty

A light snow was falling, and the temperature hovered somewhere around thirty degrees. Not bad for a February day in New Jersey. City smells were slightly deadened by the cold air, and the most vivid scent was that of passersby, hurrying one place or another, their blood leaving a rich red spoor that lingered in their wake. Desmond stood on the sidewalk in front of the main entrance to his office tower, eyes peeled for his visitors.

He had called Oliver right after setting up the appointment with Charlon and Denis. It had been, Desmond admitted to himself, awkward. He had not wanted to say too much, to sound too confessional. But he had made it clear that he wanted to get together. Oliver had seemed more than willing and had asked no questions. They had made a date for Friday evening. He was going to pick Oliver up at the museum and from there they'd figure out their plans. In his own mind he was unsure of what he was going to do; but he knew he wanted some time with Oliver, if only to talk, to make amends, to correct the mistake he had made.

A large black car swept around the corner from Raymond Boulevard and pulled up to the entrance. Desmond recognized it as the Maybach that had delivered Denis to his housewarming party. This time, however, the chauffeur emerged from the driver's seat and ran around the front of the limousine to open the rear passenger door. Desmond was startled to recognize Ivan, the wizened old manservant who had been with Charlon when he had lived in Paris in the 1790s. Ivan, as Desmond remembered, had served Charlon since they were made vampires together centuries before that. As he rounded the vehicle, the ancient vampire raised his hand to his cap in a salute, nodding as he passed.

Desmond's shock at seeing Ivan again was shunted aside at the sight of Denis's long Armani-clad legs unfolding from the limousine's front passenger seat. The handsome blond climbed out gracefully, straightened up without giving so much as a glance in Desmond's direction, and motioned to Ivan to return to his post as he held the rear door open.

Another pair of legs emerged from the darkened compartment. These were also dressed in what was patently an expensive suit, but they were neither slender nor long. The body that followed was corpulent, and wrapped in a black cashmere overcoat. Thick gray hair, elegantly cut, was brushed back off a high forehead. The clean-shaven jowls of the elderly face were pale; the glittering dark eyes that turned toward Desmond as the old man straightened his back were just as he remembered them.

"Monsieur Charlon," said Desmond, keeping his

voice neutral as he approached the car and extended his hand. He wore no overcoat, just a dark blue suit. A blood-red necktie contrasted with the white of his shirtfront. The Beckwith signet glinted dully on his right hand. When he had first met Charlon he had been unnerved and somewhat in awe of the old vampire. Not this time.

He could not help but feel a flash of surprise when Charlon reached out to take his proffered hand, clasped it in both of his ungloved hands, and smiled up at him with an apparent gladness that was entirely unexpected.

"So, my dear Mr. Beckwith, at last we meet again."

He shook Desmond's hand in his double grip as if greeting a long-lost friend.

"It has been far too long."

Dumbfounded by Charlon's evident sincerity, Desmond could only motion them to the entrance and escort them silently to the elevator. He glanced sideways at Denis, who looked back fleetingly and gave him a small smile before casting his eyes downward. They rode up to the Beckwith Investments offices in silence. A mysterious smile hovered on Charlon's lips, while Denis Schroeder's face remained determinedly blank.

Once seated in his office, having refused the coffee and water offered by Jane, Desmond turned to his guests. His pale, slim hands lay quiet on the mahogany surface in front of him. His back did not touch the back of his chair. There was no smile in his voice or on his lips as he spoke to his old nemesis and his former lover.

"Thank you, Monsieur Charlon, for coming all this way. And thank you, Denis, for arranging it so quickly."

Denis inclined his head in acknowledgement. Desmond could see sorrow in those blue eyes, however he might try to disguise it. He turned his attention back to Charlon, forcing himself to look away from Denis's face.

"At first, when I discovered how I had been deceived, it was my first instinct to cancel all further negotiations and to bring an end to any idea of our firms' financial collaboration."

He saw Charlon's brows rise, but the old man's expression didn't change, his eyes fixed on Desmond.

"However, having spoken to my partner, Robert Delacourt – you of course remember him as Roger Deland, Monsieur Charlon –" The gray head nodded slightly. "After talking it through with Roger, I have decided that we perhaps need not end things after all."

At that moment, as if on cue, the door opened and Roger entered the office. Desmond was sure he had been listening. He was, if possible, more beautiful than usual. He wore a bottle-green serge suit, which set off his deep red hair and dark green eyes. He towered over the seated men, his usually sunny expression absent as he eyed the visitors coolly, as if they were hostile strangers.

Desmond looked down at his hands, suppressing a smile. Roger was never this way in business situations. He was the affable, relaxed one. Desmond tended to be the uptight member of the team during negotiations. But this was not about business; this hauteur was nothing more than Roger remembering his own betrayal by Charlon and defending his lifelong friend. He was letting these men see that he knew what they had done, and that he was not pleased.

A wave of warm emotion suffused him as he looked up at his friend's face. "I'm sure you remember Gregory Charlon, and of course you know Denis."

Roger shook hands with the mildly intimidated men, who scrambled up from their chairs to greet him. Then he motioned for them sit back down, positioning himself behind Desmond's chair. To Desmond's barely hidden astonishment, he placed one hand gently on his shoulder.

Desmond continued. "Every indication, from the research our staff has done on Chillon Investments, is that a financial partnership between our companies would be mutually advantageous and in all likelihood profitable." He allowed himself a small smile.

"However," he continued, "Mr. Deland uncovered some disturbing real estate speculation practices associated with the dismantling of Yugoslavia; and those in turn led our researchers to still further business dealings that shared a common unsavory, um, essence."

Charlon's only response was to raise his eyebrows slightly. His eyes were on Desmond, never wavering.

Roger took the reins, his voice measured and resonant. "We noted similar activities to those that had occurred in Bosnia in other parts of Eastern Europe during the 1930s, particularly in the years paralleling the rise of the Nazi party in Germany and Austria." He directed his gaze at Denis. "A young representative of yours named Denis Schroeder appears to have been instrumental in these transactions."

At this, Denis's expression became visibly pained. Roger turned his attention back to Charlon.

"This pattern, which became increasingly difficult to discern, nonetheless, repeated itself on several more occasions, each of them with a particular historic resonance. Russia in 1915 and 1916. France in the early 1870s, and before that, in the late 1840s."

He looked back at Denis, who dropped his eyes to his lap. "Of course these were all before your transformation in 1921."

Desmond chimed in. "All of this, Monsieur Charlon, was unpleasantly reminiscent of the man I met in Paris in 1793."

Charlon spoke now, his voice low and carefully controlled. "Every one of these activities was carried out fully within the law of the time and place, Mr. Beckwith. I trust your researchers discovered that as well?"

"They did," Desmond answered. "But it is not the exacting legality of your business practice that I am troubled by; it is the abuse of your unnatural insight into human nature that skirts the edges of immorality. It is your willingness to prey upon the misfortune of others to expand your profits."

He glanced at Denis, who did not raise his eyes. His voice softened as he added, "It is the fact that you ensnared Denis in your schemes that bothers me most,

Gregory. The fact that you took advantage of a damaged boy who revered you for saving his life: that is what deeply offends me."

Charlon's mouth dropped open, but he said nothing. Denis looked up at Desmond, who could see his eyes shimmering with tears.

It was Roger's turn again, and Desmond felt him tighten the grip of the hand on his shoulder. "In spite of all this, Monsieur Charlon, there were a great many other interesting activities that were brought to my attention. I am nothing if not thorough."

Desmond allowed himself to relax against the back of his chair, steepling his fingers in front of his chest as Roger continued, the strong hand still gripping his shoulder.

"What ultimately pushed our decision in favor of continuing our business relationship was the substantive amount of information that came to light regarding your more generous behavior."

Denis glanced over at Charlon, whose own gaze never left Desmond's.

"The fact is, we found a great deal of good done in your name, which, I might note, was rather more difficult to hit upon. Indeed, good works and public largesse seem to be a hallmark of Chillon Investments and its founder going back quite a long way."

Charlon leaned his bulky frame forward in the deep leather armchair.

"Denis has told you that I am not what I was when we last met, Mr. Beckwith. I presume Roger has now given you reason to believe this to be the case."

"Denis only told me that you said what happened between us had changed your perspective on life."

"As indeed you did, Desmond." The old vampire's voice trembled slightly. "You defeated me, but without malice, all those years ago. You rescued Roger and took him away, out of my influence. You thought nothing of revenge, only of saving your friend. You gave no sway to my closed little world of the undead; but sought instead only life, free of the secrecy and macabre pantomime in which my own life had become mired."

Charlon paused, as if to catch his breath. Denis's look was locked onto his mentor, his hands clasped in his lap.

"I dared not contact you. Years slipped by and still I could never quite shake my anxiety that you would desire to revenge yourself and Roger on me. So I left Paris. I took those of my little family who would come with me, and moved to Germany, then to Switzerland. I established a small banking office there. I've been there ever since."

"So I understand. But it was not your business methods that surprised us, Gregory," said Desmond quietly, and Charlon registered the switch to his given name.

"Of course," interjected Roger, "there were no records beyond a certain time. But the name Charlon appears in a surprising number of historical contexts. It becomes associated increasingly with hospitals, orphanages, homes for old soldiers."

Charlon shrugged, his face enigmatic. "It seemed the thing to do at the time."

Roger spoke. "During both World Wars, your name appears repeatedly in association with various resistance movements." Roger's pose was challenging, but his voice had lost its coldness. "Even as you carried on with your deceitful profiteering, you seem to be simultaneously working for good."

"War is a horrific waste of money and life," the old man said. "Particularly the first World War. Every player in that game was guilty of stupidity, but Germany instigated the whole mess. As you know, Desmond, I had my fill of war long before you knew me."

"And during the Nazi occupation of much of Europe, in spite of your profiteering, you assisted Jews in escaping. You sequestered Jewish money in your bank – disregarding Swiss neutrality – and you helped scores of families get out of Europe and to America or Palestine."

Desmond had leaned forward, forcing Roger to let go of him. He placed his elbows on the desk, his chin on his clasped hands.

"Ah, well, that." Charlon shrugged again. "The Jews, you see, had become my friends. I understood their marginal status, relegated to shadows, to the fringes of society. I shared in their business of banking, and also in the opprobrium heaped upon them in times of financial duress. Unlike most of my fellow Christians – or presumed Christians – I refused to vilify my Jewish peers to improve my own position when others did. After all, if mortal humans treated each other with such gross injustice over something as insignificant as religion; how would our kind have fared?"

"When I met you in Paris ... " Desmond began.

"I was already two centuries old, and well on my way to becoming the monster you imagined me," sighed the old vampire, flicking an imaginary bit of dust off the lapel of his gray suit. He looked up, his eyes moving between Desmond's face and Roger's.

"My arrogance was at its peak then. You walked into our family circle, a mere pup in my eyes, just past your first regeneration; and you looked at us not with awe, but with contempt. You challenged my authority, you dismissed the carefully constructed fantasy I had built around myself and into which I had drawn other, younger vampires, equally adrift and appalled at their earthly condition."

Desmond allowed his eyes to flicker over to Denis again, and was surprised to see a look of wonder on the young vampire's face.

"My act of vengeance upon Roger Deland was my last futile attempt to maintain the control I'd built over all those years. But when you outsmarted me, instead of feeling anger, all I felt was relief – relief that my own idiocy had not caused the death of one of my own, my creation. My vanity had endangered the life of one of my ... children." At this last word his voice dropped to a whisper and he glanced at Denis.

Desmond spoke hesitantly. "Your life seemed entirely alien to me. My … my own experience had been so very different. Baron Tsolnay had changed me as an act of mercy, reluctantly. The life he had lived seemed so noble, so much the opposite of my own pampered youth."

"Do you know Tsolnay's fate?" Charlon interrupted him.

"Ah, no. I never saw him again after I left him, after I left Jeffrey behind in his village."

"I kept in touch with him over the years, in fact more and more as my own life changed. During the second war we did resistance work together, but you won't find any records of that on Google, I'm afraid." The old man sighed heavily.

"What happened to him?"

"In 1943, after the Nazis reoccupied Split in Croatia, they spread their nasty work into the countryside, and eventually to Tsolnay's own village. The people of the village resisted – to protect their baron, the man who had cared for them and their ancestors for centuries." Charlon paused, swallowing. His brow furrowed.

"The Germans massacred the population and torched the village. They made a special show of dynamiting and burning the castle, dragging Tsolnay's library into the square and setting it alight."

Desmond gasped and put a hand to his mouth. He remembered all too clearly the beautiful books that had lined that ancient paneled library, each with their blue leather binding and the Tsolnay crest in gold on the spine. It was in that room that the old baron had taught him everything he knew about being a vampire.

Desmond felt Roger gently caress the back of his neck.

"There is no accurate account of what actually became of Baron Tsolnay, Desmond. Among the few survivors – a handful of women and children who hid from the carnage and made their way to neighboring villages – there were rumors that my old friend simply walked into the burning castle and was swallowed up in the flames."

Desmond groaned softly, covering his face with his hands.

"There are no documents attesting to what happened in Tsolnay. It was a rare instance in Nazi history where records were not kept. The village today is nothing more than a ruin half reclaimed by the forest."

As Charlon finished his testimony, Desmond composed himself, pushing aside thoughts of the beautiful castle, that prosperous, picturesque village; that benevolent life that had endured so long – all vanished as if they had never been. He cleared his throat.

"I am sorry to hear it. I never knew."

"Tsolnay's death shook me to the core, Desmond. It was because of you that I rekindled my old friendship with him. Of course, by the time of Tsolnay's death, I had already taken on Denis."

He looked over at the young vampire, who met his gaze with steady blue eyes.

Desmond saw his opportunity. "And that brings me 'round to my final reason for calling you all this way to meet with me, Gregory." He cleared his throat again, and both Denis and Charlon fixed their looks on him.

"I had already determined, based on our research, to set aside your less admirable actions and to continue our financial relationship. Your firm is sound. You have run it wisely and well. But it has been made clear to me that you, personally, might possibly become someone with whom I would be proud to associate my name and my firm's reputation."

This last comment drew a smile from Charlon's thin lips.

"Possibly?"

"However, we do have one condition," Roger said, moving to stand beside Desmond, and leaning forward to place his hands on the desk.

"Yes?"

"We need to have your guarantee, and will indeed

have our contracts so written, that all shady dealings of the sort to which I have alluded will henceforth cease. I will not have Desmond's name tarnished after two and a half centuries of unblemished integrity, Gregory."

Charlon merely nodded, and Desmond took this as acquiescence.

"There is one more thing," Desmond interjected. "I need to understand – to have you explain to me – your relationship with Denis Schroeder." He saw Denis's eyes go wide at this. The blond vampire looked over at his employer, whose own face betrayed only the slightest surprise at Desmond's request.

"I'm not sure what you wish to know, Desmond." The old man looked over at Denis, and kept looking at him as he continued. "Denis is like a son to me. Nothing more than that."

"Nothing more than a son?" asked Desmond, his voice rising slightly. "It would seem to me to be more than enough to preclude doing what you did to him."

"What I...?" Now shock registered in Charlon's eyes, and Desmond could see Denis's expression shift as well, to something like sadness.

"Denis has told me what you did for him, and why. Clearly you care about him, have cared about him through more than a lifetime now. Do you love him, Gregory? Do you love him as a father might love a son?" Desmond fought to control a tremor from entering his voice.

Charlon's mouth opened, but no words emerged. He looked at Desmond, and then back at Schroeder. He took a breath.

"I believe I do love him, as a father might. Yes."

Desmond's voice was very soft, almost a whisper, but he knew the three other vampires would have no trouble hearing him. "Then why, Gregory, would you use Denis that way? First to enlist him to do your dirty work for decades, knowing he would never question you, so strong was his devotion and his gratitude. And then engage him to lure me into a commercial alliance as if it were just another of your money-making schemes? Why would you allow this young man, whose life you seem to have saved, to so corrupt himself in the name of making money? Why would you allow him to disgrace his beauty and endanger his emotional health by sending him off in such a calculating and cynical way on a fool's errand to seduce me? Why would you let him dishonor himself in this way – take advantage of his obvious love for you – when this sort of duplicity smacks of your old ways?"

Charlon looked back at Desmond. His eyes had softened. He did not speak. Desmond thought he saw tears shimmering once again in Denis's eyes.

"If you and I, if the houses of Charlon and Beckwith are to do business in future, you must understand from the start that neither I nor Roger will tolerate this sort of underhanded scheming. You cannot play games with people's lives, Gregory, especially if you claim to care for them. You cannot do this if you expect to be part of our world."

"But ... of course ... I wouldn't ... " Charlon sputtered softly.

"So to begin things," Desmond interrupted again, "I believe you need to speak honestly to Denis. You need to help him understand what he is to you."

He looked with rising fierceness into Charlon's face.

"And you need to apologize to him for what you've done, for misusing his trust and his gratitude to unworthy ends."

He rose and walked around the desk. As he grasped the doorknob, he turned to the two silent men, still seated in the leather armchairs. "We will leave you two alone for a moment. When we get back, we can discuss the final arrangements. My administrator has drawn up the papers, and Mr. Deland – or rather, Mr. Delacourt – has approved them."

He quickly left the room, Roger close behind, shutting the door and moving several yards down the hallway. There he stopped and turned, putting a hand on

Roger's arm to keep him there.

The partial glass wall of his office didn't allow total visibility, but he had intentionally designed the space so that he was not shut off from his employees and his assistant. Jane liked to be able to glance over and see what he was doing at his desk.

From where he stood, he could not see Charlon, but he could see Denis, who sat in the chair, his head down. As Desmond watched, Denis lifted his head, as if being spoken to. Then he rose – tentatively it seemed – pushing himself up by the arms of the chair. Even to his acute senses the words spoken were muffled through the closed door, but he could see that Denis was talking, and presumably so was Charlon.

And then Charlon appeared, having walked across the office. Desmond saw the old man wrap the younger one in his arms, pull him into an embrace. Denis buried his face in the old vampire's shoulder, and even at this distance Desmond could see that his shoulders shook as he did so.

Desmond turned and smiled into his old friend's face. Together they continued down the corridor, heading to the conference room to wait.

Chapter Twenty-One

"Oliver? Mr. Beckwith is here to see you."

The museum's receptionist replaced the phone in its cradle and looked unsmilingly up at Desmond. "He'll be right down. It's been a long time since we've seen you here." There was a faint chill in her voice, making Desmond wonder exactly what she knew.

"Thank you." He smiled hopefully at her, feeling oddly guilty at this reminder of how absent he'd been these last few months. To escape what he now was sure was a judgmental stare, Desmond turned and surveyed the high-ceilinged lobby. People stood in line to pay admission, while a flat-screen monitor offered images of exhibitions and events at the museum. A pair of large abstract circular murals by Sol LeWitt adorned the upper part of the walls, providing splashes of brilliant color to the pale, skylit space. He moved toward the staircase and slowly climbed to a small rotunda, where he absently studied a model of the museum that was intended to show visitors how to navigate the complex of buildings strung together over a century of expansion. The Ballantine house formed the eastern end of the museum's northern section.

His thoughts had drifted to that dinner in 1893, and to Robbie, when the sound of footsteps suddenly echoed in the rotunda behind him. He turned in time to shake Oliver Cameron's outstretched hand, and to appreciate the cheerful smile and the blue eyes that went so well with his coppery hair. The familiar scent, a mixture of his own unique blood-fragrance with a hint of lavender soap, filled Desmond with a sweeping sense of happiness.

They strolled through the galleries for a while, and Desmond let Oliver talk about exhibition plans he was working on. Although he was in charge of just the decorative arts collection, he seemed to know a great deal about the other departments as well, and showed pride in his familiarity with the entire museum. The two men ended up back in the Ballantine House, its Gilded Age opulence a startling contrast to the cool modern galleries that made up the rest of the institution. Desmond marveled at how much it felt like the house in which he had been a guest in 1893; while most of the objects were entirely different, the rooms were furnished and arranged authentically, reflecting the eclectic taste of that period that Desmond remembered so vividly. On the second floor, at the top of the elaborate carved oak staircase, they once again came to the room with the ornate marquetry bed, in front of which they had met for the first time months ago.

"I remember you were quite mesmerized by this bed," Oliver teased gently. "It was like waking you from a trance when I tried to get your attention."

Desmond looked closely at the older man's face. "How exactly did you figure out that this particular bed had come from this house when you found it at auction?" He cocked his head to one side. "Surely it was long gone after the family moved out in 1920?"

"Oh, yes, of course." Oliver looked slightly abashed at the unexpected cross-examination. "It seems so simple, but there was a reference to an invoice from a 'Mr. Herter' among the documents that came from the family in the 1940s relative to the decorating of the house." He looked directly at Desmond, his expression oddly defensive. "The family used a mix of local craftsmen and a New York decorating firm back in 1885 when they first did the house. They were torn between being fashionable and being loyal to their own city's economy." He gave a little smirk. "And there was a chalk inscription on one of the side rails of the bed that reads 'Washington Street, Newark,' which sort of clinched it for me. It was probably part of some delivery notation made when it was shipped over from New York."

"That's all?" Desmond was surprised. He had immediately recognized the bed, of course, but this seemed like fairly meager evidence for such a firm attribution.

Oliver looked at him, an odd little moment of panic flickering across his handsome features. "Well, not exactly, but I can't really explain it entirely." The redhead almost absently ran one of his strong hands across the headboard, his fingers skimming across the polished surface.

Desmond saw the blue eyes widen, as they had when he and Oliver first shook hands; but the look wasn't directed at him. It was as if Oliver was seeing something that Desmond couldn't see. Then he gave his head a slight shake and turned his gaze again to Desmond.

"Why don't we go? It's been a long day, and I had an idea for someplace we could talk."

They left Desmond's Volvo in front of Oliver's house and took Katrina for a short walk. Then they walked the few blocks into the village of Maplewood. As they strolled down the main shopping street, a double-decker commuter train pulled into the station at the heart of the village, disgorging its load of suburban commuters, who scattered like ants fleeing a disturbed anthill.

"That's the train I usually take to work," Oliver commented. "One of the reasons I love living here is that I don't have to take my car to Newark every day."

"I envy you. Even though Oakwood is closer to my office than the New York flat is, I have to use my car – but I leave it in Newark and take the train when I go into the city."

They made their way down the curving street, and turned into a small storefront restaurant. The sign above the plate glass window read "Very Cute Panda" in illuminated red letters. Desmond caught Oliver's eyes and gave him a quizzical smile.

"Oh, that's Fayt's sense of humor," said Oliver as he held open the door and let Desmond precede him.

The restaurant was still fairly empty, since the dinner crowd had not yet arrived. A few couples with small children occupied booths along one wall, but Oliver chose a table by the front window. They hung their coats over the backs of their chairs and sat, smiling at each other shyly, but feeling comfortable with the silence.

"You remember I don't really eat much of anything."

"I remember. If you'd rather leave ... " Oliver looked concerned and made as if to rise.

"No, no, this is fine," Desmond assured him, motioning for him to sit back down. "I'll have some tea. You eat." He smiled at Oliver, eliciting another shy smile from the curator. "I like to watch people eat."

A tall muscular Asian man suddenly materialized at their table, his wide smile shining down on Oliver with aggressive benevolence.

"So, Oliver, you brought me a friend tonight, yes?"

"Hi, Fayt. Yes, I did. This is my friend Desmond."

The two shook hands, and Desmond could feel the strength in the other man's grip. The man, broad-shouldered and barrel-chested, was handsome; hair cut short and waxed up in front. He fixed a gimlet eye on Oliver's new friend. Behind the delicious cooking smells, Desmond could detect his blood scent. He noted, not for the first time, that while every person he encountered had a unique fragrance; there was no difference among the so-called races in the way their blood smelled generally. To Desmond, it was all good.

"It's good to meet you, Mr. Desmond. Oliver comes in here all the time, but it's been a long time since he came with anyone else." He turned his glance sharply to Oliver, who lowered his eyes to study the menu. There was something almost protective in the way he regarded Oliver, and Desmond was surprised to feel a little tremor of jealousy tingle through him.

Without further comment, Fayt took their drink orders and disappeared as quickly as he'd arrived.

"I take it you and Asa used to come here."

"It was one of our regular places. Actually, it's only been here for about six years. Fayt was very young when he emigrated from Malaysia and opened this restaurant here. Asa and I started eating here as soon as it opened. That was a few years before he got sick." He gestured with his head toward the kitchen, where Fayt could be glimpsed giving orders to the staff.

"He was beside himself to discover an obvious gay couple in his restaurant. The main reason he left Malaysia was because it's so unfriendly to gay people. He became our instant friend and always made a fuss over us when we walked in. Asa's illness and death were very hard for him."

He paused, and took a long drink of his water, then blinked a few times and looked back into Desmond's eyes.

"After I lost Asa, going anywhere outside the house was very difficult for a while. I got very reclusive. Dealing with people at the museum every day drained me, and I holed up at home at first. Then one day Fayt shows up at my front door, with an armload full of Thai curry." Oliver chuckled softly. "After he fed me, he made me promise to come by at least once a week, so he'd know I was all right."

"Do you think he had feelings for you?" Again, a pang of jealousy pinged in Desmond's heart.

Oliver laughed. "Oh, no; Fayt made it clear he didn't fancy white men. I told him he was a shameless racist, but he just chided me that who he wanted to love was none of my business because that was the American way."

"I see." Desmond smiled in spite of himself. "Quite the patriot, isn't he?"

Oliver just grinned at him.

At that moment Fayt arrived with Desmond's tea and Oliver's Diet Coke. Oliver gave him an order. When Desmond demurred, he puffed up his chest in pretend umbrage.

"My food isn't good enough for you, Mr. Desmond?"

Blushing, Desmond stammered out his standard excuse. "It's just that I have these complex allergies, and I've found it's just better to avoid food when I'm out and eat what I know is safe once I'm home."

Well, I'm not lying exactly, am I?

The subterfuge about his strange and delicate constitution had been his smokescreen for many decades. Tony Chapman had seen through it, but other than him, people just accepted it as another of Desmond's eccentricities.

"Well, you're going to have to drink a lot of tea to make it worth my while, then. I assume I'll be seeing you here again with Oliver?" Desmond had to stifle a laugh at his arch expression, and he cast a beseeching look in Oliver's direction.

"He will if I have anything to say about it, Fayt, whether he eats or not." He searched Desmond's face briefly after his answer, an unasked question on his lips. In response, Desmond reached over and placed his hand over Oliver's, which lay before him on the menu.

At this, Fayt's eyes went wide, and his face split into a satisfied grin. "All right, then. As long as you take care of my friend. He is not to be trifled with, Mr. Desmond."

"I promise," he said, looking up into the Asian's dark eyes, feeling strangely like he was taking an oath, his hand still on Oliver's.

After their meal – which had smelled amazing – they stopped in at a local bar a few stores further down the block for a drink. Oliver ordered a brandy and soda, which struck Desmond as wonderfully old school, while Desmond ordered and downed two gin martinis in quick succession. He was feeling unaccountably nervous and wanted to numb himself with alcohol.

As they returned slowly to Oliver's house, they occasionally stumbled into each other, bumping shoulders and giggling like a couple of teenagers, their breath making ephemeral clouds in the cold night air.

Approaching the house, Oliver stopped and turned to Desmond, putting his hand on Desmond's arm, squeezing slightly.

"You're coming in, right?" The note of uncertainty made Desmond's heart flutter.

"If I may."

A smile spread across Oliver's face. "You may."

They opened the door and were greeted with enthusiasm by Katrina, whose tail wagged furiously as the two men entered the small hallway and removed their overcoats.

"She seems happy to see you," remarked Desmond, unsure of where to begin the conversation.

"What's more important, I think, is that she seems happy to see *you*," replied Oliver, hanging the coats in a closet by the passage to the kitchen.

"Do you think so? Could she possibly remember me?"

"I do think so. Your last visit certainly made an impression on her."

"And you think she senses that you're pleased to have me here?" Desmond's lighthearted question masked the fact that his heart was beating far too rapidly for an old vampire.

"I think she does, yes." Oliver's gaze shifted, not focusing on Desmond's face. "Because I *am* very glad to have you here. It's been far too long since you were here, and you didn't, um, stay." He closed his eyes, inhaling slowly. When he opened them, he looked right at Desmond. "I was afraid I'd missed my chance. That wasn't a happy thought."

Desmond swallowed, his mouth suddenly dry, the gin making his head buzz.

"Ollie, I'm sorry. I know I hurt you, and I wish I hadn't. I don't know what there is to say to make it up to you. I …."

The redhead placed a strong index finger across Desmond's lips, silencing him.

"Don't say anything. You're here now. And I've had enough friendship."

His eyes locked onto Desmond's, sending a shudder down his spine.

Good lord, he's beautiful. How could I not have seen?

He leaned in and tentatively pressed his lips against Desmond's. A sigh escaped Desmond's mouth as he returned the kiss, raising a hand to caress the ginger beard that framed Oliver's strong jaw; running his fingers through the coppery waves of his hair.

Oliver smelled good: the spicy richness of his blood, that little undertone of lavender soap; the warm, human fullness of his skin and hair. He wrapped both arms around Oliver's torso and pulled him tight, deepening their kiss until Oliver had to pull back to catch his breath. Desmond didn't need to catch his breath. He didn't need to breathe at all, and had never realized this particular advantage of that fact before. He looked into those big deep blue eyes, now regarding him through half-closed lids, with wonder.

How could I have turned my back on this?

Oliver took him by the hand and pulled him up the stairs and into a dark bedroom. Desmond could make out a large high-posted bed, its pencil-slim posts supporting a short canopy crocheted in a fishnet design, trimmed with little white tassels. Big pillows covered in crisp white cases leaned against the wooden headboard. A plain white down comforter was folded across the neatly made bed. Then Oliver hit a switch by the door and small brass lamps on the nightstands blazed brightly, illuminating the soft grass green of the walls and the warm fawn of the carpeting. Oliver gripped Desmond's face in his strong hands and pulled him back in for another kiss.

Even though Desmond could easily have overpowered the mortal, it felt right to let Oliver take the lead. To him, Desmond was still barely more than a boy, and he was approaching middle age. He was, for all he knew, the one with experience, the one who had lived a life already. Desmond let his body loosen up, let Oliver's strength control him. He allowed Oliver's tongue into his mouth, moving his hands over his chest, undoing his buttons with graceful efficiency. When he pulled Oliver's shirt open and slipped his long fingers inside, a little moan escaped the redhead.

Oliver's skin was silky and warm. So different from Denis's firm velvet coolness. This was not the taut body of a twenty-one-year-old, but the softer musculature of a mature man. He ran his palms up over the broad pectorals and down the redhead's ribs, feeling Oliver quiver beneath his touch.

Pulling away suddenly, Oliver gasped softly, his eyes boring into Desmond's, with an expression of hunger Desmond had not seen before.

"Desmond, I really really need you."

"Good."

"I'm sorry to seem so desperate. It's been forever." His voice trembled slightly.

Desmond didn't answer him. He simply held his gaze as he quickly stripped off his clothes, letting them fall wherever they landed – shirt, slacks, socks and shoes – all lay carelessly rumpled on the soft wall-to-wall carpeting. He stood there, eyes still locked on Oliver's, naked and relaxed. Ready. At long last, it seemed.

He knew what Oliver saw. Broad shoulders and slim hips. Long slender arms and legs with feet and hands to match. A lean muscular torso lightly furred with dark hair that contrasted with his ivory-pale skin. His hair was full and wavy, although not as long as he sometimes wore it. He knew he was handsome; but he knew that Oliver was seeing something more than that.

Oliver performed a similar striptease for Desmond, revealing his own pale, hairless torso, arms and legs, thicker and stronger-looking than Desmond's, his shoulders and arms sprinkled with freckles. The broad flat belly ended in a patch of brilliant rusty hair, against which his pink half-hard cock contrasted invitingly.

Without a word they opened their arms to each other, coming together, skin against skin, mouth to mouth, sighing and moaning quietly as they embraced, their hands exploring fervently as if trying to memorize by touch what they had known only by sight and imagination for too long.

Intuitively taking the more submissive role, and slyly pleased with himself for his own versatility, Desmond allowed Oliver to lift him, wrapping his own legs around Oliver's smooth, ample backside, and carry him to the bed.

Holding Desmond with one strong arm as if he weighed nothing, Oliver pulled back the covers with his other hand and gently laid Desmond down on the cool cotton sheets. He climbed onto the bed and pulled Desmond into a fierce embrace that allowed them to feel their cocks against each other's stomachs. His strong hands roved over Desmond's back, moving lower until they found the blood-warmed crevice between his buttocks. There, his fingers paused, their gentle probing an unspoken question.

Desmond broke their kiss and looked into Oliver's eyes.

"Whatever you need," he whispered. "Anything at all."

Oliver's look, shimmering with inarticulate tears—desire? relief?—said all Desmond needed to know. He kissed his lover again and, heart pounding like a bride on her wedding night, gave himself up to joy.

Chapter Twenty-Two

Following a leisurely Saturday morning, and another less fevered round of lovemaking, Desmond had left Oliver on his own for the rest of the weekend. Oliver had eagerly reversed roles from the night before, and Desmond had taken delight in discovering that the thirty-eight-year-old, for all his scholarly reserve, could turn into a whimpering, needy boy again under the vampire's time-honed ministrations.

He had thrown what he considered a clever smokescreen around his deathlike six hour sleep, simply by making a show of taking a small pill to help overcome insomnia and warning Oliver that it put him so deeply under that he couldn't be woken. Such subterfuge was the only way he could comfortably call sleep upon himself in the presence of a mortal. Sharing a bed with a non-vampire for an entire night was something Desmond had done with no other mortal since Tony Chapman, preferring to slip quietly out into the night on those infrequent occasions when he combined sex and blood-taking in the same person.

As winter began to morph discreetly into spring, and Desmond was seeing more and more of Oliver, he reversed his established pattern by spending the weeknights at Oakwood and only the weekends at the Dakota. He and Oliver would routinely share a midweek dinner and then spend the night together; either at Oliver's house or in the big master bedroom in Llewellyn Park. Desmond was especially pleased that, once he had seen it, Oliver reveled in the Victorian overkill of the Dakota flat. New York City quickly became their weekend getaway.

After their initial sexual encounter, Desmond had found himself increasingly hungry for Oliver's presence, physical and emotional, but felt he ought to restrain his enthusiasm for fear of scaring the redhead away. Leaving himself open nights each week also accommodated Desmond's need to hunt, and he came to realize it was more difficult in suburbia than it had been in the city. Newly regenerated, the young Desmond needed blood more frequently than he had in the later years of his last lifetime, but as old as he was, he could still go for days without drinking. Since that first night, he had shied away from any temptation to drink from Oliver, and thus needed to slake his thirst elsewhere. He managed to find a couple of gay bars in New Jersey in which to hunt, eliminating the need to go into the city during the week. The Cage in Hoboken, catering to the young professional crowd that filled the densely-packed little city across the Hudson from Manhattan, was one; while Feathers in Bergen County brought in all those gay men who had moved to the northern suburbs and, like Desmond (if for different reasons) didn't want to go all the way back into the city for a drink in friendly surroundings. Thus it was that Desmond instituted a pattern of hunting at one of these of a Monday night, leaving him sated for his Wednesdays with Oliver; and the other on Thursday evenings, so that he would not be distracted by bloodthirst for their weekends in New York.

It was late on a Saturday evening, as they lay in Desmond's ornate ebony bed in the flat, when Oliver raised a topic never before broached between them.

"Desmond?" he asked, running his fingers idly through the hair on Desmond's chest.

"Hmmm?" he responded through half-closed eyes. Had he been a cat, Desmond would have purred. He loved the warm intimacy of moments like these.

"I was thinking of going to church tomorrow."

Desmond's eyes opened wider and he looked at Oliver, noting the hesitant expression and the half-smile framed by his russet beard.

"You know, it's Palm Sunday."

"I hadn't thought of that." Desmond remembered that Oliver and Asa had been members of a church in the suburbs, but they had never discussed religion. He just regarded Oliver quizzically, waiting for him to continue.

"Well, my parents have invited us up to Connecticut next weekend."

"What? When?" This news really woke him up. Meet Oliver's family? He had never met Tony Chapman's family; and Jeffrey's family had been employees on his father's estate two centuries before that.

"They just called me yesterday, and I told them I'd have to ask you." He hesitated, his eyes downcast, his face turning adorably pink. "I was rather afraid to bring it up."

"Why ever would you be afraid?" Desmond reached over and ran his hand across Oliver's cheek, scratching lightly at the curls on his chin.

"We've never talked about religion. Or church, or anything like." Oliver returned his eyes to Desmond's, encouraged.

"I was raised Church of England. I haven't been in a very long time."

Oliver cocked his head at this, and Desmond winced internally, realizing again that he was speaking as if he were an old man, and not just twenty-one.

"Do you believe in God?"

Desmond paused, fearful that they were stepping out onto thin ice. He took the hand that Oliver had laid on his chest and gripped it.

"Would it matter?" He tried, unsuccessfully he supposed, to keep a note of worry out of his words.

Oliver smiled, his eyes lighting up with understanding.

"Don't freak out about this, Des. We might be asked to go to Easter church with my parents, and I was just trying to find out how you'd feel about it."

"I wonder about God, Oliver." He chose his words carefully, not wanting to fall into anachronism. "As a child I believed without thinking. As an adult, well, it got more complicated."

Yeah, living for 250 years tends to mess up your worldview.

"So would being in church upset you?" Oliver raised their clasped hands to his lips and gave the back of Desmond's a small kiss, his beard tickling.

Desmond smiled, genuinely, relieved.

"Of course not."

"I was thinking of Trinity Wall Street."

"Why that church in particular?"

"It's small, old. A beautiful gothic revival building. Historic." Oliver's smile broadened, enthusiasm sparking in his blue eyes.

I remember watching them build that church.

"If you wish, I'd be happy to go with you tomorrow."

"And my parents' invitation for next week?"

"I'd love to meet your family. I'm flattered you want me to. Slightly terrified, but flattered."

"Don't you think it might be time?" Another sort of question lay behind this one, and Desmond was all too aware of it. Fortunately, he realized, he knew the answer.

"I think it's time." And he pulled his lover to him, reassuring him with a kiss and the strength of his arms that it was, indeed, time.

The next morning found them tucked into a stiff wooden pew, surrounded by smiling Episcopalians as a procession of priests and choral singers moved past, palm fronds waving and pale bluish clouds of incense wafting about them in the luminous gothic interior of Trinity Church at the end of New York City's main financial avenue.

Desmond looked over and felt a small shiver of pleasure at Oliver's happy face. Clearly this man liked being here. Church was a home of sorts for him. In his last lifetime, he had encountered very few gay friends who were comfortable in church; or who could attend any sort of service without attendant guilt and painfully mixed feelings. But this beautiful old place, replete with signs of affirmation and welcome for people of all kinds, was far different from what he had experienced in the 1960s, and in an entirely different realm from the formal, ritualized ceremonies of his own childhood in the chapel at Beckwith House.

So Desmond allowed himself to relax, listened to the music, joined in the hymns, and held onto Oliver's hand for comfort.

As the congregation was called forward for communion, Desmond unthinkingly followed his lover up to the altar rail and knelt alongside him, holding his hands up as Oliver did. To his horror, the smiling woman priest uttered the soft words "The Body of Christ, the bread of Heaven," and placed a small round white wafer in his upturned palms. He stared at it, wide-eyed, as if it were a poisonous spider or a ticking grenade.

He turned and looked at Oliver, who just smiled at

him as he took his wafer into his mouth, whispering "Amen" as he did so.

Heart beating fast, Desmond followed suit, leaving the wafer on his tongue, daring neither to chew it nor make any move to swallow it. This was solid food, spiritual or otherwise, and he knew from unpleasant experience what happened to anything solid that made its way into a vampire's system. It was rejected. Violently.

His panicked thoughts were interrupted by another smiling person in a white robe; this time a pretty young man with a pierced eyebrow and a spiked blonde haircut.

"The Blood of Christ; the Cup of Salvation," he murmured, offering a silver chalice of what smelled like sherry. Automatically, Desmond leaned forward and took a small sip, letting the familiar tang of the fortified wine flow across his tongue, where he could feel it start to dissolve the simple flour-and water wafer.

He felt Oliver rise next to him, and numbly followed suit, vampire eyes scanning for exits to which he could run when his body started to reject the sanctified bread. The thought of doing this at the height of this crowded religious service, in front of Oliver, sent waves of shame, and he could feel the blood from his Thursday night outing suffuse his face.

He hesitated in the main aisle, as Oliver took his seat in the pew and knelt in prayer, while first casting a concerned look up at Desmond. Desmond simply gave up, and knelt beside his lover, hands clasped as if in prayer, while his mind frantically evaluated escape routes and excuses. He shuddered, pressing his forehead into his folded hands, wondering how he could apologize.

And then ... nothing.

The congregation continued to file past to the communion rail. The choir started a beautiful French chant, providing a musical background to the sound of shuffling feet and murmured prayers. Desmond's mouth was empty, and he could still feel the tingle of the wine on his tongue and down his throat. But there were no tremors from within. No sign of physical distress. Nothing but – and Desmond noted this with some surprise – calm, and a sense of peace that filled him with its tender warmth.

He reached over and put his hand tentatively on Oliver's arm, prompting his lover to raise his head to look at him, and then to lean over and give him a quick peck on the cheek, feeling for all the world like a child who had come through an ordeal with flying colors.

Chapter Twenty-Three

Oliver's brother, Hugo, was taller than his elder sibling, and had brown hair that fell charmingly across his forehead. Hazel-brown eyes smiled along with his generous mouth as he greeted Desmond. In his early thirties, he was still substantially older than Desmond purported to be, and he and his pretty wife Morgan had three suitably attractive and more-or-less well-behaved children. The eldest of these was a serious redheaded girl named Ella who seemed far wiser than her eight years. Desmond wondered at the difference between Oliver's niece and Jane's younger daughter, Cassandra, who at eight was as insouciant and flighty as one could imagine. The boys, Scott and Sean, were a matched set, identical twins who shared their father's coloring and their mother's features. Desmond found them eerily cooperative and eager to please this mysterious young stranger in their midst.

Mr. and Mrs. Cameron, on the other hand, not only looked uncannily like each other, but both reminded Desmond vividly of Oliver. They greeted him warmly and both embraced and kissed their son as if they hadn't seen him in years rather than months. Desmond noted that Hugo also kissed his brother in greeting, and felt curiously moved by that fraternal intimacy.

It was just the Camerons and Desmond who sat down to dinner that evening. Desmond trotted out his allergy to smooth away Mrs. Cameron's crestfallen expression at his refusal to eat her delicious-smelling cooking. In return, he gratefully accepted several glasses of wine – all the while not wanting to appear like a heavy drinker to his lover's family – and did his best to distract them with a conversation that didn't slip into anything inappropriate for his apparent age. Fortunately, between his work, his house, his apartment, and the apparently exotic nature of everything in New Jersey to these Connecticut Yankees, he felt he acquitted himself well.

As a family they attended the Easter Vigil, the late-night service on Saturday. Desmond was sure he saw Oliver's father wink at him as he reported that the Vigil allowed everybody to sleep as late as they wanted on Easter morning. A stolen glance at Oliver, and the redhead's bland "I told you so" smile, seemed to confirm this.

The Vigil service made dramatic use of candles to symbolize the light of the Resurrection. Congregants were given small hand-held tapers, which were lit at the back of the church from a brazier burning outside the red-painted entry doors, and then used to kindle the candles of the people in the pews in front of them – until the entire space was aglow with muted golden light. Only then were the altar candles lit by white-robed teenage acolytes wearing inappropriate athletic shoes as the minister and the small choir entered singing.

While the pageantry and even some of the music was familiar to Desmond from amongst his distant memories, the accompanying sense of fellowship that swept through the small rural New England church like electricity was something he had never encountered. Favoring men had always given him sufficient reason to shy away from religious institutions and their attendant moral politics.

This time, he only briefly studied the communion wafer before popping it in his mouth and looking around for the wine chaser. He experienced the same momentary anxiety, and once more felt himself bathed in the odd spiritual glow he'd felt at Trinity Wall Street the week before.

Immortality had never given him any sense of having insider knowledge on things sacred and profane. Seated in the pew with this close-knit family, he felt his own heartbeat, steady and strong, as he clasped Oliver's hand, joining his clear tenor voice to those raised in joy around him.

They returned to the Camerons' Greek Revival house near the center of the town, after sending Joshua and Liz and their brood off to their own house somewhere not far away, promising to see them all again for brunch the next day.

At first their lovemaking that night was muted by Desmond's diffidence. Not in over a century had he had sex while someone's parents slept just down the hall, and while it didn't unman him, it certainly unnerved him. In spite of this, Oliver managed to tease him into a near frenzy, and as he finally drove himself home, his lover's strong legs wrapped tightly around his hips, he fought to stifle an ecstatic moan. As he focused on adjusting his thrusts to maximize Oliver's pleasure as well as his own, he could see a smirk nestled in the ginger beard.

"What?" he muttered in a rough whisper, kissing away the smirk while keeping up the rhythm he'd tentatively begun.

"You don't have to restrain yourself," replied Oliver, voice low and husky. "You look like you're about to have a stroke." Desmond was sure there was a faint giggle, but he stopped that with another aggressive kiss.

"It's called arousal," he growled, slamming into Oliver harder and forcing a small gasp out of him.

He felt Oliver's hands on his buttocks, gripping hard and urging him on. Oliver was able to articulate a hiccupping sentence as his partner drove into him, his beard scratching against Desmond's jaw. "There's a bathroom and a bedroom between us. Just let go, love. Let go."

"What if they hear?" Desmond breathed, his lips fluttering against Oliver's.

"More fun than they've had in years, I'd guess," he answered before lacing his fingers into Desmond's hair and pulling him into a deep kiss, ending the conversation.

And he did let go, sending up a silent prayer that his cries wouldn't wake his hosts and render him unable to face them at breakfast.

As they lay snuggled in each other's arms, spent and rubber-limbed, Desmond listened to Oliver's breathing, planning to stay awake until the other man dozed off before letting sleep overtake him. He could feel Oliver's body quiet, hear the redhead's heart slow to match the steady beat of his own low pulse. The blood seemed to flow through their veins in tandem, and the coppery musk of their sweat and skin and blood soothed him, let him doze lightly without fully sleeping, without ever losing awareness of the feel of Oliver's warm body beneath his cheek, his hands, his legs.

"I love you."

The words were barely spoken, nearly inaudible, but they ran through his brain like a brilliant blade, pulling all of his senses into full alert. He raised his head, pushing himself up on one elbow, and looked down at Oliver's face. His eyes, vividly blue to Desmond even in the darkness, were wide open.

"What?"

This time Oliver spoke clearly, but still softly. "I love you."

Desmond looked at him, wonder filling his heart, his whole body starting to tingle as a silvery thrill seemed to run up his spine and explode invisibly out of the top of his head. He moved a hand up and traced Oliver's lips with his thumb, feeling the ginger whiskers in contrast to the silken skin. He smiled, eyes brimming with emotion.

"Any particular reason?"

It was Oliver's turn to smile; a small smile of happiness and, Desmond could tell, relief.

"You know why. You know what you mean to me." He lowered his lashes in a slow blink, then gazed back up at Desmond.

"And why this exact moment?"

Oliver's smile widened, his lips parted, showing even white teeth.

"I thought it was time."

"Because we're here? In your parents' house? Defiling your boyhood bed?"

Oliver chuckled quietly. "Exactly."

"Or perhaps it was because, lying here, so close, so still, next to me, you could hear me thinking how much I love you and you wanted to beat me to it?"

With a sharp intake of breath, Oliver reached up and pulled Desmond onto him in a fierce, bone-crushing hug.

"Oh my God, Des. I never thought it would happen again. I was so afraid I'd be alone. I couldn't believe it when I ran into you that day, staring at the bed in the Ballantine House. It seemed so – I don't know – *significant*."

"Ah, love at first sight, eh?" Desmond asked, his teasing words muffled by Oliver's warm bare shoulder.

"Well, lust first, I have to confess. But really, it didn't take long. And then it looked like I'd gotten it wrong way round ... "

"Never mind," Desmond interrupted. "It all came

right in the end, didn't it?"

They fell silent, wrapped in each other's arms, face to face, letting the unexpected happiness wash over them. Desmond felt Oliver's body tremble, and then go still. After a few minutes, Oliver released him, and sat up, sitting up and leaning against the maple headboard. Desmond saw that he was calm, but there was something in his face that had changed; as if he'd made a decision.

"So, now that we've gotten that out of the way …."

Desmond sat up, too, moving to the middle of the bed so he could see Oliver fully. "So 'I love you' was just a preamble to something really important?" His voice was joking, but a faint thrill of alarm shimmered through him.

"I just wanted you to be sure of how I felt. To understand what being with you means to me, to my whole life."

"Yes?"

"Before the more awkward question."

Uh oh, where is this going?

"I know *who* you are, Desmond. You're smart, you're beautiful, you're kind-hearted and loving and generous." He reached out and took one of Desmond's hands in both of his own. Desmond could feel the tremble again.

"But…?"

"I want you to tell me *what* you are."

"Excuse me?" Desmond's eyes widened.

"It's not just your lack of eating or your bizarre sleeping habits." He shook his head as if in dismissal, continuing to hold Desmond's hand. "Those I could explain. Sort of, anyway. And then there was that odd way you kept talking as if you were my age or older even. As if you'd lived life somewhere else–and I don't mean growing up in London."

Desmond found he couldn't move, couldn't speak. He felt locked in place, his heart pounding, his eyes unable to leave Oliver's.

"But the strongest hint I had that you were

something else, something I'd never met before, was when I first shook your hand in the museum that day."

"Shook my hand?" Desmond barely croaked out the three short words.

Oliver looked away, as if searching for his own words. He lifted Desmond's hand, then let their shared grasp fall back to the bed. He finally looked back at Desmond, an almost fatalistic deadness in his eyes, as if he were about to cross a line beyond which there would be no turning back.

"Desmond, when I touch things, I can see into the past. *Their* past. It's been something I've been able to do since I hit puberty. I know it sounds stupid, but it's as if I have this *power*." He lifted one of his hands, and held it up as if cradling an object in his palm. He studied the invisible thing, whatever it was.

"When I touch an inanimate object, something man-made, I can see its entire history flash through my mind, like a movie. I can see the moment it was made – where and by whom and when it was made. I can see it change hands through time, from shop to owner, from house to house. When I hold something created by human hands, I *know it*. Completely." He paused and took a deep, shuddering breath.

"That's how I knew about the table in your front hall that David bought for you. That's how I knew that the Herter Brothers bed had come from the Ballantine family. Because I *saw* it in that room." He moved his free hand over to cup Desmond's chin.

"And when I touched that bed the last time we were in that gallery, when you were with me, I saw *you* in that bed."

"Holy God," muttered Desmond. Still, he could not take his eyes off Oliver. "What happens when you touch living things?"

"I'm just getting to that. With plants, almost nothing. With most animals – living animals anyway – I get a very quick snapshot, a sense of a life, finite, vibrant. With humans it's a bigger, more complex snapshot, but without any detail. It's very non-specific compared to the way I respond to inanimate things. Children are smaller, more intense; old people give a bigger, fuller projection. But there's no detail. I can sometimes get a glimpse of joy or sorrow, or some other overwhelming trait in a person's life. Most people are pretty much the same within a very predictable range – I've shaken lots of hands in my thirty-eight years."

He was silent a moment, his brow furrowed. "I've always wondered if Hitler would have felt evil; or if Gandhi would have exuded some sort of saintly thing."

"And Asa?" Desmond asked softly.

Oliver looked deep into Desmond's eyes. "Asa was just a regular person. Nothing traumatic. You see, it's gotten so I usually don't really notice. It's become so much a part of my daily world. Most people don't register at all because they're all the same to me."

"And me?"

"Ah, you. You're entirely different from anyone I've ever met." He looked down at their clasped hands. "There's no snapshot when I touch you. No sense of a life the way I have with everyone else."

Desmond shivered slightly. "That doesn't sound good."

"When I first shook your hand, I saw . . . I don't know how to describe it. A vast cavern. I don't want to say empty, because that suggests there was nothing there. I got an instant sense of something huge, something unfulfilled in some way. As if there was enormous potential, but untapped, unbounded. Limitless."

Oliver dropped his gaze. He once again placed both hands around both of Desmond's, and pulled them to his lips to kiss the knuckles. Then, stretching his shoulders slightly as if preparing for the final round, he looked up and continued.

"So, my love, I want to know: how old are you really?" Oliver cocked his head to one side, just as he himself always did, Desmond realized, when he slipped up; when he said something that didn't quite fit.

His mind went still. What else could he do? He owed his lover the truth. Tony had accepted it. Oliver would, too.

"Physically, I am twenty-one." Oliver moved as if to speak, but Desmond silenced him with a small shake of his head.

"Literally, or maybe historically, I am two hundred eighty-five years old."

"That explains the portrait."

"The painting at Oakwood, the one that David found?"

"Yes. When you caught me inspecting it, I'd had my hands on the surface. I saw you sitting for it – or at least it looked so much like you I couldn't explain who else it could have been."

"And the spoon you gave me at Christmas?" Desmond asked softly.

"Ah, that was a disappointment." He smiled at Desmond. "A lot of people handle spoons over the years. I could see the silversmith in London who made it; and the gentleman who bought it – probably your father." He lowered his eyes and sighed. "But after that it was really just a blur." Oliver fell silent again and didn't move. Desmond realized he was expecting more from him.

"I regenerate back to my twenty-first birthday every forty-four years, when I hit sixty-five years in my life cycle."

"Life cycle?" A look of keen curiosity furrowed his brow. No fear. Just interest. He continued to hold Desmond's hands, turning them in a lover's gentle clasp, his thumbs playing across the Desmond's palms.

"I'm a vampire, Ollie. I drink blood to live."

Oliver's eyes became big as saucers. His thumbs stopped moving.

"Really?"

"Yes."

"Wow." Oliver cocked his head again, and Desmond decided he loved that.

"Whose?"

"Huh?"

"Whose blood?"

"Nobody's. I mean, nobody's in particular. Whoever I can find."

"Mine?"

Desmond froze. Then, very softly: "only once."

"That first date?"

"Yes. Never since."

"Why not?"

That surprised him. "It didn't seem appropriate."

"Is my blood good?" Oliver suddenly sounded like a child seeking approval.

Smiling at the absurdity of it, Desmond nodded. "Your blood is wonderful. I just didn't want to take advantage." He pulled his hands away from Oliver's and placed them on either side of Oliver's face.

"I didn't want to mix what was growing between us with my need to drink."

Oliver grinned at him, and his evident comfort thrilled Desmond more than he could comprehend. Then the big blue eyes widened again.

"Holy shit." Oliver gently clasped Desmond's wrists, holding his hands where he'd placed them.

"What?"

"Anthony Chapman was *your* lover, then, wasn't he?"

Oliver's face was a mask of affectionate concern. That his lover had just revealed being a vampire to him was entirely secondary to the realization that his lover had suffered a terrible loss in the past. Desmond felt his heart would shatter from the love he felt toward his man.

"Yes, Ollie, Tony was my lover. But that was a long time ago."

"Will you tell me about it sometime?"

"About Tony?"

"About Tony, the blood drinking, everything. But not now, I still have more to tell you."

With that, Oliver rose gracefully from the bed and padded over to where his clothes lay on a chair. He pulled on his briefs and slipped out the door into the darkened hallway. Desmond wondered briefly whether to follow him, deciding in the end to remain where he was.

Only a minute or two had passed before Oliver reappeared, his pale body glowing faintly in the twilight. He held something in one hand, something he handed to Desmond as he settled himself back on the bed.

"This is how I found out about myself," he said softly, closing Desmond's fingers over the small oblong object.

Oliver had handed him a small rectangular case, perhaps three inches by four, of some dark brown material ornately molded with rococo scrollwork in low relief. Desmond opened the case. There was a black and white photographic image of a lovely young woman, under glass, in an elaborate gilded metal frame. She wore a small cross at her throat, her tightly corseted bodice partly covered with a black lace shawl. Her dark hair was pulled into two smooth bands that framed an oval face that looked unsmiling into the photographer's lens. Facing the portrait was a panel of maroon velvet stamped with a design like that on the covers.

Desmond looked up. "It's an ambrotype. Mid-nineteenth century."

"Don't you want me to turn on a light?" Oliver had cocked his head again, and Desmond had to repress an impulse to grab him and kiss him.

"I can see well in the dark." He offered a slightly sheepish smile, and found it returned with an impish grin.

"How convenient," Oliver smirked. "Then you'll know that it's in its original gutta-percha case."

"Vulcanite," said Desmond softly.

"Excuse me?"

"These cases are all vulcanite – a kind of heat-treated natural rubber mixed with sulphur. The earliest form of plastic, essentially."

"You don't say." Oliver's dry tone almost made

Desmond laugh.

"Most people today mistake it for gutta-percha, which was far too fragile to use for cases like this." He matched Oliver's supercilious voice, playing along.

"And you know this because…?"

"I was in New York when Charles Goodyear invented this material and it first appeared on the market. I visited those photographic studios and watched the artists at work."

"Shit." Something between shock and awe flickered across Oliver's handsome face.

"You were going to tell me about the image?" Desmond prodded gently.

"Oh. Yeah." He looked at Desmond with an odd sort of wonder in his eyes. "Sorry, love. It just sort of hit me … um, the historical implications of being, um, as old as you are." A weak smile flashed in his beard.

Desmond held up the ambrotype, caressing Oliver's bare arm with his free hand.

"Tony was rather nonplussed by that, too. So why don't you just tell me your story for now?"

"Yes. Right. Well – I was twelve. Already a little object nerd, always rummaging about in boxes in the attic, looking through all the old things my grandparents had left. I found this in one of those boxes."

He cleared his throat.

"I can remember sitting in the attic, holding it up to the light from the one little window in the roof peak. At first I was just fascinated by the pretty young woman, and by the case itself. I loved the way it felt, too, sort of heavy and substantial, for all its small size."

His gaze drew inward, and Desmond could almost see him searching his memory for details.

"As I sat there, I began to see other images. I didn't understand what they were at first and it scared the shit out of me. I threw the ambrotype back in the box and ran downstairs. But I kept going back. Each time I'd hold it for a little longer, and each time the images came to me more clearly. The longer I held it, the more I saw."

"What did you see?" Desmond prompted after a few moments of silence.

"I saw the photographer's studio – of course that didn't make sense at first. And I saw the woman. I saw her smile, and take a seat. But then the scene changed quickly. The next thing I remember is the image of a young man, clean-shaven – as pretty as the woman. He was dressed in a uniform – a soft dove gray, with gold buttons and braid."

Desmond let out a low whistle. "Confederate soldier."

Oliver glanced up at him. "Yes."

"Then what?"

"You can probably imagine what comes next. The next images that popped into my brain were of the young man lying dead, a great hole torn in his chest, and of another young man, with a beard and a mustache."

"Who was that man?"

"I didn't know. But I found out later, in another photograph taken years later. It was my great-great-grandfather, Elihu Cameron. My dad's great-grandfather."

"Let me guess. He took the ambrotype from the corpse of the dead Confederate."

"I'm pretty sure he's the one who killed him. There was always a sense of darkness with this."

"The Civil War was pretty dark for everyone, Oliver."

Oliver stared at him. "Was it hard for you?"

"Less than for most. I bought my way out of it. Sent some poor Irish immigrant to his death by paying $300 to get out of it."

At Oliver's look of horror, he continued. "Perhaps not my proudest moment, but I have no regret. A vampire on a battlefield might not have been the best idea. I didn't particularly think this war noble or worthwhile on either side. No war is really worth the cost."

"But slavery … "

"They could have ended slavery without killing all those people. Mortal men tend to avoid peaceful solutions. But aren't we getting off topic?"

"Oh. I guess. What more do you want to know?"

"Do your parents know?"

"About what?"

"Your, um, *gift*."

Oliver beamed at him, his teeth showing lighter than the rest of his face in the dim room.

"Actually, no. I've never told anyone. Before tonight."

Desmond couldn't keep a small sigh from slipping out, but held his silence.

"Oddly enough," Oliver continued, "I somehow equated this, this special power, with the early inkling I was having about being attracted to boys. I hid the ambrotype in my room. It was only when my mother and I were going through boxes after I was in high school that we ran across the picture of Elihu Cameron, and I made that connection. By then I'd come to understand my ability to read objects was generalized. That ambrotype was just the trigger that started everything flowing."

"It was a powerful story. I can see that acting as a catalyst of sorts."

"Yes. Modern things don't give me much feedback. Everything we owned here was more or less from my parents' life as a married couple. Not a lot of history bubbling about in that stuff."

"Not yet. I'll bet this bed has some more history than it did yesterday morning."

Oliver looked at him blankly for a second, and then Desmond could scent the blood as it rushed to his face as he understood.

"Yikes. Remind me never to touch my parents' bed." He shuddered comically. Then he carefully set the ambrotype on the nightstand and crawled over to Desmond, kneeling in front of him and pulling him up into a long searching kiss. Slowly they let themselves subside onto the pillows, entwining arms and legs, hands moving lovingly across flesh, arousal growing until they could feel each other's excitement.

"Des?" whispered Oliver, breaking their kiss.

"Hm?" He regarded his handsome redhead through half-closed eyes.

"Does anyone know? About you?"

"Way to kill the buzz, sweetie," he growled softly, then yelped as Oliver grabbed his cock rather more roughly than was necessary.

"Just answer the question, blood boy."

"Oh dear. Just Bill Lawrence." He grabbed for Oliver's penis only to find himself tumbled over on his back with Oliver pressed fully upon him.

"Not Roger?"

"Of course Roger. He's a vampire, too."

"Really?" asked Oliver, wriggling his groin against Desmond's, making the younger man groan.

"And Denis."

"Denis? A vampire?"

"Yes. Long story. Not now. I have a better idea," he murmured, locking his gaze onto his lover's shadowed stare.

"What?" Oliver sighed, grazing Desmond's lips with his own.

"It's your turn on top."

"Oh goody," Oliver moaned, and let Desmond distract him.

Chapter Twenty-Four

The S70 swept off the still-busy streets of West Orange's more urban east side and through the gates into the magical rural illusion of Llewellyn Park. Desmond lowered his window to allow the nighttime fragrance of New Jersey spring fill the cabin. The pale green tang of new leaves, wet earth, and the ever-present richness of resurgent animal life filled his lungs. He glanced over and saw Oliver, his head back against the seat, a half-smile lingering, his beard glowing darkly in the flickering light.

"Have a good time?" Desmond asked softly, knowing the answer.

Oliver turned and regarded him dreamily. "It was

wonderful. Better than I could have imagined." His smiled broadened. "You surprised the shit out of me, Des."

Desmond just grinned as he negotiated the curves in the narrow lane leading toward Oakwood.

The Newark Museum's annual fundraising gala was always held on the first weekend in May. Whatever wisecracks the wider world might make about Newark, the museum knew how to throw a party. The garden behind the main building was filled with a tent, and the committee in charge of designing the gala transformed the space into a ballroom elegant enough to impress the glamorous and powerful – who paid handsomely for the privilege of spending a Saturday evening in downtown Newark and never once regretted it. This year the theme had been the museum's famed Japanese collection, and the gala tent had become a fantasy of old Kyoto.

Desmond had unhesitatingly purchased a table for ten guests at the top price. The most expensive tables were normally corporate purchases by the big New Jersey corporations such as Prudential or Johnson & Johnson; to have a relatively small New Jersey financial firm weigh in at this level was unprecedented. When Oliver had tried to protest the extravagance, Desmond had made him blush by commenting on the benefits of fucking the CEO, and then had kissed away his mortification and told him he loved him.

Wanting to fill their table at the gala with friends, they invited Alex and Bill, David and Jeffrey, and Jane and Dotty. Vivien and Luke Lake had been unavailable because of a business trip, and when Desmond had been casting about for guests to fill the last two he had been startled when Oliver had suggested Denis Schroeder.

"He's a business partner, Des. You can't just ignore him because of me."

Desmond had studied his lover's face and found only earnestness in those blue eyes. "It wouldn't bother you?"

"I figure he must feel fairly isolated now – without you there for him," Oliver's voice was thoughtful. "And I don't mean just the former boyfriend thing."

"You mean…?"

"The vampire thing. I've been thinking of how alone you must have felt – how truly alone he must feel, cut off from you as he's been."

"Denis has Charlon. I have Roger. One gets used to being alone, you know, Ollie."

"I realize that," he answered, his face serious, forcing Desmond to suppress a smile.

"But after you explained to me how you, um, hunted together, I couldn't help feel that, after having that sort of companionship, it must, well, hurt a little." He turned to Desmond and gripped his arm. "I'm not saying I'm sorry you love me and not Denis. I just think he needs friends like you more than ever. I'm willing to go there if you think he'll be willing to accept the gesture."

Desmond's only response had been to kiss him and hold him close for a long moment.

"Besides, I have a date for him," Oliver had continued with a sly smile, "So our table of ten is full." He would say no more, leaving Desmond mildly unnerved.

Desmond had driven directly to the museum from New York, resplendent in a new tuxedo, leaving the Volvo with the parking attendant and causing heads to turn as he came down the short flight of steps into the museum's main gallery. He had turned even more heads when, upon spotting Oliver – also dapper in evening clothes – he had walked over and pulled him into a kiss that would never have been mistaken as merely friendly.

"Jesus, Des, blow my cover why dontcha?" Oliver gasped as they separated, unable to disguise the delight in his eyes.

"Your fairy wings gave you away long ago, Ginger Man." He moved away from Oliver, taking him by the hand and pulling him into the museum's main court where cocktails were being served and uniformed waiters carried about trays of delicious-smelling hors d'oeuvres. It was early yet, and only about a quarter of the expected six hundred guests had arrived. The mingled smell of expensive clothes, perfume, and well-heeled blood made Desmond's pulse speed up.

"Anyway, for what I paid for that table, I suspect I could bend you over it right now and no one would say a word." Ignoring Oliver's choked laughter, he added, "No sign of our band of Theban warriors?" he asked.

"No one yet – oh, wait. Here's two of them."

Desmond turned, and his eyes widened at the sight of Jane Ashmun and Dorothy Brown, looking like movie stars in shimmering evening gowns at the top of the stairs. Both of them wore their hair up, and no jewelry other than the thin gold bracelet Jane had given Dotty for Christmas. Jane had chosen a simply cut gold lamé gown that set off the golden-brown tone of her skin, while Dotty had opted for an equally simple dress of deep blue taffeta that complimented her fair complexion. Appropriately, she looked rather fierce, a splendid guardian angel, as Jane floated gracefully down the steps and came toward her friends, Dotty protectively at her side.

"You two are fabulous!" exclaimed Oliver, as both women allowed him to brush their cheeks with his lips.

"I have to say, Jane, Dot – I've never seen you like this. It's pretty amazing," added Desmond, eliciting shy smiles out of both women. "Were the girls duly impressed?"

Dotty laughed. "Janay tried not to show it, but Speck was beside herself, going on about princesses and so on. I don't think they've ever seen us dolled up like this."

Desmond went to get his friends drinks, returning with four glasses of champagne on a tray he'd snagged from the bar – only to find four more handsome men in dinner jackets exchanging kisses with Oliver and the ladies. Alex and Bill looked distinguished, their evening clothes conservatively cut, while David and Jeffrey looked extremely pretty and very young-couple-like, with matching pink bowties and cummerbunds.

"We hired a car and driver," Jeffrey burbled, his big-jock frame uncharacteristically sleek and polished in his tuxedo, hair slicked back like a 1940s matinee idol. "I've never been in a limo before."

David rolled his eyes and patted his lover on the shoulder. "Don't get used to it, darling. We had to do it so Desmond wouldn't be ashamed of us."

"I could never be ashamed of you," Desmond answered, voice serious as he took the young men's hands and looked them each in the eye. "I'm so glad you're here, I can't tell you."

He took a glass of champagne for himself and handed the remaining three to Oliver, Jane and Dorothy. "I'm done being waiter. You four'll have to fend for yourselves at the bar."

The quartet cheerfully headed into the court to find drinks, while Oliver clasped his hand briefly before leading Jane and Dot on a little tour, happy to show his friends the museum of which he was so justly proud.

Desmond idly sipped his champagne, thinking he would probably need a martini next. He scanned the increasing crowd of elegantly dressed museum lovers, feeling an inordinate sense of pride, as if he'd had anything directly to do with this event.

He was startled out of his thoughts by a warm hand on his shoulder and a familiar scent filling his nostrils.

"Mr. Desmond, you are very dashing, and I thank you for asking me."

He turned to gaze up into the handsome face of Fayt, the owner of the Asian restaurant in Maplewood, transformed by his well-tailored evening suit into a glamorous incarnation of the Very Cute Panda eponymous with his place of business. Desmond was immediately crushed in an enthusiastic bear hug, and narrowly avoided spilling the remains of his drink on the marble floor.

"Fayt!" He smiled at Oliver's friend and protector.

"This is such a nice surprise." At Fayt's puzzled look, he added, "Oliver didn't tell me who he had invited. You were his special treat for me."

Seeing Fayt's beaming pleasure at his patent flattery, he intoned with mock seriousness: "But I warn you, I think he's trying to set you up."

At just that moment his eye caught a familiar figure at the top of the stairs, and he turned, taking Fayt's arm to direct his eyes in that direction.

Denis Schroeder, immaculate and chic, stood uncertainly, his pale blond hair glowing in the light, as he surveyed the chattering throng. His eyes quickly caught Desmond's, and giving them a tentative smile he came down into the gallery and moved over to them. The cocksure confidence of their first meeting was absent this evening, although his slim body and perfect face were as striking as they had been then. Desmond could feel Fayt's arm stiffen beneath his hand, and realized that the other man was holding his breath.

"Oh my, Mr. Desmond, he is truly beautiful," sighed Fayt.

"Hmmm, didn't think you appreciated Caucasians, or so Oliver told me." He squeezed Fayt's arm and felt it relax beneath his grip.

"Racist nonsense, Mr. Desmond. Oliver is just wounded that I don't slobber over his pathetic ginger carcass." He turned and grinned at Desmond. "One must keep an open mind, after all. America is a great country."

Denis now stood before them, even more charming in his hesitation.

"Thank you for coming, Denis. It's so good to see you." Desmond gave him a fraternal kiss on the cheek before introducing him to the tall Asian. He held his former lover's hand firmly, looking deeply into the blond vampire's eyes. He could see and smell Denis's rising blush, an indication that Denis had satisfied his need for blood recently. His blood-hunger would not complicate things.

He left the two men getting to know each other,

realizing that the time for a martini had indeed arrived.

The rest of the evening was, from Desmond's viewpoint, perfect. The circle of friends at Desmond's table had all danced with each other to the sound of the jazz orchestra and, encouraged by the dashing young CEO of Beckwith Investments, with their partners. It gave him particular joy to sway to the music, Oliver in his arms, all eyes on them. At one point, as they moved together to an upbeat swing number, Oliver gestured with his head, making Desmond turn. There, amidst the well-dressed revelers, Denis and Fayt made a dashing duet, as the slim blonde moved with incandescent glee around the stately figure of his new acquaintance, Fayt watching him with rapt pleasure.

The women had slipped out early, anxious to get back to the babysitter and their children, leaving the men to carry on without them. Alex and Bill were the next to bow out; but at Denis's offer to drive them back into the city, David and Jeffrey were able to keep on dancing until they were all staggering with exhaustion.

At last, tipsy with drink and dancing, the friends waited patiently for their cars to be brought to them by the valets. Of course, the two vampires weren't truly exhausted, but Desmond was awash in a sort of euphoric contentment he hadn't experienced for many years. His emotional glow was enhanced at seeing Fayt and Denis talking intently, heads close together, just before the Maybach pulled up to the door and Fayt, along with Jeffrey and David, disappeared inside.

Denis came over to Desmond, kissing him lightly on the lips and pulling him into a brief hug.

"I promise I'll get Fayt back to Maplewood safe and sound tomorrow morning. I'll have Ivan bring him back so he won't have to ride a commuter train in a rumpled tuxedo."

Desmond looked at his friend, a question in his eyes.

Denis shrugged. "You never know. I'm thinking I need to follow your example, the way Gregory did in

Paris." And with that he joined the giggling crew in the back of the limousine and it purred away into the quiet Newark streets.

As the Volvo's headlights swept the gravel drive on the oak allée, Oliver put his hand on Desmond's arm.

"The house is dark."

"So? It's nearly one a.m." But even as he said it, Desmond felt something was off. Dotty always turned on the front lights, as well as the lights in the master bedroom when Desmond and Oliver were going to be there. The entire front of the house was in darkness.

"Maybe Dotty forgot we were coming here tonight," he suggested.

"No, before they left the museum she told me she'd have breakfast for me in the morning."

Desmond slowed the car before it reached the end of the allée, coasting to a halt well short of the entrance to the garage parking area. All of his senses on alert, he cast a quick glance over at Oliver, who silently followed his lead, opening and shutting the car doors with as little noise as possible, and minimizing the crunch of their shoes on the gravel.

They crept around to the kitchen wing, and peered in the windows. The kitchen was dark; no signs of any activity. No lights showed in the apartment windows upstairs either. The two men moved around to the media room window, through which light spilled out onto the back lawn. Seeing movement, but not wanting to reveal themselves, they backtracked to the kitchen entrance and found the back porch dark, the door ajar.

Desmond glanced back at Oliver, whose eyes were wide. The smell of fear rose off the redhead, stirring Desmond's anger.

What the hell is going on in our house?

The kitchen door retreated noiselessly on well-oiled hinges and the men slipped off their shoes before tiptoeing down the passage. Low voices came from the open family room door, and Desmond could make out

Jane's higher pitch, and could hear a distinctive pleading tone to her voice. Holding Oliver back with a gentle hand on his chest, Desmond peered around the doorjamb.

Across the room, on the sofa, facing the big-screen television, sat Dot and Jane, dressed in jeans and t-shirts, each of them holding one of the girls at her side. Opposite them, on an ottoman in front of the wall-mounted TV, sat Dane Ashmun. He looked disheveled and exhausted. In his shaking hand he held a handgun loosely pointed in the direction of Desmond's family on the sofa. Janay and Speck were half asleep, but their little hands were clenched on their mothers' clothing.

"Dane, honey, put away the gun," said Jane, her voice taut with fear in spite of her effort to sound calm. "You're scaring the girls."

"I'm not going to shoot anybody. I just want to talk to Beckwith."

"Can't it wait till tomorrow, or Monday even?" Clearly, Jane was buying time, unsure of what her ex-husband was capable of doing. Dotty just glared at him, anger and fear mixing equally.

"No. I wanna talk to him now. He took you away. It's not fair." The blond man shook his head slightly, as if trying to clear his vision.

Dotty's lip curled. "You stupid son of a bitch. *Took* them away? What the hell are you talking about? You *threw* away your family!"

"I didn't *mean* to," he slurred, and Desmond realized he must be drunk, too. At that moment Dane lurched to his feet, raising the gun, although not aiming it.

Desmond didn't bother to see what would happen next. He straightened and stepped into the doorway.

"Put down the gun, Dane."

Dane wheeled toward the unexpected voice, and staggered back against the ottoman. His knees gave way and he sat heavily. The gun went off, its report deafening in the confined space, waking up the girls, who began screaming. Dane let it fall to the carpet.

Before he even registered the noise, Desmond felt

the bullet hit him square in the chest. He could feel the blood start pouring from the wound as his eyes lasered in on Dane's bewildered face looking at the gun as if he didn't know what it was, then up at Desmond. Ashmun's bloodshot stare registered horror at the spreading stain on Desmond's white shirtfront.

"Oh my god, oh my god. Desmond!" Oliver's voice came from close behind him. "I'm hit."

Desmond didn't turn. "Get the girls out of here!" roared Desmond, throwing himself forward as Jane and Dot dragged the girls out the door, pinning Dane to the floor like a lion taking down a gazelle.

A wave of sickening terror washed through him as he stared into Ashmun's face, contorted with confusion and fear, beneath him. The sound of howling wolves echoed faintly in Desmond's brain, bringing back the horror of the night his Jeffrey had died in the ancient vampire's lonely castle; the night Tony had died in the emergency room in Greenwich Village. A violent tremor shuddered through him, his hands clutching Dane's shoulders in a death grip.

From deep within his soul rose an animal sound, a wet snarl right from the pages of one of his vampire novels. Desmond felt his canines descend as waves of blood-scented fear rose off the man lying beneath him. He wanted nothing more than to sink his fangs into the bastard's neck and drain him dry, feel his heart slow and stop; feel his life flow away and into his own veins.

Just as I destroyed the man who tried to kill me in the Tuileries all those years ago.

And suddenly he found himself staring into the terrified face of a father. Not of a murderer or a criminal; the wide-eyed, tear-stained face of a young man who had made stupid choices and suffered much bad luck. A man who had lost his family and with them his reason to live.

Desmond's anger evaporated. The sounds in his mind faded away. His teeth retracted.

"Oliver?" His question was barely a whisper. He realized he was more afraid of silence than any answer he might receive.

"Des, I think I'm okay. Got me in the shoulder, but it's not bleeding too badly. Must have gone straight through you." The voice was soft, but steady. "I'm not going to die."

I'm not going to die.

He loosened his grip without giving Dane Ashmun the ability to get away from him. The other man didn't seem interested in budging in any case.

"Ollie, sweetheart? Can you move?"

From behind him came the reassuring words: "Yeah. I told you. It's just my shoulder."

"Can you see to the girls? See that they're okay?"

He forced himself not to look around as he heard Oliver get up off his knees, groaning in obvious pain, but moving readily enough nonetheless. He could smell Oliver's blood, but trusting his own assessment that the wound was not mortal, he was comforted by its familiar warmth. He heard Oliver walk into the passage outside, and then a series of whispers, details of which he couldn't make out due to the pounding of his own blood in his ears.

He sat up slightly, straddling Dane's hips. He released his grip on one of Dane's shoulders, lifting the other man's hand and placing it in the sticky mess on his chest. He turned the bloody hand so that Dane could see it. Dane looked back and forth from his hand to Desmond's face, his own expression a mask of despair. His body began to shake, and Desmond tightened his knees at Dane's waist as if controlling a skittish horse.

"Understand this, Dane." He spoke softly, his voice a low growl, full of menace. "You cannot kill me. Not with a gun, not with a knife, not with poison."

He fell silent as he let Dane digest these simple facts.

"But if you ever threaten my family again, Dane Ashmun, I promise that I will kill you. And no one will ever know."

Wide-eyed with terror, tears streaming down his

ashen cheeks, Dane managed to stammer, "I didn't mean to. I never would have hurt them. I swear, never. Never."

Desmond released Dane entirely, and stood, picking up the gun by the still-warm barrel. He could feel that the blood-flow from his chest wound had stopped; felt his body starting to heal, pushing outward from the inside. By morning, there would be no trace of it. No evidence that Dane Ashmun had ever shot him, accidentally or otherwise.

Dane just lay on the floor, eyes now closed, body limp, sobbing uncontrollably. A spreading stain darkened the crotch of his dirty blue jeans.

Desmond stepped into the hall, scanning right and left. By the doorway to the kitchen he saw Oliver, Janay in his arms, looking at him, a dark wet patch visible against the black wool of his ruined tuxedo. Jane and Dotty hovered behind him.

"What the fuck happened, Desmond?" asked Dotty, her voice shaky, belying her words. Waves of acrid fear radiated from her, and from Jane, who seemed too shocked to speak.

"Don't we have to call the police?" asked Janay, her voice calm and serious. "And an ambulance for Ollie?" She eyed Desmond curiously, and he could smell her fear, too; but it wasn't as intense as he might have expected, given her age and the circumstances. There was no fear coming off Oliver, he was surprised to note. His blood was strong and sweet.

He gave Oliver a small smile, which was returned. Even in the dimness, he could see much unspoken in Oliver's eyes. Not just love; that he had expected. There was something else. Pride? Odd, that.

"I think I'd better go get rid of my shirt and jacket before the police get here," Desmond said wearily. "I don't think he'll give you any trouble now, but you should go upstairs with your moms and be with your sister, Janay. She's probably really scared."

He turned and headed toward the entrance hall,

rehearsing in his mind what he would need to say to the authorities.

Chapter Twenty-Five

When Oliver awoke in his private room at St. Barnabas Hospital, Desmond was at his bedside, holding one of his hands, watching him. Outside the room's single window, dawn was just glimmering on the horizon, streaking the patchy clouds with pink above the pale greenery of the trees that dotted the hospital's grounds and bordered its acres of parking lots.

"Hey there," he smiled groggily.

"Good morning," Desmond returned softly. "How do you feel?"

"A little woozy. Achy, too. No surprise," Oliver

chuckled, gripping Desmond's hand tightly. Then he looked up into his lover's affectionate gaze.

"So?"

Desmond just cocked an eyebrow.

"Tell me what happened. You know, to Dane."

"Not much to tell." Desmond paused, as if considering what to tell Oliver, whose eyes narrowed at the silence.

"Come on, fess up."

"It seems that Mr. Ashmun was distraught."

"And drunk."

"That, too. And he showed up at our house, with a legally registered gun, as it happens, to talk to me."

"And?"

"As things transpired, and with some persuasive arguments on my part, Mr. Ashmun has been remanded to the psychiatric ward of this very hospital, for evaluation prior to treatment for alcohol, and possibly other, substance abuse."

Oliver's eyes opened incredulously.

"After all that he's just going into detox?"

"I thought it best for everyone concerned," Desmond concluded, a sheepish smile turning up the corners of his mouth.

"Desmond, he fucking shot me," Oliver protested.

"That was an accident."

"And what about you?"

"Alas, there was only one shot, one bullet. There's no sign of my being wounded, other than a bloody dress shirt and tuxedo that have recently been burned in my bedroom fireplace."

Oliver rolled his eyes. "Well, he surely threatened his ex-wife, her partner and his own damn children!"

"Well, there is that; but you know, Ollie, I'm fairly certain he never intended to hurt anyone. If anything, I rather suspect he would have killed himself before hurting any of us intentionally. I have convinced Jane not to press charges."

Desmond bent down and kissed the hand he was

holding, and Oliver reached up to run his fingers through Desmond's wavy black hair.

"Dane is a very unhappy young man, Ollie. I was ready to rip his throat out last night, but I found I couldn't. I realized in time that maybe he just needs some good luck."

Oliver just shook his head, unable to conceal a grin that spread across his face. "You are unbelieveable, Mr. Beckwith."

"I confess that Dorothy was, um, not entirely pleased with me when she heard of my idea."

"Good thing you don't eat, because she'd definitely start spitting in your food." Oliver suddenly became more alert, his look scrutinizing his partner's face.

"Speaking of eating; how much blood did you lose?"

"A fair bit. But the wound closed up quite quickly. I'm fine."

"Are you thirsty?"

It was Desmond's turn to cock his head at this. He didn't speak.

"Des?"

"What?"

"Drink from me."

"God! No, Ollie. For Lord's sake, you've just been shot."

"Yes, and they pumped me full of fresh juicy blood. You didn't get any refill. You need it, too."

"Really, not the time for this, Ollie. Besides, I have more serious things to discuss."

"Such as?"

"Such as our having a civil union."

"Where the hell did *that* come from?" Oliver tried to sit up, then winced at the pain in his bandaged shoulder and subsided back into the pillows. Desmond clung to his hand.

"From the trouble I had getting up here to see you. The police were insistent that we contact your parents – which I will do, I promise – but not till tomorrow – or later today, at any rate. It seems that being your boyfriend doesn't give me much standing in New Jersey."

"They tried to keep you out?"

"For a while. They relented eventually, but I rather think only because you were shot in my house." He winced slightly. "I'm afraid I might have had to raise my voice."

"So you want to marry me?" Oliver's voice had grown oddly small.

"I've wanted to marry you for ages now. But since we can't do that here, I thought a civil union would be adequate."

"Adequate for what?"

"Well, for starters, adequate for me to be able to visit you when you're in a place like this, or make medical decisions for you if you can't."

He paused, looking fondly at Oliver, running a slender hand across the pale brow and ruffling his coppery locks.

"And it would make the issue of inheritance simpler."

"Inheritance? Holy god, Des, you have forty-four years to go. Isn't this rushing it?"

"Perhaps, but all of this has made me think that being legally bound to you would create another way to transfer things next time around."

"You do realize how old I'll be by the time you hit sixty-five, don't you?"

"Eighty-two, I believe."

"And you think that's a good plan, do you?"

"I think I want to make sure you're taken care of."

"So you love me that much, then." It was a statement, not a question, and Oliver looked thoughtful as he spoke the words.

Desmond scowled at him. "What are you getting at, Ginger Man?"

"Listen, Blood Boy," said Oliver, pulling Desmond closer, so that they were face to face, inches apart. "The question is, do you love me enough?"

"I … I … " Desmond let go of Oliver's hand and collapsed back into the chair. He shook his head. "What do you mean 'enough?'"

"Enough to spend forever with me?" Oliver's expression was suddenly deadly serious, and not a little apprehensive. The big blue eyes glittered.

"You want me to … transform you?" Desmond spoke the last words so softly they were barely audible.

"Do you love me enough to do that for me? To give me that gift?"

Their eyes locked. Desmond inhaled slowly, filling his lungs with Oliver's beautiful, love-filled, life-filled fragrance.

"Tony didn't want me to transform him." The vampire's voice broke. "He chose death rather than eternity with me." His eyes burned at the memory.

"I'm sorry about that, Des." He reclaimed Desmond's hand. "But I'm not Tony. I've lived through death. I'm pushing forty. I know what life has in store for me, with or without you. I see what you've done with your many lives, what you've made of what you've been given. I know who you are, and I think I'd like to live your lives with you from now on."

"You love me enough, even for that?" Desmond murmured, a few tears finally spilling over and making their way down his pale cheeks.

"Till death do us part, like the book says." Oliver pulled Desmond's hand to his lips, closing his eyes as his beard tickled the back of the slim, elegant fingers. He murmured, "although in your case, that really does mean forever."

The sound of the door hissing open made Desmond turn. A nurse stood in the opening, as if waiting.

"Nurse, when will I next need any fussing over?" Oliver asked her cheerily. Desmond realized he must have pushed the call button while they were talking.

The nurse consulted her chart.

"Not until 5:30."

"Good. I just wanted to know if we might have

some time alone, uninterrupted."

The nurse looked momentarily puzzled before her expression shifted into one of mild disgust.

"Just don't wake the other patients," she said, turning and letting the door shut behind her, muttering as she went.

"Good grief, what does she think we're going to do?" Desmond asked, a small bark of laughter escaping in spite of the wetness on his cheeks.

"Certainly not what we're actually going to do." Oliver dropped Desmond's hand and lifted his unbandaged arm to his lover's face.

"Now, my love, do what you're told. Drink your blood like a good boy," he urged quietly, pulling the neck of his hospital gown down and turning his head, exposing the scattering of freckles on his shoulder and the pale, smooth expanse of his neck.

Shaking his head with wonder, both at Oliver's temerity and at his generous heart, Desmond rose slightly from his chair and leaned forward over his beloved's expectant form. He momentarily reveled in Oliver's smell, the warmth of his body, the unwavering trust in those lovely blue eyes. How, after all, could he refuse?

Desmond bared his fangs and bent down to accept the offered gift in the spirit in which it was given, his heart filling with happiness.

Chapter Twenty-Six

"I've got a meeting. I'll see you at Oakwood tonight," Desmond said over his shoulder as he whisked past Jane's desk and down the carpeted corridor.

"What? Wait!" Jane called after him. "There's nothing on your calendar … "

But Desmond had reached the elevator and failed to hear his assistant's objections.

As the elevator descended to the lobby, Desmond turned off his mobile phone and checked his watch. Twelve-thirty. They could be at the house by one, which would be more than enough time before the kids got back from school.

As he stepped onto the marble floor, he heard his

named called softly. Turning, he was startled to see Dane Ashmun standing by another elevator, apparently waiting to go up.

"Hi, Desmond." Ashmun's blue eyes, clearer and more alert than they had been last time they'd met, held Desmond's gaze briefly, before dropping in what looked like embarrassment.

Desmond moved over to him, holding out a hand.

"Dane. You look well."

"I am, thank you," the big blond replied, gripping Desmond's smaller hand and giving it a firm shake. His silence seemed to indicate Desmond should keep talking.

"Things going well here?" He knew the answer from Dane's supervisor, and he suspected Dane knew he knew.

"Really good. Just great." Ashmun seemed to be struggling, and he suddenly reached out and took Desmond's hand again, enveloping it in both of his.

"I know this is awkward. But I gotta tell you. I like it here. The job's great. Ted's a great supervisor, and I think he likes my work."

"So he tells me. You're good at what you do, Dane. Nothing awkward about that." Desmond's smile was genuine, but slightly strained. He was in a hurry. He wondered mildly how he could get his hand out of Dane's grasp.

A sigh brought Desmond's look back to Dane's, and he saw in the bigger man's face something so vulnerable and open that his own worry over the time evaporated.

"I'm glad it's working out, Dane," he said softly. "I really am."

"You saved me, Desmond," Ashmun blurted out. "You could have ended it that night – and you had every right to, after what I did." The big man swallowed. "But instead – this." He stared into Desmond's eyes, as if trying to find the answer to a question there. "Why?"

Desmond paused only for a second before responding. "Your girls need their father."

And you've never asked me about what you saw that

night.

He gently pried his hand out of Ashmun's grip and patted him on the shoulder. "Keep up the good work, Dane. Now, if you'll excuse, me, I have an appointment."

The up elevator arrived at just that moment, allowing Desmond to escape through the building's front doors. He could see Roger waiting in the sunshine out on the sidewalk, his head to one side, as if watching the little drama unfolding within.

Looking back hastily as he pushed through the tall glass door, Desmond saw Dane watching him. He then turned and got onto the elevator that would take him back to his cubicle on the floor below Desmond's office. Desmond strode over to Roger, and gave him a quick kiss on the cheek, wrapping one arm around him to steer him toward the garage.

"Wasn't that a lovely little scene," Roger smirked.

"Shut up." Desmond couldn't help grinning briefly, steering his best friend toward the garage where his car was waiting for them.

"I really can't believe you hired him."

"It was the only way to keep him on his program, to give him stability and a sense of self-worth after the detox. He's a changed man, you know, Rog." He glanced over at his friend, as if daring him to contradict him.

"The only way, hmm?" Roger caught his eye for a moment. "Well, I have great faith in your judgment, Des. I learned that the hard way."

The car swept down the gravel allée and Desmond pulled it to a quick stop in front of the garage area. Oliver's little Honda was parked in front of the main entrance, with the redhead leaning against it, his wavy hair glinting orange-gold in the bright day.

He came over to the two men, a look of mild surprise on his face. He gave Desmond a hug and a kiss, and turned to Roger.

"I'm so happy to see you again! I can't believe you

came all this way." He put his hand out for Roger to shake, but instead found himself pulled into a quick bear hug.

"After today we'll be brothers, Ollie."

Oliver's eyes widened briefly at both the contact and the use of the diminutive, but his face broke into a smile as he hugged Roger back.

"So Dotty's out of town?" he asked, pulling away, looking over at Desmond as he ran an affectionate hand down Roger's arm.

"Yes. Aunt's funeral in Virginia. She'll be gone two days. And the girls are in school till three-thirty, when the bus drops them off. Jane's at her desk till five."

"Because you're such a hard-ass boss," Oliver chuckled.

Desmond just stuck his tongue out at him, and together the three men went into the house through the front door, heading directly to the staircase and up to the master bedroom.

Oliver preceded them into the room, moving directly over to the bed. He sat down, bouncing tentatively, a tight smile on his face.

"Sooo ... how does this work?" He looked first at Roger, then at Desmond.

Roger moved from his position by the fireplace closer to the bed. He toed off his shoes and knelt on the carpet a few feet from the bed. "Are you frightened?" he asked, his voice solicitous.

"A little, yeah." Oliver looked abashed.

Desmond went and sat next to him, wrapping an arm around him in a sideways hug. "I can't imagine what this must feel like for you, love. It's been so long, my own memories are very distant."

Oliver locked his eyes on Desmond's. "I've never been surer of anything in my life, Desmond. But it's a big step, and it's an experience unlike anything in my world till this moment. I'm not ashamed of being a bit scared." He turned his gaze to Roger, a hint of defiance sparkling in his blue eyes.

"And we're here to make sure you're never alone. To help you through if you need us," Roger said.

"Why both of you, and not just you, Desmond?" He quickly looked back to Roger, a blush stealing up his neck. "Sorry, Roger, I didn't mean to suggest you're not welcome."

Roger just smiled. "Des and I talked about this, Ollie. It was different for him when he was transformed. Baron Tsolnay was alone. In 1789, when Gregory changed me, he had assistance, and it made the process more straightforward, and I believe the transformation happened more quickly and easily."

"Assistance? Another vampire?" Oliver cocked his head, and both of the younger men smiled and exchanged a glance. Curiosity had begun to replace anxiety.

"A woman named Emilie. Desmond met her at Charlon's house in Paris."

"She was Roger's lover for a time. And Emilie helped Charlon transform Denis as well. Not all of Charlon's coven had scattered completely over the centuries," Desmond continued. "Gregory and Emilie remained friends, although she tended to move about."

"Roger, the other redhead in your life." Oliver smiled. He looked at Roger.

"How do you feel about this? I never thought to ask."

"He actually cried a little over the phone when I told him," answered Desmond, his mouth quirking in a wry smile. "He's usually far less emotional than I. Neither of us has ever created one of our own kind."

"I told Desmond it felt like we'd be having a child," said Roger, a sheepish grin stealing across his handsome face.

"I never thought of it that way." Oliver looked thoughtful. He added, "It's a bit creepy if you take into account who I am to you, Desmond." This last produced stifled snorts of laughter from both vampires. Then he looked up at Roger. "Do you remember how you felt when you were transformed?"

Roger smiled again, eyes wide with emotion. "When Gregory and Emilie brought me over, they did it with gentleness, but coldly, practically. I was *in extremis*, and they offered me a new life. You, Oliver, come to this with a full and open heart. This time it is a commitment of love, for all of us; so very different from my case. I can't tell you how honored I am that you have let me be part of this."

A comfortable silence fell over them, as each considered the moment in his own way. It was Oliver who spoke first.

"So, how do we proceed? Who does what to whom, so to speak?"

Roger answered. "One of us takes blood from you. The other gives you blood from his veins. We do it more or less simultaneously, thus enhancing the effect and lessening the time needed for transformation."

"I have never witnessed the process this way, Ollie," said Desmond softly. "In the past, Roger and I have had only each other for our regenerations." He paused, taking Oliver's hand. "We thought we'd let you decide which of us should play which role."

Oliver looked at each of the vampires in turn; his lover and his lover's dearest friend. "No matter what happens, we shall be bound together forever by this," he said, his voice clear and steady. "On the one hand, taking my blood, from my own experience, seems a very intimate thing indeed – and yet both of you drink in the same way from all of your, um, *hosts*. Taking your blood, however; that seems somehow sacramental, the actual agent of change." His brow furrowed for a moment, and he closed his eyes. Then his expression cleared, and he looked at them each again, holding their gazes, looking deep into their eyes.

"I think I'd like to have you take my blood, Roger, to start me on my path." He turned to Desmond, cupping his lover's pale cheek in his warm, strong hand. "And you, love, I will drink your blood, so you can bring me home."

Desmond grabbed the hand on his cheek, pulling it over his mouth so he could kiss the palm. He inhaled deeply, savoring Oliver's mortal scent.

Will he smell as beautiful to me afterward?

"So," said Desmond briskly, "let us begin. We should take down the covers, and make you comfortable. Roger, I think perhaps a towel from my bathroom ... "

"Are you going to make him like you, Desmond?"

All three men's heads swiveled at the sound of the new voice in the room. There in the hall doorway stood Janay, eyes curious, wrapped in her favorite *Power Puff Girls* blanket. They gaped at her in stunned silence.

Desmond gathered his wits enough to speak first. "Janay, sweetheart, um, what are you doing home? It's barely one-thirty."

"I didn't feel good at school. The nurse called mom at work, and got permission to drive me home. I have a key, 'member?"

Desmond remembered dashing out of the office and not listening to anything Jane might have had to tell him.

"So, now, Janay," asked Roger, getting to his feet, but not moving toward her, "what did you mean by your question?"

The ten-year-old eyed him suspiciously. "What are you doing here?"

Without hesitation, Roger walked over to the girl, putting out his hand. "Hello, Janay. I'm here because I'm a friend, and I want to help Desmond and Oliver."

"Are you a vampire too?"

Roger's eyes went wide in shock, and he turned a comically panicked expression toward the two men seated on the bed.

Desmond jumped in, his voice soothing, as if talking a child out of a nightmare. "Why do you ask that, honey?"

Janay rubbed her eyes with her blanket. Clearly she had been napping at some point recently.

"Cause I heard what you said to Daddy. You know,

that night when he shot you."

Desmond exchanged a glance with Oliver, who shrugged. "When I got into the hallway, she was right there by the door. She wouldn't let me move her any farther away at first. I guess she saw what happened and heard what you said. I didn't think she'd understand the implications."

"An' I saw you, when you took my daddy down." Janay's beautiful face was alight with what looked like pride. Clearly she was enjoying the effect she was having on these three grown men. "I was looking into the room. I saw your fangs. I saw how mad you was. You looked like you was gonna tear him up."

"*Were*, not was," Desmond corrected automatically, then covered his mouth to stifle a laugh at the dirty look Janay shot his way.

Her expression changed, became thoughtful, and wondering. "But you didn't kill him, even though he was dumb-ass enough to shoot you. That bullet shoulda killed you, Desmond. If I'd been you, I woulda killed him."

"I'm glad I didn't kill him, Janay," Desmond said very softly. "It would have been a terrible thing."

"I'm glad, too. He's been a kinda shitty dad," she gave Desmond a warning look when she saw him move to object to her language, "but he's still the only dad I got – *have*." A small smile played across her mouth.

Still wrapped in her blanket, she crossed the room to stand by Desmond and Oliver at the bedside.

"So, Ollie, are you going to be like Desmond then?"

Oliver considered her for a moment. "Yes, sweetheart, I will. I hope I'll be as good and kind as Desmond, too."

"So you won't be eating Dotty's food no more – *any* more?"

"I'll miss that, for sure. But no."

"And you and Desmond, and," she turned her head to Roger, "and you – you'll all just need blood from now on?"

Faced with the bald fact of their lives, and the life

Oliver was choosing, the men said nothing.

Desmond finally took a deep breath. "Yes, just blood."

The girl looked at each of them, turning in place, her delicate features locked in a fierce expression of concentrated thinking.

"Yuck. That's nasty." She shook herself slightly as if to dismiss her distaste at this thought. "I guess that just means more good stuff for me," she finished, breaking into an impish grin and throwing her arms up, flinging the luridly colored blanket into the air.

She then bent to pick the blanket up, and turned, heading toward the door. "I'm going back to bed." She made it as far as the passage, then turned back to the three men, who remained frozen in place.

"I know Mom and Dotty 'been thinking about this since that night, 'cause they saw you get shot, too; but they didn't see what I did, and I think I'm not going to bring it up with them, if you don't." And with that she disappeared down the dark corridor, heading to her little-girl room at the opposite end of the great silent house.

The three men stayed motionless for a few minutes, digesting both the enormity and the absurdity of what had just happened. Finally, shaking his head as if to awaken, Desmond spoke.

"I think you'd better lock the door, Roger."

As Roger went to do this, Desmond and Oliver rose, and together folded back the silk coverlet and the cool white sheets.

Oliver removed his shirt and tie, pulled off his shoes and lay down on the bed, watching the two vampires.

Roger went into the bathroom and came out with a large bath-towel. He got Oliver to sit up so that he could cover the pillows with it.

"Just in case you're a sloppy drinker the first time out," he said, smiling warmly.

Then, removing his shirt and shoes, Desmond climbed onto the bed, sitting cross-legged at Oliver's right side, as close to his head as possible.

Vampire in Suburbia

Roger took off his shirt, too and knelt at the bedside on Oliver's left.

"Hmm," Oliver murmured, caressing his lover's bare chest while placing his other hand on Roger's shoulder. "*This* is weirdly kinky. I guess I should still be nervous, but instead I'm, well, sort of aroused."

"Are you ready, Ollie?" asked Desmond, brushing the rusty tresses off his lover's brow, leaning in close.

"I'm ready." He kissed Desmond quickly on the lips, then turned his head into the pillow, away from Roger, exposing his neck and looking up at Desmond, who had already lowered his canines and raised his wrist, poised to begin.

"Roger will start to drink first, Ollie; then as soon as I'm ready, you drink. Can you do that?"

Oliver just sighed deeply and nodded, trusting the two men beside him to bring him through.

And so they did.

Chapter Twenty-Seven

When Jane came in through the kitchen door at five-thirty, Desmond padded barefoot into the kitchen to greet her, just as Janay and Speck came bouncing down the back stairs, calling at the top of their voices.

Waiting patiently while the girls greeted their mother, Desmond felt oddly serene. Oliver was upstairs asleep in the big bed, Roger at his side. The transformation would probably be complete by the end of his first six-hour sleep cycle – a remarkably quick turnaround. Everything had gone smoothly. Oliver had been perfect. It had, however, been surprisingly upsetting to see him slip into his first death-like vampire slumber, drained of his own blood and filled with Desmond's. Visions of Jeffrey and Tony, lying lifeless and pale before him, had swirled in his mind, and he had begun to weep as the pain he had held captive for so long had surfaced. Roger had held him patiently, until the tears had subsided, replaced gradually with the nascent happiness at what had happened to all of them on this warm spring afternoon.

Straightening up from her daughter's embrace, Jane looked at him quizzically.

"Everything all right, Des?"

"Yes, everything's fine." He glanced quickly at Janay, who continued to watch him, Speck having already wandered off to the family room to watch TV.

"Oliver's feeling a little under the weather just at the moment," he started, and could see Janay's face break into a grin. "He came over earlier this afternoon, and I made him go right to bed." He slanted a dirty look at Janay, who squelched her smile, but otherwise didn't budge. "I'm just going down to the cellar to get some wine for me and Roger … "

"*Roger* is here?" Jane's brows went up.

"Yes. He's upstairs sitting with Oliver."

"Oh. You mean *Robert*. Who looks just like a very young Roger. In the same way you look *exactly* like your father." Jane offered him a small smile and began to take off her jacket, clearly not wanting to probe any further into whatever circumstances had led to her boss's business partner playing nurse to his boyfriend. "Well, fine."

She turned and went to hang her coat in the closet by the family room, leaving Desmond standing dumbstruck as Janay beamed at him.

When she came back into the kitchen, Jane reached out and gently took Desmond by the arm. "Look, why don't you just call him Roger, instead of carrying on like I'm too dim to notice? Think you can do that for me?"

Desmond simply stared at Jane for a few seconds, then managed to nod before skirting past Janay and her mother, heading toward the basement stairs. As he turned to start down the staircase, he looked over at the little girl. She winked at him, before turning to join her mother and sister in the family room.

Roger and Desmond sat silently in the library, on either side of the fireplace, staring into the flickering gas flames. Each held a glass of ruby port – not the first of the evening. It was a congenial silence, each man lost in his own thoughts, but both of them still faintly exhilarated at what they'd done.

Roger sat up straighter in the big armchair and checked his watch.

"Eight o'clock," he said, swallowing the last of his wine and standing up. He set the glass on the marble-topped coffee table and then stood, stretching, his lithe form thrown into relief by the fire.

"Going up to check on him again?" Desmond asked.

"No, going out and leaving you to it."

At Desmond's shocked expression, Roger laughed softly and stepped across the hearthrug to plant a loud kiss on Desmond's upturned forehead.

"Sweetheart, he's fine. And I've got a date in the city."

"A date? You planned a date for *tonight*?"

"Don't be self-righteous. I knew it would all go swimmingly. Besides, he's your boyfriend, not mine." He leered down at his friend, waggling his eyebrows. "I've got nothing to look forward to when he wakes up."

At Desmond's grinning assent, he added, his tone sincere, "I could swear he looked younger last time I checked. I didn't expect that. Perhaps it's an illusion."

"I'll make sure to look closely. He's only thirty-eight. The change purifies the body. Possibly it erases some of the flaws, no matter what the age at which it happens."

"Well, just make sure you take notes and tell me all about it later. But I must fly."

Desmond stood up, somewhat uncertainly, and looked at Roger.

"I don't know how to thank you."

Roger put a finger to Desmond's lips. "Shush. Of course you do. You've made a special place for me in your life. And I think Oliver has as well. That's thanks enough. We'll never need to be alone, will we?"

"But meanwhile?"

"Meanwhile I have a date, and I'm not thinking past tonight."

"That's my Roger."

Roger just smiled at him, and, with a final peck on the check, he was out the door before Desmond could move to say goodbye.

As the sound of Oliver's car crunching down the drive receded into the distance, Desmond climbed the spiral staircase to the second floor, unlocking the door to his bedroom and locking it again behind him.

I guess Oliver won't be needing his car tonight, anyway.

Oliver lay, as they had left him, pale and still, under the silk canopy. The redhead's normal pale skin had taken on a starker, porcelain whiteness. Freckles still showed faintly across the bridge of his nose, on his strong shoulders and long muscular arms. But the deathly stillness, absent all of the tiny, subtle signs of life a sleeping figure offered, still made Desmond shudder.

He sat down on the bed next to his lover's supine form, and gently placed his hand on the broad flat belly. It was smooth and cool, and Desmond felt a sudden twinge of fear that he would never again feel the Oliver with whom he had fallen in love: the warm, vital *living* Oliver. He gazed at the peaceful face, and indeed, it did look somehow younger, leaner. Turning his gaze to Oliver's naked torso, he thought that there, too, was a leanness he didn't remember from before. The skin was taut, silky to the touch.

Beneath his palm, he could feel Oliver's heart begin to beat, and sensed his own heart starting to follow its rhythm, as if by instinct. As Desmond sat there, looking down at the sleeping features, about to run his hand through the tight auburn curls of the beard, Oliver opened his eyes.

Are they bluer than they were before?

He wondered briefly if he saw a slight green tint to the blue, giving them an ultramarine depth that hadn't been there earlier.

"Hello, lover," he said softly. "Welcome to my world."

Epilogue

Desmond steered the S70 through the afternoon traffic of suburban New Jersey, the girls blessedly silent in the back seat, happily poring over comic books he'd bought them at a shop in South Orange. He turned on a Maroon 5 CD, rolling down his window to let the music and the warm summer air flow over him. As he wended his way through the leafy streets of Essex County, Desmond's mind scrolled back to that first night, when Oliver had awoken for the first time in his new form. Desmond had expected fear, perhaps, or at least some disorientation.

But Oliver's only response to Desmond's tentative greeting had been a soft gasp of astonishment.

"Oh my God, Des," he had whispered, awestruck, "you're so fucking beautiful!"

And that had been the end of their conversation. Oliver had grabbed him – startling in his strength – and pulled him into a kiss that, had he needed to breathe, would have taken his breath away.

In less than a minute they had both been naked, clothes cast wildly across the room in their shared urgency. Skin to skin, belly to belly, legs entwined, Desmond's hazel eyes locked onto Oliver's newly-intense blue ones, he felt his fears melting away. This was his Oliver, handsome as ever, thrilling, alive, and lying beneath him, eyes wide with wonder at the novel intensity of each sensation as they rocked into each other.

There had been nothing hesitant about Desmond's actions this time. He had known what he wanted from the first instant, and Oliver had complied instinctually. With the minimum preparation he was inside him, Oliver's legs locked tightly about his hips, pulling him deeper as if there was no end to his need. Their mouths were clamped one to the other, neither of them breathing, desperate to swallow each other up in their hunger.

As he had neared the moment of release, Desmond had pulled away from Oliver's kiss and, staring deep into his eyes, had managed to articulate two words with a low guttural moan.

"Bite me."

In response, he had watched Oliver's canines extend for the first time, two razor sharp scalpels of purest white contrasting with the deep rosy pink of his lips. Only then had he turned his head, exposing his throat to the man he loved, the man he trusted with his very soul. And Oliver had pulled him down, following the instincts of his race, his new world, and as the blood had flowed, they had become one as only vampires could.

Oliver stood waiting for them at the front entrance as they pulled up to the house, blinking lazily in the sun, leaning against the carved stone frame of the massive doorway. He gave a little finger wave and sauntered down the steps toward the car as Desmond shut off the engine. The girls jumped out of the back seat, running past him with the briefest of acknowledgements, and disappeared into the house.

Before Desmond could speak, Oliver began.

"Dane's here."

Desmond paused. "Oh? Everything okay with that?"

"Pretty good, actually. Dotty's kind of giving him stink eye, but Jane's being very gentle with him."

"How does he seem?"

"Honestly? He seems great. A little cowed, but given what happened the last time he was here, I guess I'm not surprised."

"It's Janay's eleventh birthday, I just thought he needed to be here."

Oliver kissed him, lingering more than was strictly necessary.

"You thought right. And that's why I love you."

Desmond could only smile at this.

"Could you help me with the groceries? I have a half hour till I have to head to Newark airport to pick up Roger. Janay's little screaming friends will be arriving in an hour."

Oliver beamed at him. "No need. Roger's here already."

"What?"

"Caught an earlier flight. Got here about ten minutes ago in a cab. I put him up in the chintz room." He took several plastic shopping bags from Desmond's hands.

Desmond looked at him, questioning.

"What?" Oliver asked, smirking.

"What do you think of Roger?"

Oliver cocked his head, and looked fondly at his partner, amused at his ill-concealed anxiety. A sly smile crept over his handsome face.

"You know I love him." He turned and headed back toward the house, weighted down with half of Dotty's shopping list. As he reached the steps he stopped and turned.

"I think, because he was with us that night, that I understand why you love him the way you do, Desmond." Then he continued on inside, leaving Desmond alone in the afternoon warmth.

Desmond followed his partner up the front steps. He paused at the wide stone threshold and turned. Before him sprawled Oakwood's huge front lawn, stretching in a smooth green expanse to the distant road. All around him the summer leaves fluttered in a light afternoon breeze. Birds flittered about, their songs vying for attention with the silvery shimmer of cicadas. He could smell the newly-cut grass, the drifting scent of phlox and roses and day lilies from the back gardens; even the faint fragrance of chlorine from the swimming pool. And below it all, he recognized the thrumming essence of life in the small creatures that scurried unseen in the fresh greenery all around him.

He took a deep breath, savoring it, letting it fill him with a sense of well-being. Turning once again, he adjusted the grocery bags in his grip, and stepped into the cool darkness of his home.

As he crossed the octagonal hall, Oliver came to meet him from the kitchen passage, and took the remaining grocery bags from him, disappearing back into the dimness. Desmond could hear the chatter of voices, sounding far away in the big house. The squeals of the girls, the deeper feminine sounds of their mothers. No hint of Dane's voice in all the hubbub; he was probably either slightly overwhelmed, or simply content to sit and watch. Desmond could make out Roger's sonorous voice as Oliver brought the groceries into the room.

There they all are, waiting for me. The ones I chose. The ones who chose me.

He stood in the comparative silence of the hall for a moment, listening to the tick of the clock in the library,

Vampire in Suburbia

his thoughts unspooling into the past. Then he turned and moved quickly in the other direction, taking the curved staircase two steps at a time to the second floor.

He crossed the bedroom to the mahogany chest of drawers in which he kept his socks and underwear. Opening the top drawer, he felt around at the very back, pulling out a small cream-colored cardboard box with gilt edges. He stared at it for a few moments, then removed the lid, and carefully withdrew a flat square parcel made of folded writing paper, bound with a black silk ribbon.

A small sound behind made him turn, and there was Oliver, standing hesitantly in the doorway.

"Everything okay, Des?"

He smiled reassuringly at the handsome redhead. "I'm fine, Ollie." He looked back down at the box. "I suddenly remembered something, and couldn't resist coming up to get it."

Oliver came across the carpet to stand at his side, placing a hand on the small of his partner's back. "What have you got there?"

Desmond glanced at him, then back at the little parcel. "I'm not exactly sure. I think it's a portrait."

Oliver shot him a quizzical look. "What you mean you *think* it's a portrait?"

Desmond looked up, locking eyes with Oliver. His answer was almost a whisper. "I've never opened it."

"How long have you had it?"

"Since 1745."

The redhead's blue eyes went wide with surprise. "I ... I don't understand."

"The day of Jeffrey Chapman's funeral, in Dalmatia." He set the box and the folded packet down on the dresser, then took Oliver's hands.

"One of the village women gave it to me as I was leaving the castle that day, heading towards the church for the funeral service. She said that she had made it for me, as a remembrance of my friend."

Oliver cocked his head. "And?"

"And I never opened it."

"What?"

"I didn't think of it for the rest of the day, and then I forgot about it completely until I was readying myself to leave. I was by then a vampire, and my new life lay before me. I found the packet in my coat pocket, and couldn't bring myself to open it."

"You've had it for two and a half centuries and haven't ever looked at it?" Oliver's expression was both incredulous and concerned. "You must open it, Desmond."

The dark-haired vampire only nodded, releasing Oliver's hands and picking up the package. He gingerly pulled at the silk ribbon, letting out a small breath of relief when the ancient fabric slipped its knot without much struggle. He carefully unfolded the heavy, cream-colored paper, revealing the contents that had lain so long in its protection.

Oliver let out a low sigh when he saw what Desmond held in his hand.

It was a portrait of a young man with radiant blond hair. He appeared to be sleeping, and had been depicted in profile, his pale skin as cool and smooth as the ivory on which the picture was painted. Deep golden lashes fringed his high cheekbones, and his full lips were of the palest pink.

"Is that Jeffrey?" Oliver asked in a voice so soft that no mortal could have heard. When Desmond didn't answer, he looked up and saw unshed tears threatening to overflow the hazel dyes.

Desmond nodded slightly. His voice trembled as he spoke. "I never dared look at it. I didn't want any remembrance other than my own memories. By the time I got back to England, it had become almost an object of superstition to me."

He turned and looked into Oliver's eyes again. A couple of stray tears had managed to escape and worked their way down his cheeks.

"I was afraid if I ever looked at it, my memories of

Jeffrey would fade away."

"Desmond, they wouldn't. You know that," murmured Oliver soothingly.

"But they have, you see." A small wry smile quirked Desmond's beautiful mouth. "First there was Tony, and now you. Especially you. Standing in the hall downstairs just now, I realized that I haven't thought of Jeffrey in weeks."

He turned and gestured to the mantelpiece, where framed photographs lined the marble surface. Among them was the ambrotype of the Civil War widow that Oliver had brought with him from his parents' house.

"You've seen pictures of Tony and my other friends from my last lifetime. But I have never had an image of Jeffrey other than the one in my mind." He looked at Oliver again, his gaze searching.

"Jeffrey was my first boyhood friend. My first lover. But he was my servant. When he lived, it would never have done to have a portrait painted, even a small one."

He held up the miniature for Oliver to see closely.

"When that woman gave me this, I was overwhelmed with shame that, in life, I had never honored Jeffrey, truly honored him, as the one I loved. I couldn't bear the thought that someone else had understood his importance to me better than I myself had."

"Desmond, you can't blame yourself for this. You can't use hindsight to second-guess what you did so long ago."

Reaching up with his free hand, Desmond stroked Oliver's beard. "I know that, Ollie. I really do."

"What, then?"

"I just realized that I was, finally, ready to see this." He held the miniature, nestled in its paper covering, out for Oliver to take.

"She must have painted it while Jeffrey was lying in the Chapel at Tsolnay Castle, before the coffin was readied. Tell me what you see, Ollie."

Oliver took it from him, and cautiously lifting it by

its edges, picked up the tiny portrait and held it in the palm of his hand. Seconds passed in silence, and at length Oliver turned his gaze back to his lover's.

"I can't."

"Can't what?"

"Can't see anything."

"What? I don't understand."

"I've lost it, Desmond. Lost the power I had with objects."

"How long? Was it the transformation?"

"Yes, I'm pretty sure." He placed the miniature back into the paper and set it down on the bureau. "At first I didn't notice, because I was so wrapped up in all my new sensations and, well, *you*."

"My god, Ollie, you should have told me." Desmond softly gripped Oliver's shoulders.

"I wasn't sure at first. I thought that it would come back, you know, the way it started when I was twelve." His own big, strong hands went up to cover Desmond's. "But it hasn't, and I'm pretty sure it's gone for good."

"Your gift. Gone. Oh, Ollie, I'm so sorry."

Oliver closed his eyes for a moment, shaking his head.

"No, don't be sorry," he said, his voice thick, but his eyes clear. "The gift you have given me is greater than any I could ever have." He smiled, radiant, pulling Desmond to him for a kiss.

Pulling back, but not letting Desmond go, he continued. "So now I just see things the way you do. I think that's more than enough, don't you?"

Desmond chuckled softly.

Oliver let go of Desmond and moved over to the mantelpiece, picking up a small photograph in a silver frame. It was of a handsome young man with dark blond hair, a dazzling smile lighting up his face. He brought it to Desmond.

"This is my favorite picture of Tony. You still think of him, don't you, Desmond?" He wasn't really asking.

Desmond looked deeply into Oliver's eyes, finding

there the trust he expected to see. He took the picture from Oliver's hand, and returned it to its place on the mantelpiece.

"I think of him every day, Ollie. I miss him. And I think of how much he would have liked you, what good friends you would have been."

Oliver took his hand, pulling him gently toward the bedroom door. He smiled at Desmond, a gentle, knowing look warming his face and making his blue eyes sparkle.

Turning, Oliver led Desmond as if he were guiding a child, pulling him out into the passage and toward the staircase. They paused at the top step, and Desmond kissed Oliver briefly, running his fingers in a teasing caress through Oliver's auburn hair.

Then, hand in hand, they started down the staircase together, to join their family in celebration.

The End

Author's Note

The characters and events in this book are, for the most part, creations of my imagination. However, there are a few people and one event that are in fact historical. The Ballantine family is real. John Holme Ballantine and his wife Jeannette did indeed build the great brick mansion at 43 Washington Street in Newark in 1885. It is part of the Newark Museum, and is the core of the decorative arts department at that wonderful institution. It is also true that Robert Ballantine, one of John and Jeannette's children, committed suicide in that very house in 1905, at the age of 35. He was unmarried, and apparently killed himself as the result of ongoing blackmail. All of this was reported in the newspapers of the day. Ever since I became the curator of the Ballantine House in 1980, at the age of 24, Robert Ballantine's story has haunted me, because the presumed reason for the blackmail was that he was gay, and feared the impact the scandal would have on his family. His suicide eliminated the threat to his family's social standing, but ended a young life tragically. I wish Desmond could have saved him.

About the Author

Ulysses Grant Dietz grew up in Syracuse, New York, where his *Leave it to Beaver* life was enlivened by his fascination with vampires, from Bela Lugosi to Barnabas Collins. He studied French at Yale, and was trained to be a museum curator at the University of Delaware. A curator for thirty-two years, Ulysses has never stopped writing fiction for the sheer pleasure of it. He created the character of Desmond Beckwith in 1988 as his personal response to Anne Rice's landmark novels. Alyson Books released his first novel, *Desmond*, in 1998. *Vampire in Suburbia* is his second novel.

Ulysses lives in suburban New Jersey with his partner of 37 years and their two teenaged children.

By the way, the name Ulysses was not his parents' idea of a joke: he is a great-great grandson of Ulysses S. Grant, and his mother is the President's last living great-grandchild. Every year on April 27 he gives a speech at Grant's Tomb in New York City.

Printed in the USA
CPSIA information can be obtained
at www.ICGtesting.com
LVHW021147160424
777556LV00030B/265